A DETE

A QUIVER OF
SORROWS

NEW YORK TIMES #1 BESTSELLER **TONY LEE** WRITING AS

JACK GATLAND

MEDIA

Published by Hooded Man Media.

First Edition: September 2022

PRAISE FOR JACK GATLAND

'This is one of those books that will keep you up past your bedtime, as each chapter lures you into reading just one more.'

'This book was excellent! A great plot which kept you guessing until the end.'

'Couldn't put it down, fast paced with twists and turns.'

'The story was captivating, good plot, twists you never saw and really likeable characters. Can't wait for the next one!'

'I got sucked into this book from the very first page, thoroughly enjoyed it, can't wait for the next one.'

'Totally addictive. Thoroughly recommend.'

'Moves at a fast pace and carries you along with it.'

'Just couldn't put this book down, from the first page to the last one it kept you wondering what would happen next.'

Before LETTER FROM THE DEAD...
There was

LIQUIDATE
THE PROFITS

Learn the story of what *really* happened to DI Declan Walsh, while at Mile End!

An EXCLUSIVE PREQUEL, completely free to anyone who joins the Declan Walsh Reader's Club!

Join at bit.ly/jackgatlandVIP

Also by Jack Gatland

ROGUE SIGNAL

ELLIE RECKLESS BOOKS

PAINT THE DEAD

STEAL THE GOLD

HUNT THE PREY

FIND THE LADY

BURN THE DEBT

DAMIAN LUCAS BOOKS

THE LIONHEART CURSE

STANDALONE BOOKS

THE BOARDROOM

For Mum, who inspired me to write.

For Tracy, who inspires me to write.

FOREWORD

I don't usually do a foreword, but as this is all set in one location, I won't be doing my usual *'Locations in this book'* section at the back, and because of that, I decided to instead place a foreword into the book, where I could thank both Mark Ryan and his beautiful wife Lutine, for the inspiration they gave me here.

Mark is known in film and TV as the voice of Bumblebee in the *Transformers* movies, as well as many other roles over the years, including Mac in *Who Dares Wins* and Mister Gates in *Black Sails*, but is best known to many as Nasir in the 1980s ITV show, *Robin of Sherwood*.

I've been lucky to know Mark for close to thirty years now, due to other, more esoteric areas of interest, and through my love of *Robin Hood* and *Robin of Sherwood*, I've also worked with many of the other cast members, releasing (under my real name of Tony Lee) full-cast *Robin of Sherwood* audio dramas with them in.

At a *Robin of Sherwood* convention earlier this year, I was enamoured with an idea of creating the story you're about to read, partly because of the lore, and the visual idea of the opening scene death, but also because, for the last couple of decades, I've been a mainstay of many *Doctor Who* and comic conventions, and I've seen every aspect of these shows, both from in front, and also from behind the curtain. Therefore, a death at a convention of some kind seemed a perfect idea. And, when I said this at the *Robin of Sherwood* convention, I had a lot of support, and in the end offered (in the event's charity auction) a chance to be in the book - maybe even die in it - if the winner of the auction so wanted.

Lutine Ryan immediately placed her hand up and won the bid, purely so she could have *Mark shot and killed with a speargun.* (her choice!)

I didn't do that, as "Mark Ryan" isn't a character in the story, but I hope both Lutine and Mark enjoy what I *did* do.

However, and more importantly, I wanted to head off any confusion resulting from this novel.

Every character in this book is nothing more than a cypher, a make-believe persona. In the same way the rock band *Alternator* was fake, but created from many different "eighties bands" in book seven, **Killing The Music,** and all the celebrity chefs were fictional in book eight, **A Dinner To Die For** - hell, we have *Charles Baker* as Prime Minister in this world, and currently, as I write this *Liz Truss* has just gained enough nominations to take on that role from Boris Johnson.

I cannot express enough that no character in this book is based on anyone, alive or dead.

And, being completely frank, pretty much every guest, appearance manager or event organiser I've ever worked with - whether it's been a comic con or a film and TV event - have all been amazing, super-friendly and are genuinely loved by fandom for valid reasons. And if I did have beef with anyone, I'd actually *avoid* writing them into the book, just to be a little bit spiteful. This is completely a work of fiction, a peering through the looking glass, as such.

I do place a *speargun* in it, though.

That's *your* fault, Lutine. X

Jack Gatland / Tony Lee,
London, September 2022

CONTENTS

PROLOGUE

RYAN GATES REALLY HATED MONTGOMERY PRYCE.

As far as the crowds were concerned, at conventions and event meetups, or when together at Blu-Ray releases and book launches, they were best friends, always laughing, ribbing each other, making sure the fans had the best times ever.

But behind the scenes, it was pretty *toxic*.

Montgomery had played the role of Robin Hood for longer than anyone else in British television. In the mid-seventies, he'd starred in *"Young Robin"*, a show that had lasted fifteen episodes in total, and starred the teenage Montgomery, then calling himself "Monty Pryce" as the titular character. The show had been for kids but held a lot of the classic folklore the shows and films of today stole mercilessly from.

There was a larger lad, Michael Bailey, who played a young Little John, there was Felicity Marshall who played a teenage Marian, and the whole thing was, quite frankly, cringeworthy, as they tried to explain how Robin was Robin *before* the legends all had him *start* as Robin. It was like a show showing a young Sherlock Holmes, while he was training to be the great detective, but also showing him as the Holmes that Doctor Watson wrote about at the same time.

As far as Gates was concerned, whatever its fanbase, it simply wasn't faithful to the core legend, and it had died pretty quickly; two short seasons, never seen again, apart from when the occasional episode was aired every time the cricket was delayed, and to be honest, they probably lost most of the episodes in the BBC archives with a ton of *Doctor Who* episodes, and a few *Steptoe and Son* and *Dad's Army* classics thrown in for good measure.

But then, in the late eighties, they'd created a sequel series. The "Young Robin" was now the right age, in his late twenties, to play the *actual* Robin Hood. The BBC were excited about this, there was still a love for the old show because of these random episode airings, and the BBC brought in people to create this new show around the already established cast, hiring the lead director of the original show, Robert Standish, back as show creator, mainly to make sure the bloody thing worked for the money they were paying.

Although, this was where "Monty" became known as "Montgomery", or more accurately, *"that bastard Montgomery"*, because he'd made a crafty contract alteration with Robert Standish before he signed, one which the BBC lawyers didn't notice before accepting the contract, stating *he would be the only original cast member returning for the show.* Which basically meant the other parts would be recast. On his own, they wouldn't have agreed, but Standish had championed the project from the start, and the BBC were over a barrel. However, by this point Michael Bailey was a useless drunk who couldn't hold down a job, so there weren't many tears shed there.

Forced into a corner, the BBC had agreed, but added a little wrinkle of their own. If new actors were being cast, then their characters would have to be re-introduced. And if this was the case, then the show would have to be reimagined, as you couldn't have a sequel to a show where half the cast ignored their predecessors. And, although Montgomery Pryce was Robin Hood still, Robert Standish decided the show, now called *The Hooded Outlaw,* would be a complete "from the ground up reboot" with no connection to *Young Robin*.

Montgomery hadn't been bothered about this. He was still the lead star, and still playing Robin Hood, he still made his agreed money, and he was once more on the covers of *Look In* and *Radio Times*. And, after the four seasons that followed finally ended, Pryce had technically been associated with the role for over fifteen years, rightly claiming the title of "longest ever TV Robin Hood".

It was on the set of *Hooded Outlaw* that Ryan Gates had met Pryce face-to-face. He'd been brought in personally by Standish as a kind of lore consultant, as the folklore of Robin Hood had been a key reason for the creation of the show, and, after stepping in when the actor cast as Will Scarlet was fired, Gates was cast in his stead, purely to appear and die in the first episode, removing the problem of "what to do with Will" pretty much immediately.

Weirdly, Pryce had liked Gates though, during read throughs and rehearsals, and had petitioned for his addition into the cast, so Will not only *didn't* die, but became one of the most beloved characters in the show, even if he barely spoke.

Years later, Ryan Gates had learned this was purely because he wasn't classically trained like the other actors in the show, and Pryce, a child-actor who also didn't have this "elitist" background, in his own words, used any scenes with Gates in as a stick to poke the other, more trained actors with. If Will Scarlet had a better scene than Little John, for example, *then Little John was shit and should quit acting altogether, as the runty little boffin-turned-actor was doing a better job.*

For Gates, it was nothing more than a pay cheque. He was an ex-soldier who'd taken night courses in English Folklore and History when he demobbed out of the service. He'd taken the job to help Robert Standish "nail the tone", after they'd met during a military job in Prague a couple of years before the show even began filming – one connected by pure coincidence to Pryce and Bailey, the now ex-Little John – and to this day most people believed he'd been cast as Scarlet purely to "punch the living shit" out of Montgomery Pryce during the first week of filming, when the two characters met for the first time in a rowdy brawl scene.

It was an order that seemed legitimate, following the issues Pryce had given the production up to that point.

And then the show had finished, and the cast had moved on; although they'd been in each other's pockets for years, they simply drifted away, apart from the occasional catch up in Soho when one was in town. Gates had realised he enjoyed this, and carried on acting, if only on the regional stage. Alex Hamilton, the actor who played the new Little John, had gone to Hollywood, playing villains against people like Stallone and Van Damme, while Pryce had, well, done nothing of worth, compared to his peers.

For *years.*

Gates recalled seeing him at a *This Is Your Life* show in 2002, when they honoured Margot Trayner, the new Marian of the show, after she'd won the *Best Actress* Oscar the previous year. Gates remembered how drunk Pryce had got at the afterparty, and how furious he was that his "supporting cast", to quote the man, had snagged "his" awards and roles.

Margot had told him, very calmly, to "piss off before I turn you from bitching actor into bitching eunuch", and Pryce had stormed out, stating *they were all beneath him, and he'd prove this to them.*

Gates hadn't seen him for another five glorious years.

And then, while playing the role of Christopher Wren in the touring production of *The Mousetrap,* Ryan Gates had found himself sharing the stage with Montgomery Pryce once more, as he took on the role of Detective Sergeant Trotter for a limited run before taking the part further at the West End.

Surprisingly, the takings had shot up. And, as they finished the show every night, both Gates and Pryce would be bombarded by *Hooded Outlaw* fans, all wanting them to sign the recently released DVD box set of the show.

It seemed the fans, realising that 'Robin and Will' were in the same show, were actively attending. And the promoter at one of the tour venues, seeing this, had created a "Twenty Year Reunion" event for the next year, even though 2009 was technically a *twenty-two-year* gap from the beginning.

The promoters had claimed it was twenty years from the end, rather than the start, and this had been accepted by pretty much everyone. They also claimed this was the "first time the cast has reunited", although they'd met up several times during US conventions. In fact, several of the smaller character actors were mainstays of the US convention network and had been for decades.

It had been a spectacular success. Margot Trayner had turned up for the Sunday afternoon only, but everyone else had agreed to do the entire weekend. Even Terry Leighton, the show's Friar Tuck had appeared, and this had been a coup for the event as Terry had been in a rather public and vicious blood-feud with Sheriff of Nottingham actor Nigel Cummings since the nineties, when they'd both fallen in love with the same young man, a sad, confused wannabe actor with some vague connection to them, who'd eventually taken his own life in LA, years later.

Neither had ended up with him, and at the 2009 event, both men seemed to bury the hatchet, playing to the crowds and genuinely looking to be having a good time.

And, of course, the money was *stellar*.

So, for the next decade, sporadic events would turn up; sometimes it was a fan-panel for a large event like the *London Film and Comic Con*, or *Birmingham Memorabilia*, and other times it was a more focused event, aimed purely at the show, with the cast, crew and a bevy of semi-famous friends and one-shot guests who would turn up, sign autographs, take photos and talk about *how great things were* back then – even if they weren't – to hundreds of people who not only loved the show, but would often dress up like characters from it.

They'd even had other Robin Hood actors turn up, some from the ITV show that happened a couple of years before theirs had, some more from the mid-2000s BBC reboot. Even a couple of extras and featured characters from the films arrived, more-so with each progressive convention. In fact, by the current event, a good twelve or thirteen years on from the first, this was now a more generic "love for the folklore of Robin" show than actual *The Hooded Outlaw* fan-fest.

Which pissed off Montgomery Pryce immensely and made Ryan Gates ecstatic because of this.

It had been a good "day one", not that Pryce would know, because he hadn't bothered to turn up until halfway through it. He'd had some kind of issue with the organisers. Pryce had claimed they'd used his card to pay for the room, which meant that any additional costs he'd placed on the room including drinks, room service food and spa treatments, taken when he'd arrived, were now coming out of his own money.

While the organisers of the event had pointed out, politely, that he'd decided *not* to turn up for day one of the event he'd been paid to attend, instead spending time on drinks, room service food and expensive spa treatments they hadn't agreed on, so if he was reneging on the deal, then they weren't paying for his "holiday", especially as he'd claimed he was "poorly", and *that* was why he wasn't signing at his table or doing his photo-shoot meet-and-greet, while fans were posting on Twitter images of Pryce doing laps in the hotel pool.

In response, Pryce appeared half an hour later, claiming he'd made a "miraculous recovery" and was "fighting through his food poisoning", which of course made him even more of a hero in the eyes of the adoring fans, as they now believed the convention had actually tried to poison him. And, even though Flick McCarthy, his pit bull appearance manager had already agreed the amount of autographs and photos he was contracted to do, Pryce now made a point of deliberately extending his meetings with each fan, causing the queues to

build up, and causing attendees to miss other shoots while
stuck in the queue, happily allowing the promoters to take
the blame, like the prick he was, while Ryan Gates watched
from two tables down, fuming.

But now it was the end of the first day, and time for the
"opening ceremony" which was always a little strange, as the
event had technically been open for the entire day, but it was
a chance for the cast to come onto the stage, say hi to the fans
and promote themselves a little. Because at the end of the
day, they were all there to make money, no matter what they
said about "love for the show" and all that.

No, that wasn't true.

Gates loved the show. He was thankful for it, and he knew
Alex Hamilton, as much as he didn't like the lanky twat, felt
the same. They both agreed pricks like Montgomery Pryce
didn't realise what they had until it was taken from them.
And Pryce made more here than anyone else, as his photos
and autographs were double the cost of everyone else,
including the guy from the BBC medical show who played
Robin Hood in the 2000s. More importantly, Pryce was more
expensive than Margot Trayner, who, as the only actor there
who'd won a bloody *Oscar*, should have been on top of the
pecking order.

Although she had left halfway through season four, so
perhaps it was a "total episodes" thing.

Of course, Alex Hamilton and Margot Trayner were there
because – Margot's *Oscar* or not – they'd reached the age
where it was harder to get meaty roles in America, as
producers looked for younger, newer faces. In fact, Margot
Trayner was now better known in the UK as being one of a
group of female television personalities who drank wine and
discussed the current state of affairs at eleven on a weekday

morning on ITV, while Alex Hamilton was now on a daytime soap, playing an ex-Army Doctor with PTSD who worked with a Coroner, or something. Gates had paid little attention, as they hadn't really spoken for years now.

To be brutally honest, from what Gates had been told over the years, Alex was lucky to have any job at all, after he'd been kicked out of LA around five or ten years earlier. Nobody spoke about it, but there weren't many things that had you removed from the US and banned from returning. And Alex had always been a fan of pharmaceuticals and prescription pain meds, even rumoured to have been selling them to the Malibu Set while he was over there.

Basically, Alex Hamilton got what he deserved.

There was movement, and it brought Gates back to the present, as a young woman, no older than twenty, was waving the guests, currently standing in a corridor behind the door to the hotel's ballroom.

'Okay, everyone,' she explained softly, 'We're starting the ceremony in a moment. There's a list on the door. We'll be bringing you out in your show groups, and our three Robins will be announced separately at the end, in movie–TV–TV format.'

Everyone nodded, returning to their conversations after this. They'd done enough of these things to know how it all worked. They'd be announced, walk on in groups, be passed a wireless microphone, say how wonderful it was to be there, stand for a photo op and then walk off stage, heading for the bar as quick as humanly possible.

Gates hadn't noticed Pryce sidle up beside him.

'We should talk this weekend,' he said. 'I have a job you might be interested in.'

'Oh aye?' Gates kept his voice low and noncommittal.

After playing Will in the eighties, Gates had also returned to security work, his bread and butter before the show, and half the job offers he received were for off-the-books troubleshooting, or straight-down-the-line body-guarding.

Pryce had offered big money a couple of times recently to hire Gates to guard him, and both times Gates had turned him down. He knew this wasn't about his personal safety, and all about one-upmanship again, having paparazzi snap an image of "Will Scarlet" opening a car door for "Robin Hood", and there was no bloody way he was having that, even if the chances of such a photo even making the press these days was small.

There were still blogs out there, and a photo on Twitter or Instagram could go viral in a heartbeat.

'Yeah,' Pryce was continuing now. 'I had a chat with the Beeb the other day. BBC One.'

'I know what the Beeb is.'

Pryce sniffed, probably the aftereffects of the cocaine he'd visibly rammed up his nose in a corner of the guest's Green Room.

'Anyway, they said they're interested in my Robin and Marian idea.'

Gates looked at Pryce in surprise at this. *Robin and Marian* was a famous Sean Connery movie, where the old and war-scarred Robin returned to Sherwood to regain his lost love, and eventually died how he did in the legends, telling Little John to bury him where an arrow, fired from his deathbed, landed. A story where Montgomery Pryce, now in his sixties, could *play* the older Robin easily.

'You did, did you?' Gates replied, hiding his interest. 'In what way?'

'They think there's an audience to see Robin Hood die,'

Pryce looked around as, through the door and on the stage the sound of a few hundred people cheering one of the other show's cast and crew could be heard, as they escaped through to the sides. 'But they're not too keen on keeping some of the old cast. Hamilton's too *daytime* now, Margot doesn't act—'

'Have you asked them?' Gates shot back a quiet reply, noting that once again, Montgomery Pryce was finding ways to throw his previous cast members under the bus in favour of a re-cast.

'Of course not,' Pryce sniffed again, wiping at his nostril. 'I'm speaking to you because the producers asked about you coming back as Will Scarlet—'

'Okay, so the *Hooded Outlaw* people now,' the young woman leaned out of the door before Gates could reply, and suddenly Gates was being escorted away from Pryce, through the backstage area and aimed at the steps behind the black curtain that surrounded the stage. And then, with a wave of noise, Ryan Gates walked out into the Milton Keynes Hilton's ballroom and waved at the cheering audience, blinking at the bright lights now shining on him, the auditorium thrown into blackness by the lack of house lights, lit only by the double doors at the back, opened and streaming light into the front of the ballroom, a good two hundred feet away.

The room had to be filled with around six hundred people, maybe more. At the front was a group of cosplayers, all dressed as characters from Robin Hood; their costumes varied, and Gates realised this was likely because they were playing the characters from different shows, all bunched together. What was the term Marvel had been using in their movies? Oh yes. A *multiverse* of Robins.

That said, the Little John they had was pretty spot on as a

young Alex Hamilton, especially with his blond beard and wild hair.

Standing now beside Margot, to his left, and waiting for his chance to speak, Gates heard her voice, softly, beside him.

'Trust nothing that shitlicker says,' she muttered, her coarse Northern accent coming out as she spoke. 'If he wants you on his new show, it's because they won't make it without you.'

'He's spoken to you about it?'

Margot nodded.

'I told him to piss off,' she smiled, waving still. 'Life's too short to spend with dickheads. It's bad enough I'm here on the sodding stage with him.'

She then stepped forward, taking the microphone as it was passed to her, and stating to the cheering crowd how *wonderful* it was to be back, giving them a line from the show, her "catchphrase" as such, and then it was his turn, accepting the microphone, giving a little speech and stepping back as Nigel Cummings, on his right and irritated he was close to the side of the stage rather than centre, snatched the microphone away from him as if scared Gates was going to hog it; always the bitchy queen.

Gates was going to continue the conversation quietly with Margot, but there was a sudden scream, and he looked up to hear, rather than see the audience go wild, as Pryce walked onto the stage way earlier than he was supposed to, interrupting Nigel's speech with his own microphone in hand.

'I'm sorry, but do we *really* want to hear from the Sheriff of Nottingham?' he asked, to a resounding and excited *no* from the shadowed audience, now in full-on *pantomime* mode. Nigel smiled weakly and stepped back, knowing this wasn't the moment to kick off at the unprofessional wanker, and Pryce walked to the middle of the stage, now standing in front of Gates, blocking the audience's view of both Will Scarlet and Maid Marian, probably deliberately, maybe even because he thought he'd blocked Margot instead.

'Or do we want to hear from *Robin of Locksley, the Hooded Outlaw?*' he shouted, hands out to the side like a messiah as the crowd went wild, and chants of *Ro-bin, Out-law,* and *Locks-ley* could be heard echoing around the ballroom—

And then it stopped, and the real screams began.

Pryce, at the front of the stage, staggered slightly, as if punched in the chest. The crowd was rising now, the noise now panicked as Pryce spun to his old cast mates and the arrow protruding out of his front was visible, blood pouring from the wound, as he collapsed to the ground.

Gates shaded his eyes from the spotlights as he tried to peer at the back of the darkened room; from the looks of things the arrow was pretty much dead centre, so had to come from the end of the middle aisle, where the doors were and, there in the doorway, bow in hand, was a hooded archer, watching for a moment before disappearing into the crowd, now running in fear from the ceremony.

Gates hadn't noticed the cosplay Little John leap onto the stage, crouching over Pryce's body.

'Someone call an ambulance!' he shouted. 'And call the police!'

'Look,' the ceremony host was confused, thrown off by this. 'I don't think fans are allowed on the stage at this convention—'

'I'm Acting-Sergeant Morten De'Geer of the City of London Police,' Little John replied, pulling a warrant card out of his jerkin. 'Montgomery Pryce has been shot and killed, the killer is in the hotel which needs to be locked down, and no offence, but your convention's pretty much over.'

Gates looked down at the obviously dead Montgomery Pryce, his eyes wide, his expression one of annoyance, as if angry that someone had spoiled his speech.

It seemed, though, that Pryce had gained his wish.

He had indeed showed the world how "Robin Hood" died.

1

THE HOODED CORPSE

'So, wait, he was Little John?'

Declan looked over at Anjli Kapoor as she sat in the passenger seat, currently chuckling to herself.

'Apparently so,' she said. 'Man, I hope they recorded the convention. Not just for the murder and all that, but so I can see De'Geer in his little green tights.'

'First off, he's seven feet tall, so they're not exactly "little" tights,' Declan smiled, indicating out into the fast lane as they headed up the M1 towards Milton Keynes. 'And second, I don't know if they're actually tights, and not some kind of leather trews.'

'Leather trews,' Anjli mocked. 'Listen to the man, talking as if he knows what he's talking about.'

She looked out of the car window.

'I bet Cooper's hoping he's in tights.'

Declan considered this for a moment.

'Have you heard from Davey?' he asked softly.

Anjli looked back at him.

'Not since she walked out,' she replied. 'You?'

'I know she spoke to Bullman when Charles Baker closed her case, but that's it,' he said.

DC Davey had been suspended after Scotland Yard discovered she was connected to the Last Chance Saloon's most recent case, and because of this had perverted the course of justice, but when the smoke had settled Declan had used information gained during the investigation to effectively blackmail the current Prime Minister (and thorn in the side of Declan), Charles Baker to clear her name, or he'd publicly reveal how involved the Prime Minister's office had been in the case itself.

Davey had been cleared to return if she wanted, but the important part of that statement had been *if she wanted*. It was a month later, and nobody, not even her old mentor, Doctor Marcos, had heard from her.

'I hope she's okay,' Declan muttered, now moving into the left lane and readying to leave at the next junction. He looked over at Anjli, hoping to lighten the mood.

'Would you like to see me in leather trews?' he asked, winking impishly as he spoke. Unfortunately, the reply wasn't exactly as he'd hoped.

'God no,' Anjli almost choked with laughter. 'I'm fine. Really. All that pirates and medieval role-play bollocks is utterly wasted on me.'

She looked back at Declan, seeing his stricken expression, and grinned.

'Now, you in a uniform? Grrrrrr,' she purred mockingly. 'I'll be a naughty constable, you can be the brusque desk sergeant, annoyed that I haven't filled out the correct forms.'

Declan blushed at this; the thought of Anjli as a "naughty constable" was one he'd never had before, but now it didn't seem to want to leave the front of his mind.

'Just don't invite Billy,' Anjli finished as she leant back in the passenger seat.

'What-why would I invite Billy?' Declan stammered, almost missing the turnoff as he pulled sharply off the motorway.

'Because he'd want to fill out the forms correctly,' Anjli smiled. 'And that would be a real buzzkill. Although, I wonder what his boyfriend would look like in uniform?'

'Probably like a male model,' Declan muttered. 'Just like he does in everything else.'

Declan had only met Billy's current partner, Andrade Estrada a couple of times over the last couple of months, and for the first of those months he, like his boss, DCI Monroe had believed the Colombian diplomat to be a spy of some kind. But, as the weeks went on, the two men seemed to be happy, and Andrade was very good at fitting in when in a social situation.

Of course, Declan considered to himself, *spies are very good at that too.*

'So, tell me about the victim,' he said quickly, attempting to change the subject.

'Actor named Montgomery Pryce,' Anjli looked down at her notes. 'I saw a photo, and he's got one of those faces.'

'What's that supposed to mean?'

'You know,' Anjli turned to look at him in the car. 'You see him in a TV show and you're like "I know him from somewhere", and then you find out he was in that thing you saw a while back. And then you realise he's been in a ton of things you like, always in the background.'

'So, a character actor?'

'I suppose,' Anjli turned back sulkily. 'I mean, if you want to label it.'

'And he was at this convention because he was Robin Hood, right?'

'In a couple of shows, one in the seventies and one in the late eighties,' Anjli nodded. 'I don't think there was any narrative tissue between them.'

'Narrative tissue?' Declan scoffed. 'That sounds like something Doctor Marcos would say.'

'I mean there's no connection between the shows, although they tried their best to make out the younger Robin in the first show was the older Robin in the later one, even though they never explained how there was a second Marian and Little John and all that.'

Declan frowned.

'How do you know this?' he asked suspiciously.

'Wikipedia,' Anjli grinned. 'I read up on it while we left London.'

Declan accepted this with a smile.

'And he was fired at by another Robin? As in someone dressed as the folklore character, all hood and that?'

'So they think.' Anjli flicked through the notes. 'De'Geer was in the middle of chaos when he called. Hopefully, by the time we arrive, he'll have more information. And arrows are *loosed* or *shot*, Declan. Not fired at. "Fired" only appeared with the arrival of gunpowder. I remember that from your mental buddies in the Peak District.'

Declan glanced at Anjli.

'If you're going to lecture me, at least be dressed like the naughty constable,' he said, hoping to lighten the mood.

Instead, Anjli sighed, shaking her head.

'Jesus, Declan. Why would the naughty constable lecture someone? You're terrible at role-play.'

Declan flushed again, looking back at the road.

'Some people might want to be lectured at by a naughty constable,' he muttered.

'I'll let PC Cooper know,' Anjli grinned.

―――――

DE'GEER DID INDEED HAVE MORE INFORMATION WHEN THEY arrived at the Milton Keynes Hilton Hotel. Actually a few miles out of the town centre, it was a rather isolated location, surrounded by farmers' fields and woodlands. He also hadn't yet changed out of his Little John costume, and Declan had commented on this, asking jovially *if he'd had fun being part of the fancy-dress brigade*, meaning the people who dressed as Robin and the Merry Men at the convention.

Apparently, this hadn't been the right thing to say.

'It's not fancy dress,' De'Geer explained irritably. 'It's called *Cosplay*.'

'But you're wearing fancy—' Declan stopped as he realised he was arguing with a seven-foot tall, obviously annoyed man, who, although acting as Scene of Crime Officer had also watched one of his childhood heroes be murdered live on stage less than an hour earlier.

'So, why are you still wearing your ... *cosplay?*' he asked.

'Because the moment Mister Pryce was shot with an arrow, I had to lock down the scene,' De'Geer waved his leather-braced wrist around the ballroom, now lit up, and filled with a mixture of Thames Valley police and forensics officers. 'And when the local coppers turned up, they didn't have someone who could replace me until you guys arrived, and there was a lot of confusion as to why we were even on it.'

'They're not the only ones,' Declan commented. 'Why is it even with us?'

'Prime Ministerial remit,' Anjli replied. 'Remember? It's how we were explained to be in the Peak District during that whole duelling fiasco. Oh, wait, you were doing your own thing then, weren't you?'

She patted De'Geer's furry shoulder.

'Anyway, the remit states we can pick any case we want, as long as we have a connection. And this lad here? *He's* our connection.'

De'Geer grinned at this.

'I wouldn't worry about the furs and leather, Guv,' he said to Declan. 'The moment Doctor Marcos arrives, she'll have me in a PPE suit anyway, so nobody would know what I'm wearing underneath.'

'*I'd* know,' Declan moaned.

'Here's a thought,' Anjli leant closer, lowering her voice. 'If De'Geer's wearing that under his PPE, what does Doctor Marcos wear under *hers?*'

'Okay, time to stop now,' Declan almost placed his fingers into his ears and made *la la la* noises. 'De'Geer, tell us what we have.'

'It was the opening ceremony for the convention,' De'Geer replied. 'They have it at the end of the first day, so nobody misses it if they travel long distances, and it's a point where all the guests can be on stage.'

'And the guests are all related to this Robin Hood show you like?'

'All Robin Hood media,' De'Geer explained. 'TV shows, films, even audio dramas, anything with the characters in, are involved in this. It's more a *folklore* convention. There's three Robins here this weekend, but Montgomery Pryce was one of the principal guests, having played Robin Hood twice on TV.'

He pointed to the stage, which was really just a selection of two-foot-high blocks that raised the end of the ballroom. There, examining a rather visible bloodstain, the body long gone, were some forensics officers.

'During the speeches, Pryce came out unexpectedly,' De'Geer carried on. 'He always has this back and forth with the actor who plays the Sheriff in his show, and he continued that, I think.'

'You think?'

'I've seen it before during interview panels during other smaller conventions, but this time it seemed ... real,' De'Geer frowned. 'Like it wasn't an act. Anyway, Pryce walks out onto the front of the stage and then *shunk!* There's an arrow jutting out of his chest. Pretty much died instantly.'

'And where were you?'

'To the side, over there,' De'Geer pointed at the front right of the stage. 'We were going to announce a charity archery contest for the weekend.'

'Of course, you were,' Declan replied without thinking, turning the last word into a clearing of his throat. 'And the archer was at the back of the ballroom?'

'It looked that way, Guv,' De'Geer pointed at the back door. 'We saw a man with a bow, and he ran when the crowds went crazy. And it fits the direction the arrow came from.'

'Are all the attendees accounted for?' Declan looked around the ballroom. *There were a lot of chairs.*

'Most, mainly because the police put cars at the entrances to stop people from leaving,' De'Geer replied with what looked like a little disgust. 'But that's irrelevant now.'

'Why so?'

'Because the event organisers are carrying on with the convention,' De'Geer explained. 'They've moved some of the stage interviews tomorrow out of here, but they're still going to do photo sessions and signings.'

'You're bloody kidding me,' Anjli hissed. 'The ghouls—'

'It's not the organisers, it's the agents and managers,' De'Geer quickly interjected. 'Some of them are claiming if the show gets cancelled by the organisers, they have to still pay the guests' appearance fees, and once *one* guest gets that, then all will demand it, and that would bankrupt the organisers. So, they're calling the managers' bluff, seeing if the guests turn up to honour their commitments. If they don't, then they can hold payment legally as per the contract.'

'Great,' Declan looked back to the rear of the ballroom as he saw DCI Monroe and Doctor Marcos walk in, the latter already in her custom fitting grey PPE suit. 'So, we have a crime scene, and a murderer who could still attend the convention, thanks to an organiser–manager pissing contest.'

'Aye, it's a wonderful time to be living in,' Monroe, having heard the last part of Declan's comment, smiled. 'We get to solve a crime and hang around with outlaws! Swash buckling and all that!'

'God, not you as well,' Declan muttered, and was amused to see Doctor Marcos wince.

'He's been like this all-bloody journey,' she said. 'Bloody Errol Flynn quotes all the way.'

'Well, you sang the bloody "Hootenanny" song from the Disney film.'

'That's because it's the best version of Robin Hood,' Doctor Marcos sniffed.

She looked at De'Geer, finally realising what he was wearing.

'Your jerkin's the wrong colour,' she said mockingly. 'It should be Lincoln green. You're an embarrassment to the force, Morten. Put your PPE suit on and cover your hideous error.'

'Yes boss,' De'Geer grinned as he walked off.

Monroe looked at the stage for a moment before shaking his head.

'Bloody arrows now,' he muttered. 'Couldn't De'Geer have been into something else? Marvel movies, or *Star Trek*? Even *Doctor Who* would have meant we weren't pulled into this mess?'

'What do you want us to do?' Declan asked, ignoring Monroe's rant.

'I want statements from everyone on stage,' Monroe replied. 'Everyone was looking at them, and they were the only ones looking out at the back of the hall. Maybe one of them saw something.'

He looked around the ballroom.

'Cooper's arrived with some uniforms and they're working with the local force to gain statements from attendees, so DS Kapoor, see if anything's come out of that. And then see if we can find any CCTV.'

'And send it to Billy?'

'God no, lassie. The poor wee bugger's bringing his setup here,' Monroe smiled. 'All hands to the pump, so they say. If he's here, we can get information back quickly. So actually, after you've chatted to the security people, find a place he can set up an ops room. Preferably next to where the guests have their Green Room, so we can nick their sandwiches.'

Declan looked over at De'Geer, now pulling on his PPE suit.

'Are you sure he should be doing this?' he asked softly. 'He's a witness.'

'And a capable acting sergeant who's currently Doctor Marcos's assistant,' Monroe replied, his tone darkening as he spoke. 'So, unless you want to tell her he's not going to be assisting her as she looks for fletches on arrows and bowstrings with DNA, I'd suggest leaving him to it and seeing how he does.'

Reluctantly, Declan nodded.

'I'll start with the guests,' he said. 'What do you intend to do?'

'I'm going to have a wee chat with the organisers,' Monroe pursed his lips. 'You don't kill a man with an arrow for fun. This has to be personal. Someone wanted him to die on stage, and they risked killing a dozen people to do it.'

'How so?' Anjli asked.

'Because to take a shot from the back like that, and guarantee your target is taken out, rather than any of the gaggle of half-rate actors and has-beens behind him?' Monroe raised an eyebrow. 'That's some serious Robin Hood shite right there.'

He turned and walked off as Declan looked at Anjli.

'Looks like we're here for the duration,' he said. 'I hope someone's able to sort us a room.'

Anjli nodded her head, ever so subtly, towards the side of the ballroom, where a middle door was half open.

'You're interviewing guests, right?' she whispered. 'Well, one of them seems to be having a stand-up row over there with a volunteer.'

Declan looked over to the side. And indeed, there was a man, in his sixties, arguing with a woman in the green T-shirt of the event's volunteer staff. Nodding a farewell to Anjli,

Declan walked over to the couple who, seeing him approach, stopped their argument.

'DI Walsh,' Declan said, showing his ID. 'What seems to be the problem?'

'She won't let me check on my wife,' the man replied grumpily.

'Mister Gates is a guest of the convention, and the organiser has asked for everyone to assemble in the Green Room,' the volunteer tried to explain.

'I think you should listen to the lady, rather than walk around an active crime scene,' Declan replied.

'I know how to step around one of these,' the now identified Ryan Gates replied. 'And I've been waiting until I could speak to someone in charge, anyway.'

'Oh yes? And why's that?'

Gates pointed at the doorway at the back of the hall.

'Because I saw the bowman,' he said assuredly. 'And I think I saw him earlier, too.'

2

HUNT THE BOWMAN

'I HEARD YOU WERE IN THE MILITARY,' DECLAN SAID AS HE walked to the stage with Gates walking beside him. 'I was a redcap for ten years.'

'Royal Military Police? Hard bastards,' Gates grinned. 'Took me down a couple of times I went over the line.'

'You don't strike me as a squaddie,' Declan smiled in return, glancing Gates up and down. There was something about his manner that said he was something more. 'Special Forces?'

'Intelligence Corps,' Gates nodded. 'But they attached me to the Director Special Forces, working with the Special Reconnaissance Unit.'

Declan paused, staring at Ryan Gates.

'Hard bastards,' he said, repeating the compliment. 'You saw a lot of blood in Northern Ireland. Strange to find you here, amongst all this.'

'I was young,' Gates shrugged. 'When I got out, I was still in my twenties. Started working on sets as an advisor, which was in a way similar to what I'd been doing *before* I left, although militarily. Directors liked me, and that got me into "all this", as you say.'

He looked across at De'Geer, working with Doctor Marcos.

'And I wouldn't mock "all this", DI Walsh,' he suggested. 'One look at your Sergeant tells me there's more to the people than just childhood loves here.'

'Well, considering one of the people here's a murderer, you could be right.' Declan climbed onto the raised platform. 'Do you miss it?'

'Not really,' Gates smiled. 'I still do a little close-quarters protection here and there. Funny enough, Pryce asked me to do some recently, but it was more so they could see him with his old co-star waiting on him.'

'Yeah, I get that could be a bad image for the co-star.' Declan looked around the stage as he spoke. 'So, where were you standing?'

'Here,' Gates said, walking to the side. 'Pryce was right there, hands outstretched, gurning for the fans—'

'No love lost?'

'I think you'd be hard pressed to find anyone here who loved him,' Gates replied softly. 'Apart from the paying punters, that is.'

He pointed down the middle aisle.

'At the end are the doors,' he said. 'They're open now, but during the opening ceremony two of the three were closed. The middle one was open for stragglers, and probably for air circulation. Anyway, when Pryce was shot, there was a man at the doorway, a bow in his hand. He watched as Pryce turned and fell ... and then he ran.'

'You said you saw him earlier?'

'Yeah,' Gates nodded. 'He doesn't have a longbow, like the usual cosplayers do. He had a Hungarian recurved bow, like the Hungarian fighters used over a thousand years ago.'

'That doesn't sound very Robin Hood-y.'

Gates shrugged.

'A couple of the shows leant that way because they filmed in Eastern Europe, and the bows were cheap to buy and fix when they broke,' he explained. 'The BBC One show used one, I think, made by either Kassai or Grozer, both fine Hungarian bowyers, but they claimed in the story it was a Saracen bow. And we had the change in bows to a recurve halfway through season two when Robin's magical bow was destroyed by the Sheriff.'

'Cheaper to make?'

'Pryce hated the longbows, claimed it made him look small.'

'Could someone have used this bow to hit Pryce?' Declan was already measuring the distance by eye.

'It's not the bow, it's the arrow.' Gates was also measuring the distance, using his hands as a frame. 'The arrow which hit Pryce was a longbow arrow, so about thirty inches, that's about seventy centimetres in length, tip to tail. Which means the *draw weight* of the bow – the amount you can pull back – was also that.'

Gates stopped, looking up to the ceiling as he did the maths in his head.

'Depending on the draw weight of the bow, he could have struck a target anywhere from a hundred and fifty to two hundred metres away,' he decided. 'And this entire room isn't over seventy metres, tops.'

He frowned, considering this.

'Pryce wasn't armoured, though,' he continued. 'If he pulled the bow at its full weight, that arrow should have punched right through. It would have hit ...'

He stopped.

'You?' Declan asked, making a calculated guess.

'Yeah,' Gates replied, his voice more cautious now. 'Maybe Margot? Thank God for Pryce being in the way and stopping the bloody thing skewering us both.'

There was a moment of silence, punctuated by the conversations of the forensics team.

'You said you saw him earlier?' Declan asked.

At this, Gates's face brightened.

'Yeah,' he said, setting his jaw. 'Come with me.'

IT'D BEEN A SHORT WALK TO A HOTEL ROOM SUITE LABELLED 'PHOTOS B', and once in it, Declan saw a camera on a tripod, aimed at a long sheet of green material, stretched out on a frame and with two lights aimed from either side.

At the back of the room, pacing nervously, was a tall, thin old man, likely in his late sixties, wearing a red polo shirt and blue jeans, his dyed black hair pulled into a ponytail.

'Malcolm,' Gates smiled. 'You having a break?'

'Done,' Malcolm the cameraman shook his head, glancing back at the door as if expecting more to come in. 'Nobody's doing photos tonight. And to be honest, I'm only keeping everything up in case someone actually wants to carry on with this tomorrow.'

He nodded at Declan.

'Personal photo? You know we shouldn't.'

'One of the police investigating the murder,' Gates explained. 'I was hoping to look through some images.'

At this, Malcolm twitched visibly, and Declan frowned.

'You knew Pryce?'

'Here and there,' Malcolm replied. 'Sorry, I'm wired, I was there when it happened.'

Deciding he needed to defuse the situation a little, Declan stared at the green sheet.

'Why green?' he asked.

At this, Malcolm waved for him to stand in front of the green sheet, taking a photo on the camera attached to the tripod.

'Because of this,' he said proudly, waving Declan over to his laptop, where, on the screen, was a confused-looking Declan. 'The green screen means we can remove everything behind you and put a different image in. So, for example ...'

A click of a mouse and Declan was standing in a forest.

'You're now in Sherwood Forest.'

A second click, and the forest changed to a different one.

'Or you're in Sherwood Forest ...'

A third click, and a third image of a forest.

'Or even Sherwood Forest.'

Declan frowned.

'Why so many forests?' he scratched at his head.

Relaxing now, Malcolm grinned, clicking through the forest images once more.

'This forest is Burnham Beeches, near Shepperton Studios,' he explained as the first image paused behind Declan. '*Hooded Outlaw* and the Kevin Costner film both used this as Sherwood. This one is the Hampton Estate in Surrey, which Ridley Scott used as Sherwood for Russell Crowe's movie, and this one's in Hungary, where they filmed the BBC one in the 2000s.'

There was a fourth click, and now on the screen Declan stood, confused, in front of a cartoon jousting event.

'I even have the Disney film, if you so want it,' Malcolm continued with a hint of pride. 'I have them all, you know. This way, whichever show you've turned up for, whatever Robin, or Merry Man you want, I have the exact Sherwood Forest for you.'

Declan nodded, impressed.

'How long have you been doing this?'

'Photography? All my life,' Malcolm replied. 'As a hobby to start, then more professionally from my thirties and forties. And then I started doing these conventions about five, ten years back. Easy money, only work weekends, and the occasional Friday.'

He looked back to Gates, remembering there had to be a reason for the arrival.

'So, what did you want to look at?'

'Today's photo shoots,' Gates replied. 'I wanted—'

'Christ, Ryan, I took over a thousand photos today!' Malcolm exclaimed. 'I'm not going through all of them!'

'I did a photo shoot around two,' Gates added. 'And I did another earlier with Monty and Alex. I just want to see them.'

Malcolm sighed theatrically, opening up folders on his computer. One was labelled "HO Merry Men - Friday" and another "HO Scarlett - Friday"

'What's HO?' Declan asked, before replying 'Ah, wait. Hooded Outlaw.'

'It's because we have three Robins, two Will Scarlets, tomorrow we were supposed to get a second Sheriff ...'

Malcolm shrugged. 'Easier for me. These are the two shoots we did with Ryan today.'

Opening up the folders, Declan saw hundreds of thumbnails of photos appear on the screen.

'This is going to take hours,' he muttered. 'I can get our tech guy to create some kind of algorithm to—'

'It'll take five minutes,' Gates was already scanning through. 'Male and in costume, which wipes out all images with women, and images with people in modern clothes. Leaves about twenty-five percent of the images.'

Declan sighed and leant in with Gates, looking for men in costume as the file scrolled up. After a couple of minutes, and in the folder with the three *Hooded Outlaw* cast members, Gates paused.

'Him,' he said. 'That's the bugger.'

On the screen were Alex Hamilton, Ryan Gates and Montgomery Pryce, all with fixed smiles for the camera, and in the middle, smiling nervously, as if unsure why he was even there was a man in his late twenties or early thirties, wearing leather trousers and boots, a green tunic and a darker green hood, currently off his head for the picture, his blond hair and stubble visible as he smiled for the camera. In his right hand, a longbow arrow nocked in it, was a small, recurved bow.

'Yeah, that's a Hungarian recurved bow,' Gates commented. 'Looks just like the one we used in Season Four.'

'Can you zoom in on the face?' Declan asked Malcolm, who complied, filling the screen. Declan took a photo with his phone, immediately sending it to everyone on the team, explaining in the text as he did so that this was a potential murderer, according to a witness.

He was about to turn away when another thumbnail caught his eye.

'What's that folder?' he asked.

At this, Malcolm closed the lid.

'Anyway, I hope you get—' he started, but Declan placed a hand on the lid of the laptop.

'Open it up before I arrest you for obstructing an investigation,' he said politely, but firmly. With incredible reluctance, Malcolm opened the laptop, and Declan saw the folder appear on the screen.

'You took *crime scene photos?*' he asked as he scanned through the images. There were photos of the stage, of the body of Montgomery Pryce, of the arrow ...

'I used to be a crime scene photographer,' Malcolm insisted. 'I knew where to stand, what not to touch. I was in the ballroom taking shots of the opening ceremony anyway, so I thought I'd help.'

'And what were you intending to do with these?' Declan asked, holding up a hand to stop Malcolm from immediately replying. 'And don't tell me you were going to give them to us, because a second ago you were hiding them from me.'

Malcolm nodded, embarrassed.

'I didn't know what to do with them,' he said, placing an SD card into the laptop and pulling the images across onto it. 'I got caught up in the moment. Remembered what it was like, you know?'

'Why did you stop?' Declan accepted the SD card as Malcolm pulled it out and passed it to him.

'They said I was too old,' he muttered. 'Said I didn't have the eye for detail. But I proved them wrong.'

'How so?' Declan frowned. 'In the photos?'

Now invigorated, Malcolm opened up an image, taken

from the crime scene earlier of the arrow, protruding out of Montgomery's chest. It wasn't as graphic as it could have been, however, as it focused mainly on the end of the arrow, the feathers lit up by the camera's flash, speckled with blood spatter.

'Here,' Malcolm leant back, folding his arms. 'Bet none of your plod work that out.'

Declan stared at the arrow.

'That it's an arrow?'

'No,' Gates was nodding now. 'Yeah, I can see that. Nice catch, Malcolm.'

'Okay, so one of you has to explain this to me, or I'm going to start arresting you,' Declan snapped.

Gates nodded.

'There are a couple of fantasy novels that use similar, and a few RPGs, role-playing games, set in the medieval or fantasy world use it too, even old folklores that fletchings on arrows can pass messages without actual messages being attached. Colours of the feathers, or the positioning of the cord, notches in the shaft, all that sort of thing.'

'Is this something from history?' Declan asked. 'Something like "we need some milk" or "help help they're sticking two fingers up at us?"'

'Nah, from what I've found, it's pretty much bollocks in the real world, purely the stuff of legends,' Gates smiled. 'Most fletchings would have been natural feather colours since arrows were expendable ammunition, so why spend extra time and money on something that would be lost or destroyed quickly?'

'Because you're sending an important message?'

'And there you have it.' Malcolm's smile was irritating

Declan now. '*The romanticism of the outlaw's tale*. They used it in the seventies show, and briefly in *Hooded Outlaw*.'

'Why only briefly?'

'You'd have to ask the director, Robert Standish,' Malcolm clicked his tongue against his teeth. 'He's here this weekend, so it shouldn't be hard. But he was one of the creators of *Hooded Outlaw*, so he'd know.'

'Okay then, what message is this arrow stating?' Declan asked as he wrote the name in his notebook.

'It was used in the show, but only in one episode,' Gates replied. 'It was a plot hammer to get some exposition out there when we couldn't do it in other ways. Think of it as similar to semaphore on a ship. White was the base colour of goose feathers, but green on one fletch could mean danger. If the fletches were cut in a particular way, it could mean other things. There was an entire list of things, but we only used a couple of them in the end. I remember the production manager, Peter Crock, being pissed when it was scrapped. He spent months on this, and Monty tossed it all away because he kept improvising scripts, as he was too stupid to learn the lines.'

He trailed off as he stared at the arrow.

'The fletch has been notched out,' he pointed. 'Just here. And there's a line of red along the base, see?'

'Okay,' Declan leant in now. 'So, explain to me what these two things together tell you. What message is the killer sending, other than "I want to shoot an arrow into your chest", which we already know?'

'The message on this arrow was used in the episode "*Pretender To The King*", and means "Imposter",' Malcolm said, rising from his chair. 'Basically, someone out there shot

Monty Pryce with an arrow that claimed he wasn't who he said he was.'

'He's an actor.' Declan straightened to match Malcolm. 'Surely that's pretty much all actors?'

'Yeah, but Prycey? He was a lying shite who was always talking bollocks and making up stories,' Gates admitted. 'Maybe he'd claimed one too many lies?'

Declan opened up the phone, staring at the image of the blond-haired man.

'I wonder what lie turned this man from a smiling fan into a murderer?' he mused.

3

MANAGEMENT

While Declan had wandered off to speak with Ryan Gates in the photo room, Anjli had decided to go with Monroe to the Green Room, and hopefully speak to some of the other guests. Now, gone eight in the evening, the hotel had calmed down. They had taken the body of Pryce to a local morgue, and Doctor Marcos had said she'd visit it later, the cause of death being quite obvious for the moment. However, with the convention still technically going on, and with the cast tied down with appearance contracts, the attendees had decided to have some kind of wake for Pryce in the hotel bar.

The guests, meanwhile, hadn't seemed to want to join them.

'Why do they call it a Green Room?' Anjli asked as they walked down a hotel corridor. 'You know, the room where guests congregate?'

'Nobody knows, lassie,' Monroe replied knowledgeably. 'Some stories say it was because early actors rooms were painted green, others say "greengage" is Cockney rhyming slang for a stage ... maybe it's a calming colour, and those poor thespians were stressed out, or where the trainees and understudies hung out, so the green actors' room?'

Anjli chuckled.

'You seem to know a lot about this,' she raised an eyebrow. 'Was a future on the stage in your cards?'

'No, but Emilia was into Amateur Dramatics for a while,' Monroe replied casually, and the name of his ex-wife appearing surprised Anjli.

Monroe noticed this and grinned.

'She may have deleted me from her life all those years ago, but I never deleted her from mine,' he explained. 'And I do have an interest in the theatrical, so to speak.'

'I'd never have guessed.' Anjli grinned back at her boss, but the smile faded as an angry-looking woman stormed towards them. Slim with grey bobbed hair and thick-rimmed glasses, she looked like Velma from Scooby Doo if she'd got old, and her tweed jacket and jeans gave her the look of a country squire's wife.

'You're police, right?' she said by introduction. 'You running this show?'

'As much as it can be called a show, aye,' Monroe replied calmly. 'DCI Monroe, this is DS Kapoor. City Police.'

'City Police? As in London?' the woman was confused at this. 'Not Thames Valley?'

Monroe raised an eyebrow.

'Does it matter which police solve this murder?'

'I suppose not. Flick McCarthy, of McCarthy Premier Management,' the woman, now identified as Flick, held a hand out, almost shoving it at Monroe to shake. 'I represent some of the talent here.'

'Oh, so you're their agent?' Anjli asked but was surprised to see Flick scowl.

'God no,' she almost spat. 'Acting agents? Those useless bastards can't do anything for these clients unless it's daytime TV or rep theatre. Maybe a pantomime. Unless you're bloody reality TV or under thirty, TV companies don't want to know.'

She drew herself up higher.

'I specialise in personal management, booking celebrities and personalities into comic cons, nightclubs, private functions, all that sort of thing.'

'Gotcha,' Monroe nodded. 'So, you're the reason these guys are here, so to speak?'

'A couple, sure,' Flick nodded. 'I deal with Nigel Cummings—'

'I'll stop you there,' Monroe raised a hand. 'You can give me all the names you want, but I don't have a clue who they are. Sorry.'

'That's alright,' Flick actually smiled at this. 'Most people don't. Nigel played the Sheriff. I also deal – *dealt* – with Monty Pryce, Robin Hood. Alex Hamilton, who played Little John and Robert Standish, the director, are also my clients. And I cover a couple of the film guests, but I'm guessing they're not important to your enquiries.'

'Why?' Anjli asked.

'Because Monty was hated by pretty much everyone he worked with, and *those* people never worked with him. Ergo, they wouldn't want to kill him. Well, yet anyway. The weekend was still early.'

'Who do you think killed him?' Monroe asked. 'If everyone's a suspect?'

'Well, they're not, are they?' Flick frowned. 'I mean, half the cast was behind him when he was shot.'

'Fair point,' Monroe smiled. 'By the way, you came towards us with a purpose. Can I ask what it was?'

'Oh, yes, absolutely,' Flick flushed. 'I want you to tell the organisers they need to close the convention down. My clients can't work during this. Their friend and colleague was just killed.'

'But you said they hated him,' Anjli contested.

'Oh, I'm sure they all did,' Monroe smiled. 'What Miss ... Mrs—'

'*Ms*,' Flick hastily interjected, forcing a smile.

'What *Ms* McCarthy here is trying to carefully insinuate is that if the convention is cancelled, her clients get paid in full, and don't have to spend the weekend here,' Monroe looked at Flick. 'Am I correct?'

'They claim if they cancel, the insurance won't pay out and they'll have to refund everyone, which means they can't pay us,' Flick sniffed. 'If the punters leave of their own accord, that's not on them. But to make sure they do this ...'

'The convention stays open,' Monroe nodded. 'Look, I am sorry, but we'd be asking your clients to stay until we've questioned them anyway, so they might as well make some money. We're all in here until we get some answers.'

'Well, if there's any way I can help, DCI Monroe, please let me know,' Flick forced another smile, somewhat coquettishly as she turned and walked off.

Watching her, Monroe felt rather than saw Anjli quietly chuckling.

'What?' he growled.

'She fancies you,' Anjli replied. 'It was so obvious.'

'What's so surprising about that?' Monroe enquired with an over-politeness that immediately warned Anjli.

'Nothing,' she said, holding her hands up. 'I was just wondering how exactly Doctor Marcos is going to murder her once she finds out.'

'Hmm. Fair point,' Monroe scratched at his beard. 'Maybe we don't tell her.'

'Good luck with that.' Anjli started off towards the Green Room once more. 'One look and she'll guess. Do you think the manager was right, though?'

'On what?'

'That the likely suspects are the ones who were standing behind Pryce, and that everyone who met him hated him?'

'I don't know,' Monroe admitted. 'She's been doing conventions with him, so she must like him a little.'

'Or she likes the ten percent she gets from him,' Anjli suggested, trying the Green Room door. 'Ah. Locked. I suppose we were hopeful to find it still open.'

There was a door to the side of the corridor, and Monroe tried that, smiling when it opened.

'Aha,' he said. 'Maybe we can find a second Green Room?'

THE ROOM THEY NOW ENTERED WAS LARGE AND OPEN PLAN, AND held about fifteen mannequins inside it, all with costumes displayed on them, apart from two at the end, which were either surplus to requirements, or yet to be dressed. In the middle of the side wall was a weapons display, with a selection of vicious looking swords, axes and spears, and a couple of armoured helmets.

'I'm guessing these are the show costumes?' Monroe

clicked his tongue against the top of his mouth, a sure sign he was considering something, as he walked around them. 'There are no names, so I don't know who—'

'That's the Sheriff's costume from *Hooded Outlaw*,' a male voice spoke now, and Anjli spun to find a short, slim, bald man in a checked shirt standing in the doorway.

'And you'd know this how?' she raised an eyebrow.

'Because I was the man who wore it,' the man walked in, holding out his hand. 'Nigel Cummings. I played the Sheriff.'

'Never watched it,' Anjli admitted as she shook his hand. 'But you look familiar.'

'As a police officer, do you watch crime shows on television?' Nigel asked with a wry grin. '*Midsomer Murders*? I've been killed four times on that. I was a murderer on *Morse*, too.'

Anjli's eyes widened.

'You were the hatchet man!' she exclaimed in delight. 'I loved that episode!'

'Hatchet man? That's what I'm known as? Oh God,' Nigel looked genuinely pained to hear this. 'Of course, I'm glad you enjoyed it, but I was hoping to be remembered more than just for the scene where I waved a rubber axe around.'

'Can you tell us about the other costumes?' Monroe asked, diverting the conversation back to the convention.

Nigel nodded, waving at the right-hand side of the room.

'Don't have a clue about those,' he admitted. 'There's a couple from the ITV show, the guy with the antlers? Herne the Hunter, on loan from Nottingham Council. The costume beside it? The more recent BBC Robin Hood, and then the one beside that is from the Patrick Bergin movie. Came out at the same time as Costner's and was far more honest to the source material. I was up for the role of the father – you know, in Costner's version, that is – but bloody Brian Blessed was always going to get it.'

He waved back to the costumes on the left-hand side of the room.

'So that one is mine, as I've already said, bloody terrible string mail for the first series, but then some nice aluminium mail for the second onward, then you have Marian's dress, for the three and a half seasons she was in it—'

'Marian was only in it for three and a half seasons?' Monroe asked. 'How many seasons did it last?'

'Four,' Nigel sniffed. 'Margot got the nod for Hollywood, so left. Personally, she couldn't stand to be near Pryce anymore. So, she asked to go be a nun, like in the legends, but he demanded she die of syphilis. In the end, I killed her, five eps before the finale. Funnily enough, they did similar with the more recent BBC show, but ITV killed one of the Robins instead, and replaced him. We're all interchangeable, you know.'

He stroked his old costume.

'Amusingly, the one character that always had a legal reason for changing an actor was the Sheriff, as it was a role, not a person, but we always stayed through to the end.'

'Did losing Marian kill the show?' Monroe was examining a hooded green outfit.

'Pretty much,' Nigel nodded. 'They tried to bring in this new character, Lady Eleanor – think "Milady" from the *Three Musketeers* and turn her into a medieval woman – as a replacement love interest, but after the season four finale Pryce demanded she never appear in the show again, and that was what killed it.'

'He didn't like her?'

'Oh, I think he liked her a little too much, and she turned

him down.' Nigel waggled his eyebrows. 'At least Margot was clever enough to lead him on until she got what she needed from the show.'

He pointed at the next one along, placed on a slightly taller mannequin.

'That was Little John's tunic and pouch, but it's not completely screen accurate, as it doesn't have prescription painkillers hidden in it,' Nigel chuckled. 'Sorry, poor joke.'

'I saw online Alex Hamilton was possibly banned from America for possession of those,' Anjli replied. 'Sounds like there's a little truth to the rumour?'

'Oh, there's more than a little,' Nigel wasn't chuckling anymore. 'The dopey bastard started selling opioids out there. *Hydrocodone-Acetaminophen*, in particular.'

'That's pretty specific. Sounds like you know your painkillers,' Anjli noted this down.

'I know *that* painkiller,' Nigel replied icily, but didn't continue. Anjli assumed, as an actor, he'd known someone who'd been addicted.

'Is this the Robin costume?' Monroe pointed at the mannequin he'd been looking at; leather trousers, a green suede tunic and hood, with a quiver of arrows behind, the white goose feathers just poking out, and a recurve bow in the mannequin's hand.

'Yes, but the bow's a reproduction of the second bow we used in the show, stuck in there for the look,' Nigel waved across to the weapons. 'They're all real, though. All screen-used props. We even have the longbow too, the magic one, but some prats broke the horn notch at the top last night, so it can't be strung right now.'

'Surely *that* wasn't used in the show, though?' Anjli had walked over to the other side of the room, where a yellow-handled gun with a long, metallic-blue tube was on a display stand. It had other, weird metal cogs and tubes welded to it, but none of these seemed to do anything.

'Oh, that's not from our shows,' Nigel nodded. 'That's Ryan Gates. He did a Steampunk *Moby Dick* prequel, set in a contemporary setting about fifteen years back. He played Ahab, and that was his screen-used weapon. It's a vintage Nemrod Corbeta speargun.'

'You seem to know your guns, too?' Anjli looked back.

'It's been at every sodding convention he's been to,' Nigel replied. 'His wife insists on it. It's the show they met on.'

'Does it work?'

'Probably not. All those cogs would have gummed it up, and it's not had a compression in decades,' Nigel went to leave the room. 'I remember Ryan saying there was a special lock on it, so it wouldn't go off in shoots, but knowing him, it's just squaddie bollocks. Anyway, I only came in because I heard talking. Nobody's supposed to be in here, and I was about to lock it up. Last night when we set this all up, some of the bar staff wandered in and were buggering around with Excalibur.'

'The same bar staff broke the bow?' Anjli looked back at Robin, as if expecting to see it there.

Nigel's face darkened.

'Yeah. The bar manager wasn't impressed with them when he learned what the repair bill was, either. It's a few hundred quid to get it done properly.'

'Did you say Excalibur?' Monroe held up a hand. 'Surely that's King Arthur?'

'Oh, absolutely, but they used every bloody myth in the series,' Nigel smiled sadly. 'We raped whatever folklore we could for a viewing figure.'

Nodding at this and ignoring the visual, Monroe and Anjli followed Nigel out of the room.

'Did you know Pryce well?' Monroe asked. 'Outside of the show?'

'God no,' Nigel shook his head. 'And if I didn't need to pay my mortgage, I wouldn't be here with him. Best thing the bugger did in years was die.'

He paled.

'Not that I wanted him dead,' he stammered. 'It's just that—'

'We know,' Anjli soothed. 'Everyone he met hated him.'

'Pretty much,' Nigel smiled, locking the door.

'Who has keys to this?' Monroe frowned. 'Surely you shouldn't have to do this?'

'Oh, didn't I mention?' Nigel made a self-deprecating half-smile. 'The *Hooded Outlaw* props and costumes in there? I own them.'

He placed the key in his pocket as he continued.

'I have quite a collection, you see. All the shows I've been in, I try to keep something. But with this show, I found a job lot of costumes at Angels, the costumers, around ten years ago. And, seeing how the conventions were becoming bigger, I invested in them. They were renting them out to stag parties for Christ's sake. Cost me a few grand, but I've made use of them. Even took them to America a couple of times. The Yanks eat this shit up like candy.'

'Have you made your money back?' Anjli followed Nigel as he started walking back towards the main bar.

'Not quite yet,' Nigel smiled. 'But I reckon Pryce's costume just rocketed in value.'

Monroe was about to reply to this when his phone buzzed.

'Aye?' he said as he answered it.

'Sir, it's Cooper,' the voice down the line spoke. 'We've found the man DI Walsh sent. He's in the bar.'

'Is he now?' Monroe smiled darkly. 'Then let's go have a chat with this wee fella and maybe get off home before midnight.'

Nodding to Nigel, Monroe and Anjli walked off back towards the hotel reception and bar. Watching them, Nigel allowed his smile to slowly fade away, until his face was totally emotionless.

He hadn't wanted to speak to the police so early in the case, but he couldn't let them wander around the props unguarded.

He couldn't let them find out yet.

Luckily, he'd arrived just in time. Taking a deep breath, releasing it and shaking the tension out of his shoulders, he turned and walked towards the corridor that led to the hotel room elevators.

———

SAM HARDY SAT IN THE BAR AND NURSED HIS PINT, STILL IN shock as to what had happened that evening. He wasn't alone, as most of the attendees had congregated in the bar, some of whom, the Pryce fans, were holding a makeshift vigil for the dead man.

Sam had tried to leave after the ceremony ended in such a final way, walking calmly with the others as they went to their rooms. His room had been booked for the weekend and his bags were still mostly unpacked, having only arrived that morning, and he hoped the hotel would let him check out quickly, so he could be on the road before the police arrived.

Unfortunately, the police had already been there, it seemed. And, while in a queue to check out, the police had stopped everyone from leaving, locking down the hotel with immediate effect.

Sam had placed everything back in his room and, removing his costume, he'd thrown on a T-shirt and jeans before heading down to the bar. His plan was to blend in with everyone, but at the same time, keep to himself. If the surrounding people knew who he was, then it wouldn't be a quiet drink, that was for sure.

Sam shuddered as he sipped his pint. He had a plan, but he hadn't been able to complete it. He needed to speak to Alex to see if they could get out of this before it came out. And, if the event, as rumoured, was still going ahead, then there was every chance, if he kept to himself, that they could. Alex would understand. After all, everything was gone now, and then he could—

He looked up, as a white-haired man with a trimmed white goatee smiled down at him.

'You've changed,' he said conversationally. 'Probably a good idea.'

'Do I know you?' Sam asked.

The man, as if realising an error, slapped his forehead.

'Aye, I forget to tell people sometimes,' he admitted. 'I'm Detective Chief Inspector Alex Monroe, City of London Police.'

Smiling, he turned his phone around to show an image of Sam's face.

'And we'd like to have a little chat with you, sonny.'

'I'm having a drink,' Sam replied haughtily. 'Come back when—'

'I could just arrest you,' Monroe said, leaning in. 'Would you prefer that?'

Swallowing, and feeling his stomach flip-flop, Sam forced a smile as he placed his pint aside and stood up.

They knew.

'Of course not,' he said, waving Monroe ahead, noting the other police officers watching him from the exits. 'Let's go chat and see how I can help.'

4

TENSION STRENGTH

Billy had taken over a meeting room to the back of the hotel, and over the last hour had wired in everything he needed: three monitors connected to two portable police desktops, handily enclosed in black hard cases, two printers, one extra laptop with two hubs for various USB drives, one keyboard, one mouse and a mouse pad that showed an image of Chris Evans – the actor who played Captain America, not the DJ – shirtless, on a beach.

He hadn't asked for this. Anjli had bought him it as a joke present last Christmas, and his complete and utter stubbornness at not being the first to back down meant he still used it.

He didn't know if his present to her, a 2022 calendar of sexy Catholic priests was still being used, if at all, but considering she lived with Declan, he'd probably cut the pictures out and taped them to punchbags. After all, it was why he ended up in the Last Chance Saloon in the first place, when a Catholic priest arrested by Declan for dog-trafficking told him, live on air, that Jess, his then-fifteen-year-old daughter would go to hell now as a punishment for Declan arresting him.

Billy would have punched him, too.

As Billy considered this, Declan walked into the room, pausing as he saw the setup.

'Are those cases ...' he started, trailing off.

Billy nodded.

'Like the ones in the *Justice* case?' he asked, referencing an investigation into murders of serial killers the team had worked on around a month earlier. 'They're the same ones. Well, the same models, as the originals, you know, had bits of people in them.'

'And you stared at these hideous murder boxes and thought, "You know what? These would be brilliant for taking my computers out for trips" and all that?'

'In fairness, they're used by tour crews and roadies for taking expensive kit around the world, so why not?' Billy smiled. 'Don't tell me you've never considered a real-world application for something you've seen in a case.'

Declan sighed, deciding not to continue the conversation, instead passing the SD card over.

'Photos of the murder scene by the convention photographer,' he explained. 'Apparently, he used to be a crime scene snapper.'

Billy went to answer this, but stopped as his phone, face down on the table, vibrated.

The two of them stared silently at the vibrating phone.

After a few seconds, it went to voicemail.

'Didn't you need to take that?' Declan asked. 'You don't know who it was.'

'I know,' Billy leant back in his chair. 'It's Andrade. He's been calling all evening. We were supposed to be going to

Brighton this weekend, but now I'm in Milton Keynes and he can't work out why I get to be in a hotel while he doesn't.'

'I know the feeling,' Declan smiled. 'I have the same with Jess. I'm supposed to have her over for the weekend ...'

His face paled.

'You forgot to tell her or Liz, didn't you?' Billy shook his head in mock condescension. 'It's nine pm. She'll be sitting in your house, waiting for you.'

He tutted.

'A sixteen-year-old girl, in her empty father's house, with only a few college-aged friends in the area she knows ... your house is going to be a war zone.'

'Shit,' Declan pulled his phone out. 'Tell you what, let's make a deal. You can bring Andrade if I can bring Jess.'

'Bring Jess, she can help me,' Billy pushed his phone away. 'Andrade needs to learn his boundaries.'

'Sounds like things between you two aren't all bunnies and roses,' Declan replied. 'You want to talk about it?'

'Honeymoon period isn't so honeymoon right now,' Billy shrugged, already going through the images on the SD card. 'He's busy with some work event. I'm working long hours. It was always going to have tough moments.'

Declan observed Billy.

'What's the actual issue here?' he asked.

'It's September,' Billy sighed. 'And Andrade returns to Colombia at the end of the year. He was only here for a six-month tour of duty.'

'I think that's what soldiers do.'

'Well, whatever you call it,' Billy muttered. 'New Year's Day, he's gone. Unless I go with him.'

Declan straightened at this.

'You've spoken about that?'

Billy pursed his lips.

'Yeah, but it's untenable. He's a diplomat. He'll be sent to a new place. And I can't keep changing locations every six months. It just won't work.'

Declan went to reply as the door opened, and Monroe walked in, the blond man Declan had seen a photo of walking in behind him, with Anjli and Cooper holding up the rear.

'Guv, I might have a problem,' Declan said softly to Monroe as Anjli placed the blond man on a chair at the end of the table. 'I'm supposed to be looking after Jess this weekend. Should I get her to come here?'

'Hold on that,' Monroe replied, watching the man. 'If matey here confesses, we might have this tied up and over in an hour.'

'I didn't kill him,' the man complained.

'This is Sam Hardy,' Anjli explained. 'Acting Sergeant De'Geer is going to his room as we speak, to grab his bow and arrows.'

'Phrases I never thought I'd have to hear in this business,' Declan sighed.

'Sam here tried to check out immediately after the murder,' Anjli continued. 'And, when refused because of the lockdown, he changed out of his costume and hid in a corner of the bar.'

'I was having a pint,' Sam muttered. 'I'm allowed to have a drink.'

'No, there were a lot of people drinking, mourning the loss of Montgomery Pryce,' Monroe replied. 'However, you didn't want to join them.'

'I don't know them.'

'Aren't they – how do people say it – aren't they your

tribe?' Monroe continued. 'Surely they love the same things as you?'

'No.'

It was soft, but final. A statement rather than a reply. Sam stared at the ground.

'Is this an interview? If it's an interview, you should take me to a police station. I should have my solicitor present.'

'It's a conversation right now,' Monroe leant over the table. 'But if you'd like it to be more, I'm sure we could arrange that, laddie.'

Sam Hardy glared up at Monroe.

'I'm not your "laddie", old man,' he snapped. 'I didn't kill Monty, and I wanted to leave—'

He stopped himself before continuing.

'Go on,' Anjli moved in now. 'You wanted to leave before something happened? You were discovered, perhaps?'

Declan was watching the interview, but something seemed off.

'You didn't kill him, did you?' he asked softly. 'I saw the photo of you, Hamilton, Ryan, and Montgomery. You were happy, but almost confused why you were there. Like you hadn't intended to be.'

'I don't like the show,' Sam muttered.

'Then why come?'

'I had my reasons.'

'Was it to kill Montgomery Pryce?'

'No!' Sam looked pained to even consider it. Declan was about to ask another question when the door opened and De'Geer, now out of his PPE and costume, and wearing his spare police uniform – one Cooper had brought for him from Temple Inn – walked into the room with a curved bow and a sheath of longbow arrows in his latex gloved hands.

'These were in his room,' he said. Billy, pulling up the image of Sam from earlier, nodded as he looked back at the bow.

'That's the right bow,' he said.

'I've been told on good authority it's a Hungarian recurved bow, made famous by artisans like Grozer,' Declan said, as De'Geer placed the bow onto the table. 'I've also been told it can shoot someone easily at a hundred and fifty to two hundred metres, which is further than the arrow you fired travelled.'

'You don't fire an arrow, Guv,' De'Geer whispered. 'You loose—'

He stopped as Declan glared across at him.

'You can't shoot someone with that bow, anyway,' Sam stated, looking up. 'That's a Larp bow and only has a drawing weight of twenty-five pounds. The bows in the show could do fifty.'

'What's a larp bow?' Monroe frowned.

'*Live action role play,* sir,' De'Geer replied. 'It's like *Dungeons and Dragons*, but instead of rolling dice, you hit people with foam weapons.'

'Sounds a bit wimpy,' Declan replied. 'Nerf swords and—'

'Sorry Guv, they're not like Nerf weapons,' De'Geer said defensively, and Declan knew without a doubt the Viking officer had used one at some point. 'They're foam, but with a glass fibre core. If you don't pull your shot, you can really do someone in. There's a lot of concussion injuries at these events.'

'And the arrows?'

'Ah, well, you loose arrows with foam heads,' De'Geer admitted. 'These aren't as painful, as the lower draw weight means they bounce off without hurting. Mostly. If you really go for it, though, you can do some serious bruising.'

He frowned.

'Although, the arrows aren't right here,' he added. 'These have white and yellow fletches, and they're plastic. The one that ... well, the one used? It was definitely goose feather.'

'And this was the only bow there?'

'Yes.'

Monroe frowned, considering this.

'Right then,' he motioned for Sam to rise from the chair. 'Let's go to an archery contest.'

IT WAS CLOSE TO TEN PM BY THE TIME THE TEAM, WITH SAM walking with them, entered the ballroom, closing the door behind them, to stop any curious attendees watching. Sam held the bow in his hand nervously but didn't have any arrows. Monroe had deemed it safer, in case he was the actual murderer, a theory that was getting weaker as the evening went on.

'Okay,' Monroe said, stopping Sam in front of the door. 'You were on the other side of the door, watching in, right?'

Sam nodded nervously. Monroe worked out the distance from the other side of the door to where Sam now stood.

'So, about three feet, give or take? We'll add that into consideration.'

He now looked over to the stage, the other end of the ballroom and a good seventy metres away where, with De'Geer's help, Anjli was positioning one of the bare mannequins onto the stage, Nigel Cummings glaring at them as they did this.

'If you damage it, I won't get my deposit back,' he moaned.

'If we damage it, you can bill us for it,' Anjli replied, and at this, Nigel smiled.

'Oh, well, that's all right then,' he said. 'He was a little further forward—'

'We know,' Anjli pointed at the floor, where, amongst the bloodstains, was a small yellow stand with a number on it. 'The body was there. He spun around, crumpled to his knees and fell backwards, so lose a foot's worth of distance ...'

She stopped, staring over at the others.

'Will this do?' she shouted.

'It's not an exact measurement, but it'll do what's needed,' Doctor Marcos replied, walking to the side of the stage. 'I'd suggest you both move away.'

As Anjli and De'Geer left the mannequin alone on the stage, walking over to Nigel, Anjli looked at his jeans.

'Your knees are dirty,' she said. 'You've got grass stains.'

'I've been praying,' Nigel shrugged. 'Good for the soul. And my clothes aren't as soiled as Monty's are, I'm sure.'

He stopped speaking as a sudden thought came to mind.

'Hey,' he breathed. 'Do you think they'll let me buy the clothes he was wearing? Tonight?'

'The ones he died in?'

'Exactly,' Nigel replied with no hint of humour or irony. 'They'd be a definite addition.'

'We're ready to do this whenever you want.' Ignoring Nigel, Anjli looked to the back of the hall. 'The quicker the better.'

Nodding at this, Monroe passed Sam one arrow they'd taken from his room.

'Go on, ladd-*son*,' he said, remembering not to use "laddie". 'And know that if we think you're not doing your best, we'll arrest you anyway.'

Nodding and licking his dry lips, Sam pulled the bow back, the arrow notched into the string as he raised the tip to aim directly at the mannequin.

'Here goes nothing,' he whispered as he loosed the arrow, and the others in the ballroom watched as it sailed across the space for around thirty metres before falling to the carpeted floor.

'See?' Sam looked around. 'The draw's not enough. If I even wanted to get remotely close to the stage, I'd have to angle it.'

'Okay, do a second one,' Monroe passed another arrow. 'And this time, angle it.'

Nocking the arrow fletches to the string once more, Sam settled his nerves, repositioned his grip on the bow, and pulled the string back as far as he could. Then, angling upwards, he loosed the arrow up into the ceiling of the ballroom.

The arrow didn't hit the ceiling though; instead, it rose up and down in a lazy arc, covering the distance and striking the mannequin. However, it had lost so much momentum and force by then, it simply bounced off the figure without piercing.

'No way that would have killed Montgomery Pryce.' Doctor Marcos was already at the mannequin, checking it over. 'Didn't make a single dent. And, even if it did, the arrow's trajectory would have come from an upward angle, which doesn't match what happened with Pryce, because that arrow was jutting straight out.'

'So, it wasn't this bow,' Declan said, taking the bow from

the now grateful Sam and examining it. 'We need to find someone else with one.'

'Laddie, I don't know if you noticed, but half the bloody people here are carrying bows,' Monroe hissed. 'That's not including the people who may have already left before we could stop them.'

The archery contest over, Monroe glared at Sam.

'So, now we know you didn't shoot Pryce, would you like to tell us what the hell is going on?'

'I don't know what you mean—' Sam protested again, but by now Anjli, De'Geer and Nigel had walked over.

'You might as well come clean,' Anjli said. 'It'll come out later, anyway.'

Sam took a deep breath, and then let it out in a resigned sigh.

'Montgomery Pryce was my father,' he replied. 'My mum was Carol Hardy.'

'Lady Eleanor?' Nigel was surprised at this. Noting the confused expressions, he added, 'The one they tried to replace Margot with.'

Sam nodded at this.

'I thought Pryce petitioned to have her fired?' Anjli asked, frowning.

'He did,' Sam looked back at the stage, as if expecting to see the shade of Montgomery Pryce watching them. 'Once he had his way with mum, he didn't need her anymore. And nobody wants a pregnant romantic lead, especially the bastard who got her that way.'

'Did he ever know, though?' Declan asked Sam, who shrugged.

'Mum never contacted him, so she never said anything, but he had to, you know?' he explained. 'I didn't learn of it until I turned eighteen. But by then I had a step-dad I loved, and I didn't want to look for him. He'd never looked for me, and he treated Mum like shit back then.'

'You're aware this could also be grounds for motive for killing him?' Anjli replied. 'He never looked for you, and so you demanded revenge?'

Sam looked horrified for a long moment, but then nodded.

'Yeah, I can see that,' he eventually said.

'I don't understand,' Declan muttered, half to himself. 'Why didn't you just tell us? Why act so guilty?'

Sam blushed.

'I thought you were after me for something else,' he whispered, looking up at the officers. 'I'm really sorry. But they became really popular.'

'What did?' Anjli asked, confused.

Sam took another deep breath, steadied himself, and then told them.

5

CHECK IN TIME

'Slash fic?' Billy exclaimed with delight. 'He wrote slash fiction?'

'Apparently so, if that's the right name for them.' Declan sat on a chair, feet up on the table as he stared at his phone. 'Sheriff and Robin, mainly. There's one with the Sheriff and Will, and hints of a Robin and Little John frisson, too. Always same sex, always … explicit.'

'Fifty shades of Lincoln green,' Anjli chuckled. 'Apparently, Sam started writing them about five years ago, and put them online on forums related to this sort of stuff. Surprisingly it's super popular. People actually commissioned "Samantha" to write specialised novels for them.'

'Samantha?'

'It seems more people bought them if they thought it was a woman writing,' Declan placed the phone down. 'Anyway, Sam thought we were arresting him for pornography laws, and he also thought the BBC were about to come down on him for writing x-rated stories about licensed family-show characters.'

'Although he wasn't,' De'Geer was standing in the corner as he spoke. 'Sam never used the BBC characters as such, just the names from legends.'

'And you know this how?' Anjli spun to face the acting-Sergeant, a smile on her lips.

'I've been doing the folklore conventions for years,' De'Geer replied stoically. 'Everyone's heard of *Samantha Hardly*, the name he used.'

'Oh,' Anjli looked unimpressed. 'I wondered whether you were a secret fan.'

'No, sorry,' De'Geer grinned. 'No shipping from me.'

'Shipping is when you take two popular characters—' Billy started explaining to Declan but was waved silent.

'I really don't need to know,' Declan said. 'But if Sam isn't the killer, we're back to square one. Looks like we're here for the night.'

'We've sorted some double rooms and twins,' Monroe said. 'But we have an issue, room wise.'

'Sir?' Cooper, writing notes, looked up. 'If you need, I could check around other hotels—'

'Too late for the other hotels,' Monroe replied, holding his hands up. 'There's some kind of sports event on in Milton Keynes this weekend, so the rooms are at a scarcity. Only reason we have what we have, is because several attendees booked out before the rooms were locked down.'

He looked at his list.

'One of the open rooms is blocked, possibly because it needs to be fixed, so of the three left, I'll share a double with Doctor Marcos, and Billy will share a twin with Declan,' he started. 'Declan's daughter Jess arrives soon, coming up from Hurley, so we're sticking her with you if that's okay, Anjli?'

'That's fine,' Anjli nodded. 'All girls together.'

'But that leaves us our problem,' Monroe looked up. 'The other coppers we brought up are returning to London, and we'll use local plod tomorrow, but we couldn't get a room for you, Cooper, as with the fourth room barred from access, there simply weren't any. But we might get a cot—'

'I have a bed,' De'Geer blurted. 'I mean, I have a twin room. I had a friend sharing from tomorrow, but when this all happened, he texted to say he wasn't coming. So, it's a single bed, but you'd have to share the room with me.'

'Well, I'm not sure about that,' Monroe frowned. 'I'd rather we found—'

'I'm okay with that, sir,' Cooper replied, perhaps a little too quickly. 'It's only for a night, with luck. And Morten will probably be helping Doctor Marcos throughout the night, anyway.'

'Are you sure?' Monroe asked, and Declan glanced across at Anjli, who was trying not to smile. Esme Cooper's unrequited crush on Morten De'Geer was known by everyone except for De'Geer, apparently.

'Jess doesn't arrive until tomorrow,' Anjli said. 'Cooper can bunk in my twin room tonight and move across tomorrow. Unless Jess would rather share with De'Geer—'

'No, that's fine,' Declan interrupted. He also knew Jess had a crush on the Viking acting-Sergeant. 'If Cooper and De'Geer are okay with sharing? We can worry about it tomorrow.'

He looked across to Billy, hiding a smile as he faced his monitors.

'These rooms are available because people checked out,' he said. 'How many potential murderers did we lose before we locked down?'

'Twenty-two,' Billy pulled up a spreadsheet on his screen.

'However, seven of them had left before the murder – day passes only – and of the remaining fifteen, six checked out of their rooms and left, that's two couples and two singles with a total of four rooms, and the remaining nine were day passes who left after the event. The organisers gave us details of the names and addresses, so if we need to, we can bring them in. However, a few have already placed pictures up on social media, not of the murder, but just general ones of the opening ceremony's start, and I can make out from five of these they were in seats that couldn't have fired the arrow.'

'I think anyone in seats couldn't have *loosed* the arrow,' Declan said, nodding at De'Geer as he said the word "loosed". 'See? I'm learning. If they had, there would have been witnesses. It has to be the back of the room, but Sam was at the door and saw nothing, and they shot Pryce dead centre.'

'Actually, I might have something on that,' Billy started typing, and pulled up a series of fan-filmed videos and photos of the moment Montgomery Pryce was shot. 'The police, when they locked down, asked anyone with video of the murder to upload it to a particular server connected to HOLMES2. Details given and everything. I now have about twenty videos of various quality; all of the death.'

On the screen, one video played, and the team watched as Montgomery Pryce walked onto the stage to massive cheers, played to the crowd, and then crumpled to the floor, an arrow sticking out of his chest.

'And how does this help?' Declan asked. 'This shows the stage, not the back of the hall.'

'A.I,' Billy opened up another app, turning to face everyone. 'Artificial Intelligence.'

On the screen was a basic three-dimensional model of the

ballroom, with squares for chairs and a large rectangle, likely the stage at the other end.

'This is a to-scale map of the ballroom,' Billy explained. 'I got the measurements from the hotel, and De'Geer had someone measure the stage for me.'

He then pulled up another video, clicking on several points on the stage in it.

'I'm creating anchor points,' he said, pulling one point from the image to the map. 'The software then looks at the video, sees where the items should be placed, and ...'

On the map, a two-dimensional selection of figures appeared.

'That's not helpful,' Declan commented.

'That's only one video,' Billy replied testily. 'We have a dozen, all from different directions. This means we get to show differing widths, and the AI works out where people are in real time. Here's one I prepared earlier.'

The map on the screen changed, and now there were a dozen fully formed images on the stage.

'This is a snapshot, in 3D, of the moment Montgomery Pryce was shot,' Billy explained. 'I can't get super-detailed levels, as I took a lot from phone footage, but I can show this.'

He zoomed in on the figure of Montgomery Pryce, no more than a CGI avatar.

'He was shot, dead centre, right?' Billy looked at Doctor Marcos, who pulled up a photo of the body on her phone, passing it across.

'Shot from directly in front, yes.'

Using a cursor to do so, Billy took a line from the back of Pryce, through to the front, and then extended it to the front of the stage.

'When he was shot, he was turning slightly to his right,'

he explained. 'A back door killer couldn't have shot dead centre.'

'Could have saved us time and told us this before we scared some wee fellow to death,' Monroe growled.

'It's not legally admissible,' Billy shrugged. 'I'd rather we did things both ways. Digital and analogue.'

'Oh aye, so I'm analogue now?'

'Can you extend the line further?' Declan asked. 'Into the audience?'

Billy complied, and the map zoomed out, showing the line ending on the back wall, to the right of the doors as you faced them.

'Darkened corner of the ballroom.' Declan stood back. 'Lights shining away from them, nobody would see someone standing at the back, shooting an arrow.'

'Aye, but someone must have seen this,' Monroe muttered. 'The place was packed to the gills.'

'Hold on,' Doctor Marcos waved at the stage. 'Now extend the line the other way.'

Billy did so, and the room went quiet.

'Ryan Gates thought the arrow would have hit him, or maybe Margot Trayner, because they were both directly behind Pryce,' Doctor Marcos said. 'And if it was a straight-on shot from the back, it would have been a coin toss. But from this angle?'

She pointed at the screen, where the line could be clearly seen entering Margot's chest, dead centre.

'If Pryce hadn't walked on, there's every chance we'd have been investigating the murder of Margot Trayner right now.'

Declan considered this.

'"Imposter",' he said. 'That's what they reckoned the arrow said, the secret message on it.'

'Message?' Monroe looked confused. 'And when exactly were you going to enlighten us with this piece of knowledge?'

'It's been a busy evening,' Declan sheepishly replied, pulling out his phone as it silently vibrated. 'And it didn't mean much to start with, because pretty much everyone reckoned Pryce wasn't who he claimed to be.'

'Why would Trayner be an imposter?' Anjli mused, looking at her watch. 'It's almost eleven. Maybe we should ask her tomorrow.'

Monroe nodded.

'Aye, we're not getting anything else done here,' he said. 'We'll know more from forensics tomorrow, so De'Geer, see if you and Doctor Marcos can gain anything else. I'll stay up a little longer, chat to some people in the bar, maybe see if anyone else can help us.'

Declan rose from his chair.

'I'll join you,' he said. 'Jess texted. She'll be here in half an hour.'

'I thought she wasn't coming until tomorrow morning?'

'That was until she learned there was a murder investigation,' Declan shrugged. 'You know what she's like.'

Monroe grinned. Jessica Walsh had made it very clear she wanted to follow in her father's footsteps when she finished college, and any opportunity to help with a case was always taken.

'How did she get here so quick, though?' Anjli asked. 'The trains don't go direct from Hurley to Milton Keynes. She would have gone back into London, and then caught another out.'

'She's cadged a lift,' Declan read the text. 'Doesn't say who from.'

'Bullman,' Doctor Marcos replied, leaning back in her

chair. 'I'll put cash on the table right now. She's the one who took the last room, and that's why we didn't get it.'

Declan sat back down in the chair. It was also well known that Detective Superintendent Bullman had a lot of time for Jess and had even stated she'd be welcome in any team she ran once she was trained up, offering to be her police mentor, even offering to fire Declan to free up the budget, although he hoped that was a joke.

'Cooper could share with Bullman,' he said. 'I'm sure—'

'No, I'm fine,' Cooper quickly interjected. 'I'm not precious, I'll bunk up with Morten.'

She blushed as she realised what she'd said. De'Geer, also flushing a little, walked to the door.

'I'll go see if anything else has been found,' he said, with a hint of awkwardness in his voice. Leaving the room, Anjli looked at Cooper.

'You haven't told him yet, have you?' she asked, just loud enough for the PC to hear.

'How can I?' Cooper replied. 'He's only just lost Davey. I don't want to be his rebound shag.'

'Fair point,' Anjli smiled. 'Just don't fall for his charms while sharing the bedroom. Even if he's in his tight, leather trousers ...'

Cooper picked up her notebook and left at speed, as Anjli chuckled.

'You'll go to hell for that,' Monroe raised an eyebrow. 'Poor bloody woman.'

'If Doctor Marcos is going to be working all night, we could always see if Flick wanted to have a one-on-one interview with you tonight,' Anjli replied innocently. Seeing Doctor Marcos look over at Monroe at this, she pulled at Declan, the two of them walking towards the door.

'Let's see if room service still works,' she said with a grin. 'Before I get killed by my superior.'

As Doctor Marcos asked Monroe who "Flick" was, and Billy gathered up his items and followed at speed, Declan and Anjli left the meeting room and headed to the lobby area.

DECLAN DIDN'T HAVE TO WAIT LONG IN THE LOBBY BEFORE JESS and Bullman arrived.

'I'm really sorry,' he said to Jess, embracing her. 'I meant to email you, but all of this came up last minute—'

'It's all good,' Jess grinned. 'Bullman said I could get involved. Help Billy.'

'I think he's already sorted a place out for you beside him,' Declan replied, looking at Detective Superintendent Bullman. 'Sorry if this was out of your way, Ma'am.'

'Not at all,' Bullman ruffled Jess's hair as she walked past. 'Kid reminds me of you, back in the day.'

'You didn't know me back in the day,' Declan frowned.

'Yeah, but she reminds me how I think you would have been, but, you know, better at being a detective and all that, Deckers,' Bullman shifted her overnight bag. 'Right, I'm off to bed. They upgraded me to a suite.'

Declan and Anjli stared after her.

'I thought there weren't any rooms left?' Declan asked. 'And surely Billy would have got his butler to call ahead and book any suites for him?'

Walking into the bar area, Anjli smiled.

'Billy would have bought out the hotel,' she said. 'Probably best we keep him grounded.'

'Can I have a drink?' Jess was already eyeing up the bar.

'Sure,' Declan nodded to the barman. 'I'll have a Guinness. My partner here a white wine, and the *underage child* will have whatever soft drinks you sell.'

Jess glared at Declan. He smiled widely at her.

'It's police hazing,' he said. 'Everyone gets it on their first case.'

'This isn't my first case,' Jess muttered.

'Every case is going to be classed as your first until the day you join officially,' Declan shrugged. 'Besides, you're just starting your A' Levels, so you shouldn't be drinking.'

'I'm not sure about that.' Anjli sipped at her wine. 'I was pissed for most of my A' Level years.'

'You're supposed to be a good influence.' Declan winced as he saw the bill. 'Put it on my room, thanks.'

'I'm being an excellent influence,' Anjli replied indignantly. 'I was pissed but look at me now!'

Declan watched Anjli for a long moment, trying to work out if this was mocking or not, but was interrupted by Ryan Gates, walking over, a blonde woman around ten years younger beside him.

'Detective Walsh,' he smiled. 'Did you find the killer?'

'He wasn't the killer, I'm afraid,' Declan replied. 'Ryan Gates, meet Detective Sergeant Kapoor and my daughter Jess. She's a trainee police officer, so is here to assist.'

'Pleasure to meet you,' Gates smiled, pausing as he glanced at Jess, staring at him, open-mouthed. 'Are you okay?'

'You're Captain Ahab,' Jess rammed a hand out to be shaken. 'I love your show. It's on Netflix.'

'That's because Netflix will buy up any old crap, as long as it's already made,' Gates replied self-deprecatingly.

'I'm sure it was made before you were even born, so it's nice to see new fans are still finding it,' the woman interjected, slightly glaring at Gates as she spoke, but with a nervousness she hadn't shown when walking over. Declan assumed Jess's sudden eagerness had thrown her. And, as he considered this, Jess looked now at the woman, her eyes widening even more in realisation.

'You played Starbuck!' she exclaimed. 'The first mate on the *Peaquod*!'

'Mister Walsh, may I introduce my wife, Luna Hedlun-Gates,' Gates smiled. 'She did indeed play my first mate in the show. Would have been a PR dream, if that bloody *Battlestar Galactica* show hadn't also cast a blonde, female Starbuck at the same time. But we fell in love on set, and Luna's been with me ever since.'

'I don't act anymore,' Luna smiled, still shaking Jess's hand. 'When the show came out, it was a commercial flop. So these days I manage Ryan's appearances, mainly.'

'Hey, they have his speargun in the props room,' Anjli said to Jess. 'You could look at it tomorrow, maybe even stroke it lovingly. I mean, if you didn't want to help Billy and solve this murder, that is.'

Jess straightened, dropped the hand, and made a weak smile.

'It's a pleasure meeting you,' she said to Luna. 'I do hope you're not the killer, as that'd be a real buzzkill.'

'Montgomery?' Luna was surprised. 'I wasn't in the opening ceremonies. I'd gone to the hotel spa instead, and there were tons of witnesses there.'

'Sounds like you were planning an alibi,' Declan said, half mockingly.

'I can see that, but believe me, I wasn't having fun,' Luna

replied. 'I'd gone for some relaxation, and instead I ended up cleaning shit.'

'Do you mean actual—'

'No no, of course not,' Luna waved her hands. 'I mean the shit Montgomery Pryce left behind when he was told to leave the spa and do his job.'

She leant in, whispering so the attendees couldn't hear.

'Speak to the spa manager,' she said. 'He was … let's just say, inappropriate with the masseuse. And if it had been me on the receiving end? Pryce wouldn't have made it onto the stage to be shot.'

'Anyway, we're off to bed,' Gates said, his smile seemingly more plastered on now, his eyes no longer matching it. 'Hopefully, I can be of help tomorrow.'

As they walked off, Declan glanced at Anjli.

'Another thread to pull on tomorrow,' he said. 'Maybe we're looking in the wrong direction.'

'Absolutely,' Anjli pursed her lips. 'Guests, attendees … what if it was the hotel employees themselves?'

And with that worrying thought weighing heavily on their heads, Declan, Anjli and Jess walked over to an empty table.

BILLY HADN'T INTENDED TO CALL, BUT WITH THE TENSION IN the air between Doctor Marcos and Monroe, he thought a bit of space would be good. And, when he hit the bar, he saw Jess and Bullman arrive, and so decided a quick phone call might be an idea.

Unfortunately, Andrade's phone kept going to voicemail. Which meant he was either asleep with it on "do not disturb" mode, or he was doing something else, with it on "do not disturb" mode.

Come on, Billy, calm down, he told himself. *Andrade is pissed at you, so let him stew for a day or so. He'll call tomorrow.*

Billy was about to re-enter the hotel, typing a message into his phone, when he stopped, stepping back into the foliage beside the door as, storming through it were Ryan Gates, the Will Scarlet from the late-eighties show, and a blonde woman, pulling out a pack of cigarettes, lighting one up.

'You should have told me they were police,' she hissed. 'What if Alex said something?'

'Then they would have asked you,' Gates argued. 'Hamilton won't do shit. He knows he was in the wrong last night; you were right to kick-off back, and he's probably terrified they'll search his room and find ... well, you know.'

'But if they question him?' The woman was pleading now, terrified. In contrast, Ryan Gates was relaxed and calm.

'If Alex Hamilton says anything,' he said calmly, taking her by the arms as Billy moved back into the foliage, 'I'll kill his creepy arse myself.'

Tossing the half-smoked cigarette to the side, Luna kissed Gates passionately, and the two of them re-entered the hotel.

Now alone again, Billy walked out, staring after them.

Things were going to get very interesting tomorrow.

6

BEDTIME STORIES

De'Geer stood uncomfortably by the desk, pointing at both beds.

'You can have whichever one you want,' he offered, forcing a nervous smile. 'I checked in today so I didn't sleep in either of them yet.'

Cooper stared around the room, hefting her overnight bag over her shoulder as she took it in. Although De'Geer hadn't used the beds, the sofa to the side was covered in scraps of leather and fur, with a six-foot-long length of wood next to it.

'It's my costume,' De'Geer muttered, almost too soft to be heard. 'Little John.'

'I know, you idiot,' Cooper grinned. 'I've seen the photos.'

'There are photos?' De'Geer looked mortified. 'Where?'

'You know when Billy was looking at pictures of Sam Hardy? Guess who was also in the pile of photo shoot images,' Cooper said, placing the overnight bag onto one bed and picking up the staff, easily towering above her.

'My, Little John,' she winked. 'What a big stick you have.'

'It's um, not the size of the stick that's the issue there with a quarterstaff,' De'Geer started. 'You need to make sure the weight is balanced, and ...'

He paused as he saw Cooper's face. She was trying hard not to laugh.

'What?'

'I made a penis joke, and for a moment I thought you were playing along with your "It's not the size of the stick" line, but you really weren't, were you?' Cooper shook her head. 'You genuinely wanted to make sure I'd not got the, pardon the pun, wrong end of the stick.'

De'Geer blushed a little.

'Sorry,' he said. 'I'm nervous.'

'Morten De'Geer, I've seen you chase after Chinese hitmen with nothing but a boathook,' Cooper smiled. 'Why the hell are you nervous?'

'Because *you're* here,' De'Geer shrugged. 'I don't often have girls in my hotel rooms.'

'Oh, you have a lot of hotel rooms, do you?' Cooper sat on the bed and watched De'Geer. 'Oh, for Christ's sake, open the minibar and see what's in there. If you're going to be like this all night, I'll swap with Anjli.'

'No, it's fine,' De'Geer shook his head. 'I don't want Jess in here—'

'I meant I'd swap with Anjli, not Jess,' Cooper continued. 'You could be all Sergeant-talk. I know you're scared of her.'

De'Geer opened the minibar and pulled out two drinks: one was a bottle of lager, the other a slim can.

'I know you don't like pints, and I seem to recall you liked vodka. This seems to be the only thing like that in there,' he said, passing across a can of vodka and orange. 'I can call room service if you want.'

'No, that's fine,' Cooper flipped the tab at the top and sipped at it, looking back at the costume. 'So come on then, why the interest?'

De'Geer, struggling to find a bottle opener and eventually using his key, sipped at the bubbling froth that spilled out of the top of the bottle before replying.

'My parents,' he said. 'Freya and Magnus. They had a fascination for mythology and folktales. Loved the Viking myths, all that Ragnarok crap.'

'You're not a fan?'

'I think I had a little too much of it,' De'Geer shrugged. 'Anyway, I started looking at other folklores. King Arthur, Hereward The Wake—'

'Here-what the *what?*'

De'Geer sighed.

'See? This is what I put up with,' he smiled. 'Philistines. He was an Anglo-Saxon nobleman, and a leader of local resistance to the Normans when they invaded. "The Wake" means "The Watcher". His story was told in the *Gesta Here- wardi,* a twelfth century, Middle Latin text.'

'Sounds less like a folktale and more like a story about a real person.'

'That's the best sort of folk tales.' De'Geer sat on the other bed now, warming to the conversation. 'Robin Hood is a folk- tale, but there's half a dozen people he could have been in the real world. His story has been constantly changed. Where does he live?'

'Easy. Sherwood Forest, near Nottingham.'

'Yes and no,' De'Geer sipped from the bottle. 'He does now, but the first legends had him in Yorkshire. Barnsdale and Nottingham have argued over him for decades. His so-called grave is in North Huddersfield, not Nottingham, almost seventy miles away. When did he live?'

'End of the eleven hundreds, because King Richard's in it.'

'Again, yes and no. He started off in the fourteenth century. It was Sir Walter Scott, using him in *Ivanhoe*, which placed him in Richard's time. And there he stuck.'

'You come alive when you talk about this,' Cooper grinned. 'Almost as much as when you talk about autopsies.'

De'Geer couldn't help but chuckle.

'I suppose they're both about discovering mysteries, with a hint of dress up,' he said.

'Yeah, but I'd prefer you in leather trousers than those bloody awful PPE suits.'

Cooper realised what she'd said and blushed a little.

'Sorry. Vodka talking.'

There was an uncomfortable moment of silence in the hotel room; Cooper wasn't sure what to say next, and De'Geer was too scared to speak. In the end, it was Cooper that spoke.

'Have you heard from Joanne?' she asked, referencing DC Joanne Davey, the previous assistant to Doctor Marcos. At this, De'Geer's posture stiffened slightly.

'No,' he replied softly. 'I sent her a message, but she never responded. She also moved back with her parents.'

'Do you think she'll come back?'

De'Geer looked up at the ceiling as he pondered the question.

'I don't think so.'

'Do you want her to come back?' Cooper was more hesitant to ask this question, but once it was out there, she leant forward, waiting for an answer.

'I-I don't think so,' De'Geer shook his head. 'I mean, she's still a friend, no matter what she did, but she did bad things, whether she meant to, or whether or not she had reasons to. I know DI Walsh got her a "get out of jail free" card, but that doesn't mean she should use it.'

'Wow,' Cooper relaxed a little, sipping her drink. 'I really didn't expect that answer from you.'

'Why? Because I hold a torch for her?' De'Geer made a wry smile. 'Doesn't change the fact she went against us. And as much as I – as much as all of us – will be there for her, I think she needs time to work out what she needs.'

'And what if she needs you?'

De'Geer almost spat out lager.

'That, Esme Cooper, is extremely unlikely.'

'But what if—'

De'Geer rose from the bed, placing the bottle of beer on the desk.

'Did I like her? Yes. Did she like me? I don't know. Did I love her?'

He looked back at Cooper, and for a second his expression softened, as he bared his soul to her.

'No.'

Walking to the bathroom, he pulled off his shirt.

'I'm having a shower,' he said, grabbing a robe from the closet. 'It's been a long day.'

Blushing brightly, Cooper rose. The sight of his muscled back had been the instigator, but his honest expression moments earlier had made her breathless.

'I'm just going for a walk,' she said. 'I need to clear my head.'

'Are you sure?' De'Geer, topless, asked.

'Oh yes, absolutely,' Cooper insisted, grabbing her room

key and almost running from the room. Only once she was outside did she stop, lean against the wall and release the pent-up breath.

'You utter bloody fool, Esme Cooper,' she muttered to herself as she walked towards the elevators. 'Utter, utter, idiot.'

JESS WAS CLICKING THROUGH THE TV CONTROLS AS ANJLI clambered into her bed.

'It's gone midnight,' Anjli said. 'I know you're young enough to enjoy sleepovers and pyjama parties, but I'm old and need my eight hours.'

'I'm getting Netflix to work,' Jess smiled in response. 'I want to show you *Ahab*.'

'You can show me in the morning.' Anjli turned her side lamp off and turned away from Jess. After a moment, she stopped herself, turning around, so she was facing the younger woman again.

'What's up?' she asked.

'I don't know what you mean,' Jess replied, placing the remote control down for the moment. 'I'm good.'

'No,' Anjli sat up. 'You're more wired than usual.'

Jess looked at the duvet, sighing.

'I ... I got in a row with Prisha,' she muttered. 'She's at Henley College, I'm in Tottenham, we only see each other when I'm in Hurley, so it's difficult.'

'And you were supposed to see her this weekend,' Anjli nodded. 'Yeah, that's tough. Believe it or not, Billy's suffering with the same problem.'

'With Prisha?' Jess made a weak smile.

'How are you two?' Anjli asked, ignoring the attempt at a joke. 'You didn't spend much time with her over the summer.'

'She was spending summer in the London School of Economics, so I saw her when she had time off.' Jess shrugged. 'When I was in Hurley, she wasn't about. But now she's home, and I don't see her in London, and we were hoping ...'

'But you came here.'

'Yeah,' Jess nodded. 'I came here.'

Anjli leant back against the headboard, understanding.

'It's what broke your parents up, isn't it?' she said. 'He chose work over life with Liz and you.'

'Yeah,' Jess nodded. 'Not the best of times. Thanks for bringing it up.'

She smiled after saying this, to show she wasn't serious, and Anjli carried on.

'You think you're doing the same, choosing this case over her?'

'And I'm not?'

'It's not the same,' Anjli replied. 'Declan? He had you, he had the job, and he chose the job. And I get that. The only reason we probably work is because we *are* the job. Same with Monroe and Marcos. But Billy? Andrade isn't the police and works to Billy's schedule. But at the same time, Billy works to his own one, too. A diplomat is even harder to tie down for a date.'

She looked across at Jess now.

'Prisha and you? You're both in your A' Levels. She's second year, you've just started, but anything you do outside of that isn't about the now, it's about the future. Prisha spent the summer at LSE because she was planning for her future. And you didn't see her in Henley during that time. But you?

All this? It's planning for *your* future. This isn't *Scooby Doo* or anything. You're not one of the *Magpies*, running around with your magnifying glass and dog. You're working with your dad, helping a serious crimes unit in solving cases. You've fought with us, you've almost died with us, and you still come back to us for more.'

Anjli clambered out of the bed now, straightening her *Moomins* pyjamas as she did so, sitting beside Jess on the bed.

'If Prisha doesn't understand why you have to miss this weekend, then she doesn't deserve you,' she said reassuringly, placing an arm around Jess's shoulders. 'And believe me, your dad is going to put you to work the moment you hit the hub tomorrow.'

She sighed, as a slight realisation came over her.

'Has your dad met Prisha yet?' she asked.

'Yeah, she was in the *Red Reaper* case, and we saw her at that vegan place in Covent Garden—'

'No, I don't mean while on duty, or while you fancied her from afar, I mean, since you both became an item?'

'No,' Jess shook her head. 'Mum hasn't either. You're the only one who has, when we went to that gig.'

Anjli raised an eyebrow at this.

'You haven't introduced her to your parents, but you've introduced her to me?'

Jess smiled.

'Well, you're kinda my step-mum, so it's alright.'

Anjli made a noise at this; guttural, terrified, and horrified at the same time.

'No,' she said. 'I'm more the cool aunt.'

'Who's sleeping with my dad, so that just starts up all sorts of wrong visual images,' Jess grinned.

'Great,' Anjli muttered. 'So much for going to sleep.'

She stopped.

'Have you met Prisha's parents yet?' she asked suddenly.

At this, Jess's face fell.

'I was supposed to meet them on Sunday, for lunch,' she said. 'Doesn't look like that'll be happening soon.'

'Now listen here.' Anjli took Jess's hand, holding as she stared into the young woman's eyes. 'Your father is a very good, more than adequate detective, and I am a brilliant one. Between us, and with our supporting cast of Billy Rich, Scottie McScottish, Doctor Scary and the Viking Raider, we'll sort this case out well before Sunday arrives.'

'You forgot PC Cooper, Detective Superintendent Bullman and DC Davey.' Jess was laughing now, but the laughter stopped as she realised the last name she spoke. 'Oh, damn. Sorry.'

'No, you're right.' Anjli let go of the hand, walking over to her bed now. 'Joanna Davey's still part of the Last Chance Saloon, whether she's there or not. And as for Cooper and Bullman, I didn't name them because when things go tits up, and *they* will inevitably go tits up, those two will probably have to come and save us.'

She leant back against her pillow now, realising to her irritation that she was awake.

'Go on, then,' she said, nodding at the TV. 'Show me what you wanted to show.'

Grinning, Jess turned the TV onto the Netflix app.

'You're gonna love this,' she said. 'It's gloriously terrible, very tongue-in-cheek and called *Ahab*.'

MONROE WASN'T SLEEPING.

Doctor Marcos was still away, examining the body in Milton Keynes morgue, and he didn't want to go to bed before she arrived. There were too many things he wanted to say, too many moments he'd wasted.

He looked up from his whisky as Bullman walked over, plonking herself down in front of him.

'Christ, you look miserable,' she said. 'I mean, you always look bloody miserable. It's your terrible Scottish upbringing that did that and we all make adjustments for it, but you're even more bloody dour right now.'

'I had plans for the weekend,' Monroe muttered. 'Until the bloody Viking volunteered us for this.'

'We all had plans,' Bullman shrugged. 'I was supposed to—'

She paused, realising she'd spoken without thinking.

'I had police stuff to do,' she finished.

'You could have done it,' Monroe replied, looking up. 'We could have done this without you.'

'Nothing better at making a woman feel special than being told she's not needed.'

'You know that's not what I mean,' Monroe grimaced. 'But you run Temple Inn. You should be there, running it.'

'So, solve the case quick, so we can all go home,' Bullman smiled. 'And you can get back to doing whatever you were supposed to be doing. What was that, anyway?'

Monroe leant back in his chair, finished his drink, reached into his jacket and showed her.

7

BUFFET BREAKFAST

BILLY HAD BEEN AN INTERESTING ROOM MATE FOR THE NIGHT. After a drink in the hotel bar, mainly to gain an idea of the underlying mood of the attendees holding the wake, Declan had kissed his daughter goodnight, returned to his hotel room, unpacked his duffle bag, clambered out of his suit, folding it over a chair's back, thrown a sleeping T-shirt and some PJ bottoms on and clambered into bed, after hunting aimlessly for a plug socket to place his phone on charge. He wasn't worried about sleeping, as his years in the Military Police had taught him to pretty much sleep anywhere, but he had to admit, he found it difficult to sleep right then, as he found, lying in the bed, he had a fascination with his hotel roommate.

Billy, he realised quickly, *had a whole regimen before he went to bed.*

First, he took a small handful of tablets, most likely supplements of some kind, taking them all in one go with a swallow of water. Then, he opened his suit bag, pulling out two immaculately pressed three-piece suits, placing them in the wardrobe. They took a lot of the space up, especially after he pulled out two dress shirts, hanging them up beside them, and he turned nervously to face Declan.

'Do you want more space?' he asked. 'I could—'

'No, I'm good,' Declan almost laughed. 'Take what you need.'

Billy smiled, opening up his expensive aluminium cabin case now, pulling out underwear, socks, gym gear, and running shoes.

'They have a gym and a pool here,' he said, adding a pair of swimming trunks to the pile. 'Thought I'd bring it all, just in case.'

'Good plan, mine's in the car,' Declan replied, actually grateful for the fact that his running gear *was* in his car, if a little musty. Maybe Billy was right, and a run could help clear his head. 'Billy, if you don't mind me asking, what were the pills?'

'Melatonin, magnesium, and a couple of vits,' Billy was now pulling out a pair of perfectly pressed silk pyjamas. 'I take those at night, and the other supplements when I wake up, with some collagen powder.'

'Oh,' Declan nodded, as if knowing what Billy meant. 'I've been meaning to add that to my bulletproof coffee.'

Billy stopped, turning to face Declan.

'How will you deal with breakfast?' he asked.

'I don't usually have it,' Declan replied.

'Yeah, but it's included, and it's a full-on buffet,' Billy smiled. 'I'll be eating all I can.'

Declan frowned at this. On the one hand, he rarely ate breakfast. But on the other hand, *unlimited bacon and sausage.*

'I suppose it's only one day,' he muttered. 'I can start again on Monday.'

'That's two days.' Billy pulled on his pyjama top. 'Saturday and Sunday.'

'Well yes,' Declan sat up in the bed. 'But if I'm going to do it tomorrow, I might as well continue until we solve the case. I can't see the police keeping us here indefinitely, and the convention ends on Sunday.'

'We'll have to solve it by then,' Billy nodded as he walked into the bathroom. A moment later, the sounds of an electric toothbrush could be heard, and Declan fought the urge to get up and clean his own teeth again.

Just go to sleep, Declan. Settling back into the bed, Declan shut his eyes. *Billy has his regimen and that's fine.*

And by the time Billy walked back into the room, a moisturising sheet mask on his face, Declan was fast asleep.

That said, Declan hadn't slept well.

To be honest, it didn't help that he'd had a pint of Guinness before bed; it didn't make him drunk, but it sat on his stomach all night, and he dreaded speaking to Billy about whether there was any ... well, *flatulence* the following morning, but on and off, he managed about six hours before waking up to the sounds of wind chimes.

Billy was cross-legged on his bed, eyes shut.

'Sorry,' he said, opening an eye as he heard Declan moving, pressing pause on his phone's meditation app. 'Did I wake you?'

Declan checked his watch, seeing it was seven in the morning.

'No, it's all good,' he said. 'I'll just grab a shower and get out of your hair.'

Declan wasn't really thinking when he went into the bathroom, and, pretty much on autopilot, he showered, shaved, cleaned his teeth and, now ready for work and back beside his bed, got dressed while Billy entered for his own shower.

A split second after Billy closed the door, the scream was heard.

'You *bastard!*' Billy spluttered through the closed door. 'You put it on cold!'

'I take cold showers,' Declan started laughing as he pulled on a shirt. 'I've told you that. And with you and all your supplements and stuff, you should embrace the world of Wim Hoff!'

A few minutes later, wearing a towelling robe he'd brought himself and a scowl he'd fixed purely for Declan, Billy walked out of the bathroom.

'Invigorating,' he said with no hint of irony, but Declan could tell he didn't mean it.

'You look just like Anjli did when she first tried it,' he smiled, straightening his tie. 'I'm going for breakfast. See you down there.'

And before Billy could reply, Declan left the hotel room, laughing.

BILLY ARRIVED AT THE BREAKFAST TABLE FIVE MINUTES AFTER Declan, which impressed him, as Billy was perfectly groomed, considering he had had little extra time to make sure no hair on his head was out of place.

Opposite Billy and Declan were Anjli and Jess, already tucking into their breakfasts, although Anjli seemed to have taken the entire pastry counter for hers.

'How was your night?' Declan asked.

Anjli looked up from her croissant.

'Oh, just fine,' she said, but once more Declan could hear the slightest hint of annoyance in the tone. 'Did you know the TVs here have Netflix? Put your details in and you can watch it.'

Jess smiled.

'I showed Anjli "*Ahab*",' she said. 'That's the Moby Dick prequel Ryan Gates was in.'

'It's very ... low budget,' was the best Anjli could offer. 'What was interesting, though, was that Jess showed me every special guest in the eight episodes it ran for. You've got the Sheriff appearing as an insane captain, Little John as a mad scientist and Friar Tuck as some kind of rival monster hunter, all turning up in the show, but no Marian or Robin.'

'Margot was in Hollywood by then,' Billy said, returning from the food counter, a pile of fried food on it. 'She was probably too expensive.'

'Yes, but Alex Hamilton was also in Hollywood,' Declan said, grabbing a piece of bacon from Billy's plate as he rose. 'I'll get you another bit.'

When Declan returned to his chair, now with his own, carefully curated full English breakfast, Billy returned the favour, snatching a piece of bacon back.

'Hamilton was a B-movie bad guy,' he said, munching on it. 'Did lots of straight-to-video stuff. Chances were he wasn't making that much, so he probably jumped at the chance to be on a TV show.'

'It might be on Netflix now, but it was on some unknown US network back in the mid-2000s,' Anjli added. 'He might have seen this as a chance to move into television in the US?'

Declan nodded.

'And no Pryce,' he mused, munching on a hash brown. 'Maybe he didn't want to be upstaged by his sidekick?'

'It must have really pissed him off, too,' Anjli replied. 'That Ryan Gates got a show, and he didn't.'

'Only lasted one season, though,' Jess interrupted. 'Only reason I saw it was because Netflix recommended it to me.'

'And Pryce probably held a party the day that news of its cancellation came out,' Declan nodded across the restaurant. 'I see Monroe's fan is still around.'

Anjli glanced to the side, where, in the room's corner, Monroe sat, eating alone, reading his phone while, two tables away, Flick McCarthy stared at him like a hungry child watching an ice-cream van. At the table on the other side of her, oblivious to anything, was Margot Trayner.

'That's going to end badly,' Billy muttered, watching Flick and Monroe. 'Poor woman doesn't stand a chance.'

'You haven't said how your night was,' Anjli raised an innocent eyebrow. 'Did Billy's butler tuck you in and tell you bedtime stories?'

Billy glared at Anjli.

'I've told you before, I don't have a butler,' he said icily. 'I have a *team* of butlers. You're belittling their work. Just wait until I tell Jeeves and Jarvis what you said. They won't fluff your pillows anymore.'

Anjli snorted at this and, while Declan finished his plate, Billy looked at her.

'Declan tried the cold shower thing with you, right?' he asked, a little too innocently.

'Yes.'

'And why haven't you killed him yet?'

Anjli laughed as Declan, deciding the conversation was definitely not going his way, half-rose.

'We can go up for more, right?' he asked innocently, ignoring the conversation and noticing the amused expressions. As he said this, however, across the room Monroe straightened, glaring at his phone.

'*Bastards*,' he hissed, loud enough for the entire restaurant to hear. 'Bloody idiot buggering *bastards!*'

He looked up at Declan, plate in hand, and waved the phone.

'Have you seen this?' he half-shouted.

'A phone?' Declan looked confused.

'The bloody article!' Monroe replied. 'Good God, lad, I know what a sodding phone is!'

With this, Monroe rose from his own table, storming across the restaurant, ignoring the confused expressions of the diners, and slammed the phone on the table.

'Read,' he commanded, his face softening into a smile as he noticed Jess. 'Oh, hello, lassie, good to see you.'

Declan picked up the phone first, reading the article.

SHERIFF GETS HIS MAN - ROBIN HOOD ACTOR KILLED WITH ARROW LIVE ON STAGE

'Ah,' he said, reading down the page. 'Well, we knew it'd get out.'

'There's a picture of the bloody arrow!' Monroe half shouted in anger. 'How did they get that?'

Declan examined the photo, zooming in.

'Malcolm, the show's photographer,' he said. 'It looks like one of the photos he took. I reckon he probably sold it.'

'I want him arrested,' Monroe hissed. 'For buggering around with our case.'

'Apparently, it's not our case,' Anjli said as she now read the piece. 'Listen. "Detective Chief Inspector Sampson, currently heading the murder case, said that although the murderer was still at large, the convention attendees were unlikely to be in danger, and the event had been allowed to continue." Who the hell is Sampson?'

'Oi!' Monroe waved across to De'Geer, sitting across the restaurant, and quietly eating his own food. 'Come here.'

De'Geer nervously rose from his table, grabbing a last piece of toast to munch on as he walked over.

'Who the Bloody Mary is DCI Sampson?' Monroe asked.

'Thames Valley Police,' De'Geer replied. 'He was first on scene, started ordering everyone around until he realised I was City Police. I phoned Bullman, she phoned his boss, and we took on the case as part of the "national major crimes when needed" remit she put in when we took on the Military Police case for the Prime Minister.'

'Well, someone hasn't told Sampson he's not on it anymore,' Monroe muttered. 'Bloody hellfire. Anjli, call the paper and speak to the reporter who wrote this drivel. Find out who spoke to them.'

'They might not want to give up their sources.'

'Then arrest them,' Monroe hissed. 'Declan, speak to the photographer and find out what the hell he's up to. I'll call Sampson and have a wee chat, from DCI to DCI. The rest of you, expect a busy day, as this'll bring everyone to the convention. It's going to be sold out.'

'How so?' Billy frowned.

'It's the *Blind Beggar* cabbie effect,' Monroe scowled. 'Every bloody East End cabbie over the age of seventy reckons they were in the pub the day Ronnie Kray killed George Cornell, right? Well, everyone will want to have bragging rights they were at the sodding convention Montgomery Pryce was murdered at.'

He rapped on the table.

'Get your seconds and eat heartily because we're going to be on our feet all day. Any other surprises I should be aware of?'

'Actually, yes,' Billy said, lowering his voice. 'Last night, I was outside—'

'Why were you outside?' Anjli asked.

'I was calling Andrade.'

'Oh, is he okay? Did you tell him we said hi?'

'I didn't get through to him.'

'That's strange, right? Could he—'

'*For the love of sweet Mary, mother of Christ, could you let the wee bairn tell us his story?*' Monroe almost wailed in true, dramatic Scots fashion.

Anjli, reddening, nodded.

'Anyway, I was in the bushes—'

'Why the hell were you in the bushes?' Monroe couldn't help himself, gaining a glare from Anjli. 'Look, I get you're annoyed at me for doing the same, but this isn't normal behaviour.'

'I was in the bushes because I saw Ryan Gates and his wife walk out, and I didn't want to be seen,' Billy explained. 'They were arguing when they came out through the doors, and I thought if they didn't see me, I'd get more information.'

'Okay, and what did you get?' Declan asked. 'As you peeked at celebrities through bushes like a stalker?'

Billy held up his phone.

'I recorded it.'

'That's not admissible,' Monroe muttered. Billy nodded at this, though, opening an app.

'I was texting, and the moment they emerged, I turned it to dictation,' he said. 'It did a pretty good job of it. The wife spoke first, and it was a back and forth.'

On the screen, lines of text could be seen.

> You should have told me they were police what if Alex said something

> Then they would have asked you Hamilton won't do shit he knows he was in the wrong last night you were right to kick off back and he's probably terrified they'll search his room and find well you know

> But if they question him

> If Alex Hamilton says anything I'll kill his creepy hearse myself

'Hearse?' Monroe asked.

'Arse,' Billy replied. 'Kill his creepy arse. The software isn't a hundred percent. Hence the lack of punctuation too.'

'This must have been directly after they spoke to us,' Declan mused. 'We talked about the TV show, and also about Pryce's antics in the spa.'

'Antics?' De'Geer frowned. 'There were rumours he'd no-showed his signing around lunchtime because he was in the pool and wasn't leaving soon, but then he turned up, claiming he was being a trooper for everyone.'

'Well, the impression I got through Ryan Gates's wife, who was apparently there, was Pryce had been inappropriate with the masseuse, and there was fallout before he left,' Declan replied. 'Although nothing about Alex Hamilton and Luna. Maybe we need to look into that?'

'Maybe she was a client of his?' Billy suggested, miming knocking back some pills.

'We don't know if Hamilton still does that,' Declan muttered. 'But we should, so look into the reasons he got kicked out of America. Although the "you know" comment about what we'd find in his room suggests he still partakes.'

He looked at Jess as he spoke.

'Luna was unhappy we were police, but you were a fan, so she might talk to you. Befriend her, see what she says,' he suggested. 'De'Geer, if Doctor Marcos doesn't need you right now, take Cooper and go speak to the spa staff, see if any of them want to tell us what happened.'

Declan paused, looking around the room.

'Where is Cooper, anyway?'

'Sleeping in,' De'Geer replied almost immediately. 'She had problems getting to sleep last night.'

Declan wanted to make a joke comment but held himself back.

'Okay then,' he said, glancing at his watch. 'Let's go speak to people.'

8

OLD MAIDS

As the detectives left the breakfast area, in the far corner, another conversation was occurring.

The problem with hotels like this, Margot Trayner considered to herself, *was that you never knew who you'd end up sitting with.*

She'd come down to breakfast alone; usually at the bigger convention hotels there was a friend or two you could meet with, or perhaps old acquaintances who were there, who you could join up with once you arrived. But if there wasn't anyone, you were often at the whim of the server who, seeing a lot of single guest breakfast diners, would walk you to a two-person table, most often with one seat being a long, wall-length booth bench, and sit you down while the servers removed the other items, purely to show you were alone.

Again, Margot didn't really care about that, as she was comfortable in her own company, and had a Kindle she brought down to these meals, sitting at the table and eating her fruits and yoghurt while reading the latest spy thriller, oblivious to those around her.

Unfortunately, this morning she was placed a few seats down from the loud DCI running the case, and, worse still, beside Flick McCarthy.

Margot didn't like Flick. To be brutally honest, she also believed the distaste was mutual, as in the three years she'd known the manager, Flick had not tried to befriend her, which in a way was strange, as she was the personal appearance manager of half of *Hooded Outlaw*, and Margot had a small twinge of personal insult she hadn't been approached, even once, to be on Flick's books. She would have rejected the offer, of course. It would just have been nice to have been asked.

Flick didn't seem to have noticed Margot, engrossed in something on her phone, so Margot rose from her table, walking over to the self-service area, grabbing a coffee and a juice, returning and placing them down before returning to the yoghurt and fruit section. On this return to the chair, Margot noticed Flick look up, a momentary nod of greeting and recognition before she looked back down at her phone.

Not even a vocal "hello", Margot thought to herself as she sat herself down. *How rude.* Again, the fact that Margot hadn't offered either was forgotten here, as she started on her breakfast, only stopping as a small shadow blocked the light from the window.

Looking up, she saw a twelve-year-old girl standing opposite her, smiling. She was wearing a home-made Maid Marian dress, and Margot could see she was bursting to speak.

'Hello,' Margot smiled. 'And what's your name?'

'Maisy,' the girl beamed with excitement. 'And when I grow up, I want to be you.'

Margot raised her eyebrows.

'But I'm already me,' she said, playing the game she'd played with children so many times. The girl didn't mean Margot Trayner, actor, she meant Maid Marian. 'You can't be me.'

'Oh, by the time I'm old enough, you'll be retired, or dead of old age,' the girl said knowledgeably. 'I'll be your replacement.'

Margot thought she heard a snort from the table beside her as she forced the smile to stay on her face.

'Well, I'll watch my back,' she said. 'But should you still be here? After what happened yesterday?'

'Oh, mummy said it was all make believe,' Maisy said with a determined nod. 'Just like when you were stabbed by the Sheriff.'

To emphasise this point, Maisy looked around the room.

'He'll probably be down for breakfast soon,' she said, and the words almost broke Margot's heart. *A man, no matter how much of a bastard he'd been, had died, and there were still people who thought it was just part of the show.*

'Well, I'll look forward to seeing you play Maid Marian.' Margot's fixed smile was becoming harder to hold and faltered slightly as Maisy frowned.

'I don't want to be Marian,' she said. 'I want to be *you*.'

As she spoke, another woman, likely Maisy's mother, ran across, grabbing her daughter by the shoulders.

'Maisy, you shouldn't hassle the lady while she's eating,' she said, while making no attempt to take her child away. 'I'm so sorry. She's a big fan of your show.'

'I know,' Margot waved at the costume. 'She looks very grown up.'

'Oh no, not that,' the mother shook her head, laughing.

'That's her dad's influence. No, our Maisy, she loves your Lunchtime Ladies show.'

'Oh,' Margot leant back on the booth seat. 'So, when you said you wanted to be me, you meant be on *that* show?'

Maisy nodded her head eagerly, and Margot chuckled.

'Well, when you're older, drop me a message and we'll see what we can do.'

'How much older?'

'Say ten years.' Margot leant forward and patted Maisy on the shoulder, confident that within ten years the show would be cancelled, she would have left, or Maisy would have grown up and forgotten this.

The mother, however, was overjoyed at this, crouching over Maisy and looking down at her.

'Hear that? You're going to be on television!' she exclaimed.

'Yeah, in about a decade,' Flick muttered softly, just loud enough for Margot to hear. She decided not to comment, instead, obviously starting her breakfast once more.

'Well, if you'll excuse me,' she said, waving at her bowl, not wanting to continue chatting. However, the mother didn't get the message.

'So, what advice would you give my daughter for a role in TV and film?' she asked, Maisy standing in front of her.

Margot sighed, placing the spoon down. *She'd tried, she really had.* She'd been nice to the kid; she'd even played along. But she was going to be doing this for hours today, and the last thing she wanted was to be adding to that for free.

'Don't hassle celebrities when they're trying to be alone?' she said lightly, staring directly at the mother. 'It's early. I haven't had breakfast yet. I lost a good friend last night and

I'm still being contractually forced to be here today, so how about letting me have some alone time, yes?'

The mother stared in confusion at Margot. The woman simply wasn't getting it.

'Look,' Margot added, feeling a little self-conscious; the last thing she wanted was to be accused of shouting at a child. 'Come and meet me during my signing session. I'll have more time then to go over everything.'

'We won't be able to,' the mother replied icily. 'We're leaving this morning.'

'Well, safe journey home,' Margot nodded, already taking up her spoon once more.

'Can we get a selfie?' the mother asked. 'Before we go?'

'I'm sorry, we're not allowed to, as there are photo ops available, and we have a contract that prohibits us,' Margot apologised. 'Did you not get one yesterday?'

'We didn't pay for one,' the mother looked down at her daughter. 'We chose the one with the movie actors instead.'

'Right,' Margot folded her arms irritably. 'You want a photo for free because you couldn't be bothered to pay for one yesterday, and you want free advice from me now, at breakfast, because you can't be bothered to stay until a better time for *me*. Is that about right?'

'Take a photo with the bloody child,' Flick finally spoke. 'She's like ten years old. It's not her fault her mum's a bitch.'

'I'm sorry but what?' the mother glared at Flick, who smiled sweetly back at her.

'I saw you last night,' she said. 'You got a signed picture of Monty Pryce yesterday, paid forty quid for it. Last night, I saw you in the bar next door, selling it for five hundred. "Signed at his last ever convention", you were saying. Did some idiot pay for it? I left before I saw.'

The mother stared utter daggers at Flick, while speaking to her daughter.

'Come on, Maisy, let's leave these old crones alone,' she said, looking back at Margot. 'My daughter loves your show, but she's ten and doesn't know better. I think you're shit.'

And, this stated, mother and daughter stormed off.

Margot watched for a moment, feeling her heart thump harder in her chest, a sure sign of an oncoming panic attack. Flick, meanwhile, had returned to her phone.

'That's your problem,' she said. 'Always has been.'

'And what's that?' Margot, taking a mouthful of yoghurt, asked.

'You want everyone to like you, even if you don't like them.' Flick placed the phone down, turning to the woman beside her. 'You can utterly detest someone, and that's fine, but if you find that person even remotely dislikes *you*, you're all "what the hell" and "what did I do". You always have been.'

'You know nothing about me,' Margot sniffed. 'You've been hanging around these things for what, five years now, and you think that makes you an expert?'

'I've been doing these for close to seven now,' Flick replied calmly.

'What made you even think you were good enough to rep people anyway?' Margot snapped. 'I mean, you were nothing beforehand, and suddenly you're all "my client wants puppies to stroke" and all that bollocks?'

'I was asked to rep Nigel, and I agreed,' Flick said. 'Malcolm is an old friend. He was at a convention, said Nigel was being fleeced, and as I was at a crossroads in my life, I offered to help.'

'And steal other clients along the way.'

'If you're good, people come to you.' Flick shrugged. 'I watch how the wind blows, and act accordingly. And I've been watching you for a while now.'

'So, what, you're my stalker now?'

'More a historian,' Flick shrugged, munching on a cold piece of toast. 'But then the winners always write the history. Just ask poor Richard the Third.'

There was a clatter of metal on crockery as Margot Trayner slammed her spoon onto the plate, spinning around to face Flick McCarthy.

'Just what exactly did I do to make you hate me so?' she hissed. 'Because it's been pretty bloody blatant since we met.'

'I'll answer that if you answer a question of mine,' Flick said. 'Why do *you* hate *me* so?'

'I don't hate you.'

'But you dislike me.'

'Hate and dislike are two different things.'

Flick waited a moment for Margot's comment to sink in.

'Yes, they are,' she said. 'I dislike you because you think you're better than them. You won an Oscar, two decades ago, and ever since then you've looked down your nose at everyone else. And you've not been subtle in how you're pissed that Pryce was getting more than you this weekend.'

'All because of you, I guess?' Margot snipped back. 'Was it deliberate? Make sure he beat the *real* actor?'

'No, it was because he played the *lead bloody role*,' Flick turned away, looking at the ceiling in despair. 'It's a Robin Hood convention. He played Robin Hood. *Twice*.'

'Nobody cares about the first one he did—'

'*I* care,' Flick hissed. 'And so do his fans. And he's got a lot. Maybe not of the man, let's face it. We both know he was an insufferable prick at the best of times, but of the folklore and the character. You played a love interest who walked off the show. Even when the companion is a bigger name than *Doctor Who* at a convention, the Doctor always gets top billing, because the show's named after them.'

Flick sneered.

'And what have you done exactly recently?' she asked mockingly. 'You drink cheap plonk and bitch about things on TV as if your opinion means anything. You, who only got your break because Montgomery Pryce didn't want the original Marian in his show.'

Margot went to speak, but then held back for a moment, chewing on her words.

'You seem to know a lot,' she said. 'Pryce tell you all this, did he?'

'I don't just rep ... I *didn't* just rep Monty,' Flick replied. 'I speak to Alex, to Nigel, to Robert. They were there from the start. Robert from *Young Robin*, even. And they all tell me how you played Monty like a fiddle, getting him to fight for bigger roles and meatier lines for you, always promising to suck him off in Sherwood at some point—'

Margot rose from her seat in fury.

'How *dare* you,' she hissed. 'How dare you cheapen my relationship with Montgomery Pryce!'

'Oh, is it all healed up now?' Flick didn't move, leaning back and looking up at Margot now. 'This problem you had for years, is it all okay now he's dead? Or are you preparing your speeches for when the TV cameras turn up?'

'He wanted me back, you know,' Margot leant in now, spittle hitting Flick's cheek as she hissed at her. 'For his sequel, his third go as Robin. I was going to be back. And I said no.'

'Bullshit,' Flick now rose, refusing to wipe the spit from

her cheek. 'I've seen the receipts. I know the scripts that were being discussed. Marian died, remember? *You killed her.* You'd be a one-episode cameo as a memory, or a "what could have been" dream. You weren't returning. You weren't even wanted. But that didn't stop you from telling Alex and Ryan to back away from it, did it? You wanted him to fail because you couldn't bear to consider being second fiddle again, an "oh do you remember the last series" nostalgia act while everyone else was contemporary again. And you would kill an entire show just to do that.'

'Don't you dare lecture me about the show,' she hissed. 'You know who they thought was the killer last night? Sam Hardy. He was in the audience, and Monty never knew who he was.'

'I don't know the name Sam Hardy,' Flick frowned.

'No, you don't.' Margot picked up her items from the table, preparing to leave. 'You're so busy looking at *you*, you don't look at *them.*'

With this, Margot pushed past Flick, walking away from the table as the appearance manager stared after her in confusion.

'Who the hell's Sam Hardy?' she muttered to herself. 'And how does this relate to me?'

Looking around, Flick realised her personal breakfast time had become something public, with the attendees eating their breakfasts now staring in interest at her. Grumbling and gathering up her items, she left, trying to work out what Margot had meant about Hardy, making sure she didn't catch eye contact with anyone else as she walked out of the room.

Which was a shame, because if she had looked around as she left, she would have noticed Luna Hedlun-Gates, sitting with her husband in a corner of the restaurant, watching with great interest.

And, as Flick left the breakfast room, Luna smiled at her husband – nodding in response to whatever war story he'd been telling for the last five minutes, a story she'd zoned out of the moment he'd started with "there was a time" – sipped at her coffee and considered what she'd just witnessed.

9

MORNING GLORIES

'I KNOW WHAT YOU'RE ABOUT TO SAY, AND IT WASN'T BLOODY me,' Malcolm Stoddard held his hands up as Declan walked into the photo op room. 'I'm not a rookie, and I know what'll happen now a crime scene photo is out there.'

'So how did this image get out there?' Declan waved the article, now on his own phone, at him. 'You were hacked, perhaps?'

'I sold the image,' Malcolm admitted. 'But not to the papers. And it's one of the few that only shows the arrow, not the body.'

'Who did you sell it to?'

'Pryce's manager, Flick.' Malcolm sat down at his desk, setting up the camera app as he spoke. 'One of her clients wanted the image, said it was a good memorial for him.'

'Which client?'

'No idea. She bought it, but like I always do when I sell images, I made sure she bought the extended licence. I thought it would be for a memorial, but she'd obviously already made the deal, or her client had.'

He shrugged at this, leaning back on the chair.

'I will say though, I'd rather this than one of those shaky video shots screen-shotted,' he added. 'Because that's what they would have done. Terrible, half-arsed image of Monty dying, or an arty tribute, I know which one I'd want. Maybe that's why she did it?'

Declan had to admit that Malcolm could be right. He knew from long experience how a tabloid would fight for *the* picture, whatever it was, and if it didn't work, they'd find something just as attention-grab worthy.

'By the way, I'm guessing Sam wasn't the killer?' Malcolm asked.

At this, Declan stopped, looking back at him.

'How did you know the name?' he enquired as he started to slowly move towards the photographer.

'I heard from Ryan last night in the bar,' Malcolm replied. 'Lady Eleanor's son? Harsh. You know, there were even rumours around a while back saying he was actually Pryce's illegitimate kid, too.'

Declan didn't reply to this, sighing as he turned to leave.

'I think we'll be having a chat with Flick,' he said as he walked to the door. 'But if you hear anything, let me know.'

'Of course,' Malcolm was nodding idly as he turned on the bank of photo printers beside the laptop. 'Have you spoken to the organisers yet?'

'That's next on my list,' Declan replied.

'I saw them talking to Robert, if that helps.' Malcolm stopped what he was doing and looked back at Declan. 'He seemed real agitated, and I don't think it was because of money.'

ANJLI WAS WALKING TO THE GREEN ROOM AS DECLAN WALKED up to her, matching step.

'Paper?'

'Bought the photo from the manager,' Anjli replied. 'Claimed they did nothing wrong.'

Declan nodded at this.

'Photographer said the same,' he replied. 'Actually, made a case that this was a better result, too, as it wasn't a screen grab of the moment taken in portrait from one of the phones. It's actually quite artistic.'

'He's not wrong,' Anjli stopped, looking at Declan. 'The piece was well-written, making sure no blame seemed to fall on the organisers. If I was a cynical person, I'd say they put this out, using it as ammunition to keep the convention going.'

'Apparently, Flick bought it for a client,' Declan added. 'That's likely Alex Hamilton, Nigel Cummings, Robert Standish, and a couple of the others. You think any of them would want something like this?'

'From what we've been hearing, probably everyone that worked with him,' Anjli smiled.

'Probably the organisers as well. In fact, I'm off to talk to them now.'

'Me too,' Declan smiled. 'Apparently, they were arguing with the director, Robert Standish. I'd like to know what it was about.'

THE GREEN ROOM WAS ALMOST EMPTY AS THEY ARRIVED; IT was a small room, with a selection of round tables, with hand gel and breath mints in the middle of each. Along the side was a table, with a selection of fruits, pastries and cold meats, next to a fridge filled with waters and soft drinks, and a table with a coffee and tea urn set up beside it.

Sitting at the tables were several people Declan didn't recognise, although he knew he'd seen one or two of them on TV. However, standing by the rear door, talking to the Green Room supervisor, a woman in a green T-shirt, was Detective Superintendent Bullman.

'DS Kapoor, Deckers,' she said, as usual ignoring police procedures on nicknames, when it came to mocking Declan. 'Come for a free breakfast?'

'You get breakfast as part of the hotel deal, ma'am,' Anjli replied cautiously. 'Didn't anyone tell you?'

'Oh sure, have breakfast with the normals,' Bullman winked. 'Or come here and eat with the stars.'

'I don't see any stars,' Declan admitted.

'Yeah, me neither,' Bullman sighed. 'I was hoping Russell Crowe might be here. I saw the guy who looked after the horses in the film was turning up, so I kept my hopes high. Crowe does like horses. He might have wanted to chat about them.'

'Is this why you came, boss?' Declan grinned. 'Celebrity spotting?'

'Of course,' Bullman sniffed, and Declan really couldn't tell if she was joking or not. 'Murders bore the shit out of me. But I'm glad you're here now. You can help me talk to him.'

She pointed across at a portly, balding man with red-rimmed glasses.

'That's Derek McAfee,' she explained. 'This entire show is his. And his partner, John something, who I haven't met yet.'

Declan nodded, following as Bullman now walked over to the man. Out of the corner of his eye, he noticed Anjli, deciding three was a crowd, walking over to another guest, sitting at a far table, a very slim man in what Declan guessed would be his eighties, his still-thick white hair parted on the right.

'Mister McAfee,' Bullman held out a hand, bringing Declan back to the moment. 'Detective Superintendent Bullman, this is Detective Inspector Walsh.'

Derek McAfee shook hands with both of them.

'Probably not the most normal of cases for you,' he muttered. 'Personally, I'm stunned we're still going.'

'I heard that's because of you?' Declan asked. 'That you wouldn't pay the managers?'

'I don't have to,' there was a slight sullenness to Derek's voice as he spoke. 'Events like this, we always have insurance. Flood, fire, act of God, all that. We also point out very clearly that guests can cancel at the last minute, and we can change the refund to vouchers if we reschedule. What we didn't have was a clause that says what to do when the Guest of Honour gets skewered with a sodding arrow.'

He waved around the half empty Green Room.

'We have ... that is, we *had* around twenty-five, maybe thirty guests,' he said. 'A chunk were from *Hooded Outlaw* because that's where the fandom started from, but we have a few from the other BBC Robin Hood show, a couple from the ITV one, three from the Kevin Costner movie, two from the Russell Crowe one, and the rest are all higgledy piggledy from films, TV shows related to the legend, all that sort of thing. Three Robins, but only one people gave a shit about, as the other two were from small budget shows and films.'

He looked back at Bullman and Declan as he continued.

'As of this morning, I'll be surprised if we have more than half left,' he admitted. 'Most of them left last night before the police lockdown and as soon as the closing ceremony ended. Some disappeared early this morning, a couple have said they'll stay, but only because the police said to, and they'll be covering their own costs and hiding in their rooms.'

'At least they're still on site if you need them for a crafty photo op,' Declan replied.

'Do you think we want this publicity? The convention where actors go to die?' Derek was angering now as he spoke. 'We were hoping to close this down, but then the bloody managers started.'

'Explain to me what you mean,' Bullman pulled out her notebook as she spoke. 'Why would managers do that?'

'Money,' Derek shrugged. 'They get a percentage of what their client makes. If their client makes nothing, if the show is cancelled for example and there's no fee paid, then they make nothing as well. And most of the guests were on a standard fee with guaranteed return. Which meant we paid them a fee to appear and sold tickets to match that. Once we hit the target, then we made the rest, but even if we didn't, they kept the money their clients made at the start.'

'Let me guess,' Declan chimed in now. 'If the convention was on all weekend, you'd make the money, but you hadn't by the end of Friday?'

'Exactly,' Derek nodded. 'As I said, a lot of guests got it, but bloody Flick McCarthy started demanding payments for her clients. We'd guaranteed it, after all. We pointed out that, with all the pay-outs etc, if we cancelled the show, we'd be paying back everyone for hotel rooms, tickets, all that stuff, and that'd leave us out of pocket. We could survive that, but add some four-figure guarantees into that, and we're thirty-grand out of pocket. So, my business partner called her bluff, said we weren't stopping the con if the fans were up for it. The plan was to force them to quit.'

'Because if a guest quits, then you don't have to pay them?'

'We only have to pay a percentage of what they've made so far, up to the guarantee,' Derek replied. 'And again, a couple of actors agreed to that.'

'But Flick didn't.'

'No, and because she'd been Pryce's agent, the other managers, Matty, Larry, Sonia, all the usuals, they did the same. They called our bluff while we called theirs. It also didn't help that Pryce was hated.'

'Yeah, we've heard that.' Declan looked up from his notes. 'We understand you had issues with him. Something about the spa?'

'Yeah, he was pushing our last nerve even before he got offed.' Derek shook his head now. 'All the guests, well, most of them, arrived Thursday night. The convention started ten in the morning yesterday, so it's easier to have everyone here early. Some couldn't manage it and that's fine, but the bulk arrived, had a guest dinner on us, and then went to bed. Pryce turned up, bitching, at around seven in the evening, ordered a room service dinner for him and a friend, following it up with two of the most expensive bottles of wine the hotel did, and then the following morning claimed the hotel had given him food poisoning, and he wasn't leaving the room until he was better. Three hours later, we've got Twitter pictures going up from pissed-off fans, who'd been waiting patiently for his autograph, showing him swimming in the pool. And then the spa kicks off against him, and we end up having to dress him down.'

'How so?'

'He'd placed the food, drinks, spa treatments, all of that on his hotel room,' Derek explained. 'We cover the room, but not the extras. He was trying to get a jolly out of us. However, by not turning up, he was reneging on the deal. So, when we saw the pool photos, we sent someone down to the spa to speak to him, saying he was letting the fans down. He said he didn't give a monkeys about the fans, so we then pointed out we'd put all of his extras onto the card he'd given when checking in, an amount which was already close to a grand, thanks to the expensive wines and spa treatments he'd booked.'

'I can see him being pissed at that.'

'Oh, and the rest,' Derek's face darkened. 'He said he'd come down to the convention once his treatments were finished, but then an hour later we've got Luna Hedlun-Gates dragging him out of the spa by his hair, threatening to drown him in the jacuzzi. She then spent the rest of the day soothing egos in there.'

'We'd heard about this last night,' Declan said. 'He was propositioning a masseuse or something?'

'Worse.' Derek looked as if he didn't want to speak, but then sighed. 'I don't want to speak ill of the dead, but you can't do anything but speak ill of Pryce. He tried to shag the masseuse, that's true. And, when she said no, he pressured her. Luna was there, she knew the history and—'

'Explain to me the history,' Bullman interrupted.

'The masseuse was Jenny Moss, John's daughter,' Derek said, looking up at the two detectives and noticing their confused expressions. 'John Moss. He's my partner in the events. He lives local, and his daughter works in the spa.'

'So, Pryce knew Jenny through John?'

Derek made an awkward face, scrunching it up as if working out how much he could say.

'They met at the last Robin Hood convention we did, about three years ago,' he eventually explained. 'She was eighteen and a big fan. She became his liaison for the show.'

'What's that exactly?'

'They sit beside the talent, take the money so there's no photo of the talent doing that; moves people on when they get too chatty, get drinks, whatever,' Derek explained. 'Anyway, she does that for the convention, and a few months later, I learn they'd ended up in bed together during the weekend.'

'She's young enough to be his daughter! His *grand*daughter!' Declan exclaimed.

'I know, and I wasn't happy about it,' Derek growled. 'But she's eighteen, she's got a thing for older men—'

'There's older, and there's *older*.'

'Oh, I know, but they both claimed it was a drunken accident, even though there were rumours she was on drugs, but she was too proud to admit it, and the next day someone else took on the liaison job.'

'You're a better man than me,' Declan muttered. 'I would have—'

'I wanted to kick him out, but John said it wasn't worth the hassle, and he was the dad, you know? If he could let it swing for the moment, then so could I. We finished the weekend, paid him the money—'

'Not Flick?'

'She wasn't managing him at that point,' Derek replied. 'In fact, it was the issues with him being caught sleeping with a teenager that made his then manager, Matty, quit repping him and Alex, moving into other areas. Honest talk for a moment? I think Matty was glad to get shot of the pair of them.'

'He had issues with Alex Hamilton during the same convention?'

'Guy's a pill-head,' Derek nodded. 'Half the time he's out of his skull on oxycodone. He's not too bad, I think he's been taking this shit for so long he's like a functioning alcoholic, but it's the social side.'

'Social side?'

'He's generous with giving out sweeties.' Derek's face hardened. 'It's what got him kicked out of the States. They said he was dealing. And yeah, I reckon he was, because you get given enough of those? You want more, and he was giving them out in fistfuls, and paying out some serious rent costs.'

'He did that with other guests back then?'

'I dunno, I don't think so. He's not that stupid.' Derek shook his head. 'But I know, from reports, he gave some to one person that weekend. John's daughter Jenny.'

'Who Pryce slept with?'

'Yeah,' Derek shrugged. 'Makes you wonder whether she would have if she wasn't, well, blissed out on oxy.'

'You think Pryce got Hamilton to do this?'

'Nah, I think Hamilton was just being sociable and not thinking,' Derek replied. 'Anyway, after that, Flick took Pryce and Hamilton on, as she was already repping Nigel, but that was a couple of months after this. But us? We moved on. Jenny was mortified about the whole thing, said she'd had a few drinks with him, we couldn't prove there'd been drugs involved, and that, added to the fact she grew up worshipping the *Hooded Outlaw* show ...'

'I get it,' Bullman nodded. 'I felt the same way about bands in my youth.'

'Okay, so how does that turn into issues this year?' Declan tried to turn the conversation back onto the topic.

'Jenny's a therapist now,' Derek explained. 'Works in the spa. Pryce turns up, sees her, books a massage. But she's twenty-one, she's in a relationship and the last thing she wants is to go back there.'

'But Montgomery Pryce doesn't accept that.'

'No, he doesn't,' Derek nodded. 'According to Jenny, he got a little too grabby, and when she said no, he offered her money for a "happy ending", saying she should pay him after her shit performance last time. And then he started talking about the photos.'

'Photos?'

Derek winced.

'It'd been a rumour on the circuit for years, but never said. A running joke, that we had to keep hiring him for shows, because he had compromising photos of Jenny, and if John did anything, he'd upload them to some revenge porn site. Nobody had seen them, but Hamilton once claimed Pryce, when pissed or high on coke, would whip his phone out, offering to show photos of the "eighteen-year-old with cracking knockers" he had shagged.'

'So, what happened with Jenny?' Declan was finding it hard not to snap his tactical pen as he wrote, a throwback to his time in the Military Police, which would have been impressive, considering what it was made of.

'He said if she didn't do what he said, he'd release the photos,' Derek muttered, and Declan could see the anger in his eyes. 'When Luna luckily turned up, he was trying to pull her dress up as she flailed at him with joss sticks. Luna pulled him out, and told him if one photo appeared, his ... you know, his ...'

Derek pointed at his groin.

'... would *dis*appear.'

Declan wrote this down, wondering quietly how Pryce hadn't been killed before this weekend. *The man was an absolute scumbag.*

'Where was John during opening ceremonies?' he asked.

'You can't think he did this, surely?' Derek was stunned by the question. 'He was on the sound desk.'

'Your Guest of Honour effectively tried to rape and blackmail his daughter,' Bullman snapped. 'If it was mine, I'd find a slower way to kill him. Bastard got off with a quick death.'

Declan sighed, closing the book.

'Are you sure keeping the convention going is a good idea?' he asked.

At this, Derek simply shrugged.

'Don't have much of a choice. John's already signed off on it,' he said, but his face brightened at this.

'Still, at least we saved ourselves Montgomery Pryce's appearance fee.'

10

ARROW POST

While Declan and Bullman spoke to the event organiser, Anjli walked to the slim, elderly man on the back table.

'Are you Robert Standish?' she enquired politely. At this, the man looked up nervously.

'I am,' he said, glancing at his watch. 'Am I supposed to be somewhere? I lost my schedule, you see.'

'No, it's nothing like that,' Anjli sat down beside him. 'I'm DS Anjli Kapoor. I'm one of the team—'

'Oh, Pryce,' Robert realised, nodding. 'Bad way to go.'

'I wanted to ask you about the arrow,' Anjli pulled out a notebook. 'Nothing official, just a chat.'

'I never really saw it,' Robert admitted. 'I'm not sure how much I can help you.'

'We were told the arrow had a message on it,' Anjli said, showing an image of the fletches. 'White arrows with notches cut in, and a red line.'

'Oh, yes, it means "imposter",' Robert zoomed in,

checking the feathers. 'But that's just from the show. It's not real.'

'It's not?'

'Oh God, no,' Robert chuckled. 'We put it into *Young Robin* back in the seventies, just so we could have a little more colour. Everything was brown or green, you see. And television had just become colourful and we wanted to shout this out. So, we had blue dyes and deep reds, and we thought we could do this with the arrows. And I'd read a book years earlier that did similar.'

'So why not just have messages on the arrows?' Anjli asked. 'You see that in other movies, parchment attached and all that?'

'That's when a message needs to be seen and read,' Robert straightened, almost as if he was giving a masterclass. 'In the show, we liked the idea of a secret code, one that even the Sheriff's men didn't realise was being passed. An arrow slamming into the back of a cart could say "let this pass", and the driver could tell the Sheriff he was attacked but escaped.'

'Which meant he wasn't punished for knowing Robin,' Anjli wrote this down. 'How many codes were there?'

'As many as the story needed,' Robert laughed. 'We'd paint up an arrow, use it, and then have a character look at it and go "ah, this means ..." and then whatever expositional plot bollocks we needed.'

'And you used this in *Hooded Outlaw* too?'

'Only the third episode,' Robert nodded. 'The "*Pretender to the Crown*" one. I can't remember everything, but we needed a quick explanation as we were running out of time. And when we were writing these, back before we were filming, this was still the heir apparent to *Young Robin*. It was therefore logical to have the arrow codes continue.'

He sipped at his coffee.

'But then Monty became difficult, said he didn't want Felicity Marshall and Michael Bailey – the original Marian and John – in the show, so we had to remove anything that connected the two, as BBC heads went, *"if we're not using any connecting storylines, then we'll go with a new show rather than a sequel"*, and that reduced our deadline time even more. So, I used it in the pretender story, and then we threw the arrows away rather than cause any other problems.'

'My colleague spoke to Ryan Gates about this,' Anjli read her notes. 'Said that a Peter Crock had made a lot of them?'

'Yeah, he was really furious, too, because we'd had half a dozen different ones made, all identical to the ones in the seventies, and that was hard because half the episodes were missing, but Peter had been on the show for the last couple of episodes, had a great memory, and remembered nearly all of them,' Robert finished his coffee, leaning back. 'But I don't know why Ryan was making out he was any kind of expert there. He came in after we'd burned them all.'

'You said *had*,' Anjli replied. 'I thought Peter Crock was a guest here?'

'Oh, I mean *has*,' Robert smiled, waving a hand. 'I was saying *had* as in "back then". I didn't mean anything by it.'

'The photographer knew about these too, so maybe it's a known fan thing?'

'Yes, possibly,' Robert nodded. 'Peter makes a lot of the props for these events too, so maybe he told Nigel, and Nigel told someone else ...'

'Nigel Cummings?'

'Oh yes,' Robert smiled. 'Peter makes the arrows for the events. Nigel buys them, puts them with the costume all weekend and then signs them on the last day, selling them for fifty quid each.'

He paused.

'They'll probably go for more now, I suppose.'

'Why?'

Robert tapped the image of the arrow again.

'Because that's the arrow message Peter always puts on the fletches,' he said. 'As I said, it's the only one used in the show.'

AFTER THANKING ROBERT FOR HIS HELP, AND SEEING DECLAN finishing his conversation with the organiser, Anjli waited until Bullman and Declan were finished, before sharing her discoveries.

'We need to speak to Cummings,' Bullman glanced at her watch. 'We should hurry though, as he'll be signing in fifteen minutes.'

'How do you know that?' Declan was surprised, but Bullman shrugged it off.

'I checked the schedules on the walls,' she said. 'Actually, could you take this on yourselves? I want to speak with Cooper, get her to see if the spa have the same story Derek did.'

Nodding, Declan and Anjli left the Green Room, heading a little way down the corridor and turning into the side room where the costumes were.

Inside the room were Nigel Cummings and Alex Hamilton, the former of the two looking annoyed.

'Good,' Nigel said, turning to face the two new arrivals. 'Maybe you can help. I've had a theft.'

'Well, we *are* solving the murder of your co-star, but sure, we can look at this,' Declan mocked, but Nigel didn't understand the tone, or rather chose not to, as he walked over to the Robin Hood costume, pointing at the quiver held behind it, now twisted around to the side of the mannequin.

'Look,' he said, pointing at the arrows inside it. 'Three of them, gone.'

Declan walked over to the costume, pulling out an arrow from the others. There were seven in the ten-arrow quiver now and the shafts, when examined, looked identical to the one found the previous day in Montgomery Pryce.

'When did you realise they were missing?' he asked.

Nigel considered this for a moment.

'This morning when I came in to make sure everything's okay,' he said. 'And the time before that was probably when I set everything up on the Thursday.'

He stared at the costume, frowning.

'I didn't check it when the idiot bar staff were playing with the swords, so I suppose they could have taken the arrows then when they broke the bow. And Alex was playing silly buggers with the costume when I came in this morning.'

'I was not,' Alex insisted. 'I was waiting. I was told we were having a briefing before the show in here.'

'Why the bloody hell would we have a briefing in here?'

'I don't know!' Alex snapped. 'Ask bloody Flick!'

'Maybe you should lay off the oxy,' Nigel snapped back. 'You might actually listen to what you're being told.'

Alex went to speak, stopped himself, and then angrily stormed out of the room.

'Self-obsessed druggie,' Nigel muttered. 'So anyway, are you going to find my arrows?'

'Oh, I think that should be easy,' Declan added, staring at

the arrow. 'Personally, I'd say they were taken before Friday evening, because I think one of these was the murder weapon.'

Nigel froze.

'You don't think I—' he started, but Declan held a hand up.

'You were standing beside him on stage so I don't think you could have shot the arrow, but I do believe there's a chance your arrow was used.'

He looked around the room now, trying to recall if anything else had been removed or moved from their original places.

'How many arrows did you have?'

'Twelve,' Nigel replied nervously now, realising the level of trouble he could be in. 'The quiver holds ten, but I always have two spare. I haven't put them in yet. Peter makes them for me.'

'Why "imposter"?' Anjli asked.

At this, Nigel frowned.

'What?'

'The arrows have the code for "imposter" on them,' Declan pointed at the red line. 'Didn't you know?'

Nigel shook his head, dumbfounded.

'The prick,' he muttered. 'Probably thought he was being funny. He's done them all like that. Since he started making them for me. Bloody imposter, eh? Prick.'

He stopped speaking though, as he saw Declan's face.

'What aren't you telling me?'

Declan passed the arrow back to Nigel.

'We don't have CCTV in here, so there's every chance that three different people stole arrows, and that's why they're missing,' he said, looking at Anjli.

'Or one person stole three arrows,' she continued. 'Which means, after killing Montgomery Pryce, they have two more. Now, maybe they wanted spares in case they missed ...'

'Or the killer has two more victims they want to kill,' Declan finished, looking back at the door. 'You said Alex was in here when you arrived?'

'Yes,' Nigel considered this. 'Said Flick wanted a briefing, which is probable, considering what happened and all that, but she never told us it was in here. I was just setting up, walked in to find him playing with ...'

He slowed down as he realised what he was describing.

'He was playing with the *quiver*,' he admitted. 'Pulling out an arrow, looking at it. When I walked in, he slammed it back into place, probably broke it too, the clumsy oaf.'

Declan noted this down.

'I'm guessing you're not going anywhere today?' he asked.

'Not while I'm contracted to this death-fest,' Nigel said, walking over to the mannequin, fixing the clothing. 'I'll be around if I'm needed.'

Leaving Nigel to curate his costumes, Declan and Anjli walked out of the room.

'Maybe we should check if all the guests are still alive?' Declan suggested.

'You know, that might be a good idea,' Anjli admitted as they headed back to the room the unit had claimed for themselves. It had coffee. And today was going to be a long day.

PC COOPER HADN'T EXPECTED THE SPA TO BE OPEN WHEN SHE arrived, as the hotel was currently in the middle of a murder investigation, but as she entered through the glass doors, she found a smiling, young, blonde woman facing her.

'Here for a massage?' she asked, obviously a joke, as she looked at the police officer walking into the waiting area.

'I wish,' Cooper smiled. 'I'm looking for Jenny Moss.'

'Oh, yeah, that,' the blonde woman's smile faded now. 'She's not in today. She was supposed to be, but after the whole thing yesterday, the manager said to have a break. And I don't think it's going to be busy today.'

'You're still open?'

'While the hotel is, we are, whether we want to be or not,' the woman shrugged. 'Do you want to see where it happened?'

'Sure,' Cooper replied. It wasn't what they had sent her to do, but with no Jenny around, Cooper wasn't given many alternatives, and so followed the blonde woman down the spa corridors.

'I'm Linda,' the woman now identified as Linda explained. 'I wasn't around when it happened.'

'What did you hear?'

'Creepy old bastard tried it on, couldn't understand she wasn't interested anymore. Tried to blackmail her. Or gaslight her. One of the two.'

Now they were in a small massage room; there was a bed in the middle, a cloth on top, and a hole where the face would lie, as the person being massaged would lay face down. There was a shelf against the wall, with candles, a Bluetooth speaker and a photo frame, and to the side of the bed there was a cabinet with a selection of oils on the top.

'And he tried it on in here?' Cooper looked around. 'Enclosed area.'

'Yeah, she held the bed between them as she called for

help,' Linda pointed at a phone on the shelf. It was a small, cordless one, with what looked to be an answerphone base unit. 'Press a button on that, and reception hears you. They were here in less than a minute.'

Cooper picked up the photo of Jenny and an older man.

'Dad?' she asked.

'Current boyfriend,' Linda grimaced a little. 'Don't ask. She does like them a little more mature. He's in his thirties though, so not as bad as ...' she shuddered.

'I mean, don't get me wrong, that Pryce guy was a looker back in the day, but I'm not into granddads.'

Cooper smiled, taking one last look around.

'So, we heard that Mister Pryce was "grabby", and only stopped when another guest, Luna Hedlun-Gates arrived,' Cooper read from her notes. 'Do you know anyone here who can corroborate that?'

'No, I'm the only one in right now, but that's what I was told happened,' Linda nodded. 'John, Jenny's father was in this morning, and I asked him.'

Cooper noted that although Linda had the same story, it had been told to her second-hand.

'That's all I need then,' she smiled, closing up the notebook, and leaving the room with Linda.

'Officer,' Linda held out a hand, stopping her. 'John wasn't the only one that told me about it. There's another woman works here, Chantelle. She came in early to pick up her phone, but she was here then.'

'And?' Cooper was curious about where this was going.

'And she said Pryce didn't do anything, and was a perfect gentleman,' Linda shrugged. 'But she's one person against several, so what does she know?'

'What does she know indeed,' Cooper nodded as she wrote this down. 'Do you have her number, by chance?'

MONROE HAD LEFT THE HOTEL AND WAS IN THE CAR PARK AS HE made his call to Milton Keynes police station. He was doing his best to keep his "polite" voice as he waited to speak to DCI Sampson. Eventually, the phone connected through.

'This is Sampson,' a young male voice eventually spoke. 'Who am I speaking to?'

'Aye, is that *DCI* Sampson?' Monroe had already decided he disliked the prick and had made it his plan to be as annoying as possible.

'Yes,' the voice replied.

'Who was quoted in the national papers today as saying, "although the murderer was still at large, the convention attendees were unlikely to be in danger, and the event had been allowed to continue", *that* DCI Sampson?'

'Who is this?' Sampson was getting irritated now.

'This is DCI Alexander Monroe, laddie, and I'm confused,' Monroe snapped. 'Because the paper also claimed you were currently heading the murder case, but as I look around *my* murder case, I can't see you anywhere.'

There was a long pause on the other end of the line, and Monroe wondered whether Sampson was now looking for places in the office to hide.

Eventually there was a rustling on the phone, and Monroe realised Sampson had been holding his hand over the mouthpiece, probably while he shouted at his staff.

'I've just seen the piece,' he said to Monroe. 'I said none of that.'

'So, the journalist just added your name for fun?'

'I'll look into it,' Sampson replied.

'You're damn right you'll be looking into it,' Monroe hissed. 'Because if I hear you're telling porkies about cases you're on, I'll be turning up at your doorstep and dragging you down here myself. You know damn well what something like this does. We never comment. And your – or whomever was pretending to be you – comment on this has caused me nothing but bloody trouble.'

'I was misquoted.'

'Now why would you say that?' Monroe sighed theatrically. 'A moment ago, you said you said none of it, and now you're saying you *did* say something, but they wrote it down wrong. It's one or the other, laddie. I want to know who spoke to you, when they did it, what you said and why. And you can *come to the bloody hotel and tell me in person right now.*'

The last part of the statement was shouted down the line, and as Monroe disconnected the call, he saw two elderly women, standing outside the doors and having a cigarette, staring at him in shock.

'Police business,' he said with a wry smile. 'Move along now.'

WHILE ANJLI AND DECLAN DRANK A QUICK AND MUCH-NEEDED coffee, De'Geer had pointed out the location of Peter Crock. He wasn't a guest as such but had set up a medieval encampment at the back of the hotel where, every day, attendees could turn up and, for a nominal fee, try their hands at bowmanship firing at targets attached to hay bales. There were about six people involved, all dressed as characters from the show, and Peter himself would dress as a Lord of the Manor, since he didn't shoot arrows anymore.

De'Geer had insisted he accompany Declan, explaining he knew the people well, and Anjli had taken this opportunity to return to the Green Room and look for Flick McCarthy, to see if her story matched with Nigel's, and whether she had told Alex Hamilton to meet in the room.

'So, are these people also fancy dr— I mean, *cosplayers*?' Declan asked as they walked out of a side door, crossing across an outside bar patio and entering a wooded area. De'Geer, momentarily grinning at Declan's saving of the name, shook his head.

'These aren't cosplayers, these are full on re-enactors,' he explained. 'Peter and his team call themselves *Golden Arrow,* after the one in the legends. They do a lot of events in castles, conventions, that sort of thing. Peter still works with props, but this is his hobby. If he could, he'd do this all the time. They rent the wooded gardens at the back of the hotel, put up some bell tents and some banners, all the things you'd expect from a medieval village, and then they do sword-fight training and archery contests, for a fee.'

'But he's not a guest?' Declan asked.

'Technically he is,' De'Geer replied, opening a gate for Declan to pass through. 'Pete created a ton of props over the years so he talks about them on a panel, and he has a room in the hotel, but apart from that he's out here being a Lord of the Manor and calling contests.'

'He doesn't enter them?'

'God, no,' De'Geer shook his head. 'He has the shakes when he's not drinking. Not alcoholism, but more something to do with explosions and his inner ear now being imbalanced. And I heard he separated his shoulder a year or two back. So now he just drinks and shouts at archers to shoot their targets.'

'Nice work if you can get it,' Declan smiled. 'And in the evenings?'

'They have a massive fire pit they sit around, drinking ale and mead and telling stories until they pass out,' De'Geer smiled. 'I've joined them a couple of times. It's really magical. And, when it gets dark, they hold a night show for the convention, where they douse swords with white spirit and have flaming sword fights, and fire staffs, all that sort of thing.'

He waved at a young man, no more than twenty-years old, pale-brown hair and a wispy beard over a brown tunic and leggings.

'Alright Rory,' he said, looking around. 'We're looking for Peter.'

'Morton, I see you're in your real costume today,' Rory smiled, noting the police uniform De'Geer sported. 'This your boss?'

'One of them,' De'Geer waved at Declan. 'This is DI Walsh.'

'Any friend of Morten's is a friend of mine,' Rory said, as Declan shook his outstretched hand.

'Did you know Pryce well?'

'Not as well as Pete did,' Rory admitted. 'We all thought he was a ponce.'

'You'd be surprised how many people seem to agree with that,' Declan smiled. 'Peter around?'

Rory looked across the makeshift medieval village, staring at a white bell-tent secured with toggles.

'We've not seen him yet, but he probably won't be up

until late,' he whispered. 'His tent is locked up still, so he's not out and about.'

'I thought he has a hotel room?' Declan was shocked, but Rory laughed.

'Of course, he does,' he replied. 'We all do. We just sit out here and get pissed up on our own drink rather than spending a mortgage on a round in there. Peter didn't join us last night, though. He was in the tent knocking back some of his homemade moonshine, you know, mourning the loss of his mate, and then around nine, ten, maybe? We saw he'd locked up and gone in.'

Rory started leading them towards the tent.

'He was close to the *Hooded Outlaw* guys, and he knew Pryce well, so the death really hit him,' he said. 'Chelly, one of the "Marians" we use at events, she made a joke, and he almost took her head off, saying nobody knew the man like he did. We kept quiet, and he buggered off to drown his sorrows ...'

He trailed off as they reached the tent.

There were small patches of dried blood on the base of the flap.

'De'Geer,' Declan said calmly, as De'Geer stepped forwards, pulling on latex gloves before opening the tent's toggles. Slowly, and with great care, De'Geer opened enough to be able to peer inside.

'What do you see?' Declan asked, as Rory and himself also looked in.

On the ground, eyes staring vacantly upwards, and with a white fletched-arrow protruding out of his chest, was a man in his sixties, but with a jet-black beard and hair. He was wearing a lord's tunic and cloak, his mottled expression had turned blue, and De'Geer already knew he'd been dead and left outside for around twelve hours.

'Peter Crock?' Declan asked Rory and De'Geer, both now stepping back, the former looking like he was about to throw up.

'Yes, sir,' De'Geer replied, already checking the tent flap. 'They killed him in the doorway, he fell backwards and then it was closed up afterwards, I'd say.'

'Last night?'

'Looks like it, but I'd rather Doctor Marcos examined first.'

Declan took one more look at the arrow and stepped back.

This was the second of Nigel Cummings' stolen arrows.

Which meant there was one more potential victim out there.

11

ACCESS ALL AREAS

'TELL US WHAT YOU SEE,' MONROE ASKED AS DOCTOR MARCOS and her team examined the body of Peter Crock, a blue police gazebo now over the bell tent, as she walked around the scene in her custom grey PPE suit. 'I mean, I know it's murder, but what can you tell us about it?'

Doctor Marcos crouched beside the body, examining it, or rather, the arrow still jutting out.

'He was shot at close range,' she said, moving the shoulder, checking under the body briefly before placing it back. 'Probably the same bow. The arrow's punched through the ribcage, and it's protruding a couple of inches out of the spine.'

'The arrow?' Declan asked.

'Yes, it's the same as the one that killed Montgomery Pryce, and it's one of the three likely taken from Nigel Cummings,' Doctor Marcos nodded. 'Same markings, same notches, same lack of any fingerprints or DNA. Not even fibres from the bow cord, which is more than a little suspicious.'

She rose, walking out of the bell tent, ducking under the top of the front flap as she did so, pulling off her mask to speak clearer. Across the field, the police, including Cooper, were holding back curious onlookers, and only a couple of the re-enactors had been allowed near the tent, mainly to identify items.

'So, now we have a second murder, and any of these buggers could have done it,' Monroe muttered, looking around the crowd.

At this, however, Rory, standing with them, shook his head.

'No, that's wrong,' he blurted. 'Sorry to interrupt.'

'No, laddie, if you have something to say, let me know,' Monroe replied quickly. 'If I'm wrong, I need to be corrected.'

Rory nodded at this, as if deciding to continue.

'So, there's only two entrances to the camp,' he explained. 'There's the public one, where you guys came today when you came to find Peter—' this part was to Declan '—and the private one, for guests, over there.'

He pointed at a corner of the back of the hotel, where a door was just visible.

'During the day, everyone comes through this one,' Rory pointed at the gate to the side, and in between the crime scene and the audience. 'This way we can take money for tickets, monitor numbers, all that stuff. But we don't let the guests come through this way. Some of them don't enjoy meeting fans outside of meet and greets or photo moments. You know, times when there's nobody around to stop the fans getting "too close". This way though, they can come out through that door, which is at the end of a corridor to the left of the guest Green Room, but not everyone can use it.'

'So, who *can* walk through the door?' Monroe frowned at the statement. 'How come it's only available to guests?'

'Well technically, it's anyone out there with a guest pass, a guest plus one pass, an organiser pass or an access all areas, or AAA one.' Rory showed his own badge, which read *Exhibitor*. 'These are like hotel room cards, and all the important people have an RFID chip embedded into them, swiped into a reader. And when they get near a door reader, if they're allowed through, the RFID chip opens the door for them. I can't go through there, none of us can, because our cards haven't been upgraded to that level. But Peter could.'

'Because he was a guest,' Declan nodded. 'You know a lot for a man dressed in the 1200s.'

'I work in guest relations for another chain of hotels,' Rory shrugged again, almost embarrassed at the compliment. 'I know a little about all this, as we use them as well.'

'Can we see where a card has gone?' Doctor Marcos pursed her lips. 'As in when it opens a door?'

'No, it's not a tracker, it's really basic tech.' Rory shook his head. 'Mainly, it uses radio frequencies to provide access when someone with one is beside the lock or reader. It'd pick up the chip in the plastic and let you through. Or, you'd have to take it off and wave it beside the reader to get through. Either way, no pass, no getting through.'

He pointed at the gym area, seen through some windows on the far right of the hotel.

'It also stops people going into the pool area if they're not guests, and in cities, it stops you going up in a hotel lift or elevator if you haven't swiped the card.'

'And after the opening ceremony last night, when you all came back here, you didn't see anyone use that door?'

'The fire pit is near the gate, so anyone, well, *normal*

coming in or out through that route would have been seen by us, as we were drinking well into the night,' Rory shrugged. 'And as I said, apart from having a pass with the chip in, to get out through the door you'd have to walk through the Green Room area and the corridor beside it without being stopped and know the back routes through the hotel.'

Declan wrote this down while considering the implications. Doctor Marcos, staring at the door herself, vocalised them.

'So, any potential murderer had to come through that door, or they would have been seen by you,' she said. 'Or they hid out until later, but they'd still have to find a way back which wasn't past you. Which means any potential murderer has to have one of these special badges. That narrows the list down immensely.'

'And muddies it,' Monroe growled. 'Half the guests were on the stage when Pryce was killed.'

'But half weren't,' Declan replied. 'And we're not including managers, liaisons, organisers, crew; all of those could have been walking through. Even hotel staff could have done it, as I'm sure they have access to these doors in case of an emergency.'

'Two steps forward, one step back,' Doctor Marcos looked back into the tent. 'I'd say death was around nine in the evening. So, a good couple of hours after Pryce was killed.'

'And after we arrived,' Declan realised.

'In fairness, it's not like you'd hear an arrow being shot,' Doctor Marcos stared at the body. 'No defensive wounds, this might be because it was a surprise, maybe because Peter was pissed already by that point and too drunk to fight back, or maybe he knew his killer. Either way, it was another bow and arrow death, and the press will have a bloody field day unless we fix this.'

'Keep on it, let us know what you find,' Monroe said, nodding at De'Geer, now with his own PPE suit on. 'I'll need you working double duties if the Doctor can spare you. You're the only one here with some solid knowledge of the area.'

'We're good here,' Doctor Marcos nodded. 'Not much we can do right now. Same modus operandi, same method of murder, we need something new, so if the Viking can find that, we'd appreciate it.'

'We need to find out where every guest, crew member, anyone who had one of these exciting RFID guest cards, was when Peter died at nine pm,' Monroe muttered. 'It'll be easier to work out who was visible at the time. If they were on stage during the first murder, even better.'

'Ryan Gates,' Declan said. 'He was on stage when Pryce was killed, and was with me around nine, talking with the photographer.'

'Okay, he's one,' Monroe thought as they walked into the bar area. 'Nigel Cummings was on stage, and we saw him in the costume room around nine, but that doesn't mean he couldn't have killed Peter and then returned. And his cry of theft could be an excuse to explain why his arrows are disappearing.'

'If that's the case, sir,' De'Geer replied. 'Then we have multiple killers.'

'Aye, and I bloody hate those kind of cases.' Monroe nodded at Cooper as she walked over. 'Let's have one psycho killer, eh? Far easier all around. What do you have, lassie?'

'Just been told from one of the local coppers you have a visitor, Guv,' Cooper replied, nodding into the lobby area. 'A DCI Sampson.'

'Ah,' Monroe sighed. 'What perfect bloody timing. Give me a couple of minutes and then bring him to the hub.'

'Hub, sir?'

'It's what we're calling the room Billy's set up in,' Declan smiled. 'Why? What do you call it?'

'A few of the local officers call it the Batcave,' Cooper smiled. 'I'll find someone to take over here and then—'

'No, it's okay, just get one of the locals to bring him in.' Monroe shook his head. 'I don't want to take any friendly faces from Doctor Marcos right now, especially now I've stolen De'Geer.'

Declan smiled at this, noting how Monroe was desperate to not give any reason for Doctor Marcos to be angry at him. Cooper nodded at this, looking back at the hotel.

'Makes sense, Guv,' she said. 'I'll give you a few minutes and then get one of them to escort him to you.'

Monroe nodded, and carried on past with Declan, taking the long way through the bar area to not accidentally bump into the DCI by the reception desk.

'Claims he had nothing to do with his statement,' he said as they walked into the back corridors. 'I might have shouted at him to get his arse down here.'

'You're a people person,' Declan commented as they entered the room where Billy had set up camp. Beside him, working through a list of names, was Jess.

'Hail to the computer king!' Monroe exclaimed, as Declan nodded to his daughter.

'Anything from Luna?' he asked.

'I didn't get much, as they found the body while I was talking to her,' Jess turned on her chair to face Declan. 'But she hates Alex Hamilton.'

'Hearsay, or an intuition?' Monroe asked, making himself a coffee.

'Actual statement,' Jess smiled. 'I mentioned how the episode of *Ahab* with him in was my favourite, and she replied with "I hate that man." Full stop.'

'Hmm,' Monroe tapped at his bottom lip with the edge of the cup. 'The question here, of course, is whether this applies to our case. Does it matter that two people don't get on when there's other stuff to work through?'

'I don't think so, sir,' Jess replied.

'See?' Monroe looked at Declan. 'She calls me sir.'

'She doesn't know better,' Declan grinned. 'Sir.'

'I've been trying to get through to the newspaper,' Billy interjected, looking around. 'Currently, they're giving me the go-around.'

Monroe turned to Declan.

'You used to know someone in *The Guardian*,' he said carefully. 'Can you use any of the mutual contacts you may have gained?'

Declan frowned. He knew Monroe was talking about Kendis Taylor, the onetime love of his life, killed almost a year earlier.

'I'd more likely get traction by being Charles Baker's mate than through knowing Kendis,' he admitted.

'Capital,' Monroe grinned. 'Use that, then.'

Sighing, Declan nodded, looking at Billy, who passed him a list of phone numbers.

'I'll see what I can do,' he said, already dialling the first number on the list, walking to the end of the table as the door to the room opened, and DCI Sampson walked into the room. He was tall, slim and had thick, black-rimmed glasses under short, bright ginger hair, which looked like it was one curl away from chaos at any moment.

'DCI Monroe,' he said, holding out his hand. 'I'm DCI Sampson.'

Monroe nodded, shaking it.

'I'd asked my people to escort you in,' he said, looking around. 'But you don't seem to have them.'

'I know the hotel well,' Sampson shrugged. 'I've been here a few times before, including last night, before the circus came to town. When they said it was the Babbage Room, I knew where to go.'

Monroe nodded, ignoring the *circus* jibe, and moving on.

'When I called you in, I didn't know there was a second body,' he admitted.

Sampson smiled in response to this.

'I've had people do less to gain my attention,' he said. 'But before we start, I'd like to point out how I didn't appreciate being chewed out on the phone.'

'I didn't appreciate seeing your name commenting on our case,' Monroe squared up to Sampson.

'Which you hadn't had the decency to inform me about when you took it over after I'd left the site,' Sampson faced down Monroe. 'And don't give me that bull about your special remit, I've seen the paperwork. I also know your history.'

'Oh aye?' Monroe folded his arms. 'Do tell.'

'Your case in Birmingham, you worked with DCI Bullman,' Sampson started. 'In Hurley, DCI Freeman.'

'Freeman asked for our help,' Declan pointed out, before turning back to the phone call he was on.

'DCI Hendrick didn't though, did he?' Sampson ignored Declan, staring at Monroe. 'When you trampled all over his Edinburgh patch.'

Declan, on hold and watching, thought Monroe was about to kick off back at the DCI, but instead, he nodded.

'You're right,' he said. 'We assumed you'd been told when your uniforms assisted us, but I should have called. But, we've had our share of bad apple DCIs, and it's a tough habit to break.'

He leant in.

'Especially when the first time we hear of you, it's in a newspaper article talking about us.'

'And as I said, I do not know how that happened,' Sampson continued.

'Actually, I might do.' Billy looked around, aiming his attention at Sampson. 'I'm guessing you'd talk at a lot of these sort of cases?'

'And you are?'

'DC Fitzwarren, sir.'

'Well then, DC Fitzwarren, I don't talk at any cases,' Sampson corrected.

'Sorry, I didn't explain myself,' Billy replied, straightening. 'The article says that you gave a statement. That although the murderer was still at large, the convention attendees were unlikely to be in danger, and the event had been allowed to continue.'

'I know what it says I stated,' Sampson frowned. 'I don't get where you're going with this.'

'It's very generic,' Billy replied. 'It's not a press conference statement. More a "give the press something to shut them up" statement. And I wondered if you've given statements like this before?'

'I suppose so,' Sampson considered this. 'We've had a lot of events in Milton Keynes, and we've had issues here and there with them, so there's every chance we'd have said something like this.'

'If you were in charge, hypothetically,' Billy continued. 'Would this have been a statement you'd have made?'

'Possibly.' Sampson looked at Monroe now. 'I'm still not getting where he's going with this.'

'Aye, but I am,' Monroe nodded at Billy now. 'In a usual, real-world situation, this murder would have fallen under your remit. The only reason it didn't is my man there.'

At this, he pointed at De'Geer, now out of his PPE coveralls.

'I called it in,' De'Geer explained. 'I was here already, as an attendee. And I saw you arrive at the start, but then leave when you realised you weren't needed.'

'I wasn't needed?'

'You know what the man meant,' Monroe half-snapped back. Sampson slowly nodded as he realised what was being said.

'The person who sent this didn't expect *you*,' he replied. 'They assumed I'd come in and take the case, as I did at the start. I'd give a similar sounding statement and move on.'

'I came in at eight-thirty last night,' Monroe continued. 'That's when I officially took on the case. The murder was around six-fifteen. So, for two hours, technically, this would have been you in charge, even though the paperwork was already set. Which means ...'

'The story was sent in before we arrived,' Declan looked up from his phone as he disconnected a call. 'Just spoke to a sub-editor on the paper. Had to promise an exclusive on the case once we solve it, but they admitted the story arrived at seven-thirty, an hour after the death. Also, the by-line author,

Alan Smithee, doesn't exist. It's a name given to people who don't want their real identities given and comes from directors who hated their movies and wanted their names taken off it.'

Monroe picked up a copy of the paper, staring down at the article.

'So, someone writes up an article less than an hour after the murder, assuming DCI Sampson here will be the detective on scene, and sends it in,' he muttered. 'But why?'

'We should ask Flick McCarthy that,' Declan said from his seat at the table. 'She bought the image used from Malcolm Stoddard.'

'So now, the question is why was Flick McCarthy writing news pieces about her dead client an hour after he died, and how did she know DCI Sampson would be involved?' Monroe was pacing now. 'I think we need to have a serious chat with that bloody woman.'

12

PERSONAL SECURITY

ANJLI WASN'T IN THE ROOM WHILE ALL THIS WAS HAPPENING; instead, she'd taken the opportunity to speak to some of the other guests, now all camped out in the hotel Green Room, and all nervously watching the door, in case the murderer, with his final arrow, was about to burst through it and kill their final victim.

The only guest that didn't seem bothered, however, was Ryan Gates. And it was Gates who Anjli made a beeline for.

'Any news on poor Crockie?' Gates asked.

'You mean Peter Crock?' Anjli shook her head. 'They're still examining the scene. Did you know him well?'

'Yeah,' Gates nodded. 'He was ex-military, like me. But whereas my hobbies were more contemporary, he liked to live in the past.'

'I didn't know he was military.' Anjli didn't pull out her notebook, but subtly turned her phone's recorder on. Pulling out a notebook might actually stop Gates from speaking. 'What did he do?'

'Crockie was a bloody brilliant demolition specialist,'

Gates replied. 'Spent hours looking at things, working out how they worked, planning for every eventuality. It's why he was so good at practical effects.'

Anjli leant closer.

'Do you think he could have been killed because of that?' she whispered. 'Something from his past?'

Gates considered this, and for a moment his mask slipped, and Anjli saw concern, possibly for his own safety, cross the face of Ryan Gates.

'No,' he replied, cautiously at first, and then more vehemently. 'No.'

'You sound very sure about that,' Anjli said softly, not wanting to divert away from this. 'You mentioned to DI Walsh that Montgomery Pryce wanted you to work as close protection at one point.'

'Yeah, it was a little while back.'

'But you thought it was purely to make you look bad?'

Gates shrugged.

'With hindsight, maybe not,' he replied cautiously. 'After all, he's the one in the morgue right now. But, at the time, you took anything Pryce said with a pinch of salt. He was known for making sure his co-stars looked like shit at premieres. Did you know he once dated Margot? For a week, end of season three. They attended the BAFTAs together. Well, they were supposed to, but Pryce then turned up with some impressionist comedienne he'd met on the Bobby Davro show, and Margot didn't realise until she got into the limo. All the photos showed Pryce with a woman on each arm, and Margot was immediately downgraded from partner to dolly bird.'

'So, it was deliberate?' Anjli asked. 'Or could he have just been rubbish with schedules?'

'No, it was deliberate,' Gates was icy as he continued.

'Margot had been gaining traction with her role, and magazines like *Look In* and *Just Seventeen* were using her as an example of a strong woman. Jodie Foster had just done *The Accused*, Kylie, Tiffany, Debbie Gibson and Sinitta were pushing musical boundaries and magazines were falling over themselves to move away from the more traditional stereotypes for women. And mainstay interviews for Pryce were being held off so Margot could gain column inches.'

Gates chuckled.

'Personally, we loved it,' he said. 'But it's why Margot left. On the set, Pryce was toxic. Off the set, she was getting interest from the US. No brainer, really.'

'And you?' Anjli returned the conversation back onto track. 'He did the same?'

'Nah, he knew I'd kick the shit out of him,' Gates muttered. 'It was no secret I was ex-military. He used me as a stick on the other, classically trained actors, but never with my knowledge.'

'A stick?'

'I wasn't trained as an actor, so if I did better in a scene than, say, Nigel or Alex, Pryce wouldn't let them hear the end of it. He was a child actor, you see, so never went to places like RADA, doing his learning on sets, and always had a chip on his shoulder because of it.'

Anjli shook her head.

'The more I hear about this guy ...' she started, and Gates laughed.

'Join the club,' he said. 'And that's the problem. When he asked for my protection, I assumed he wanted to make me look stupid. We'd been on stage together in the West End, and I had a bigger role than he did. I guessed he wanted me to look like his servant. Or, knowing Pryce, he'd fake some kind of attack, with someone he knew who could kick my arse, just so he could mock those skills when they did it.'

'But nobody ever did?'

'Nobody has ever managed it,' Gates replied with a hint of pride. 'But now, maybe he did have someone after him. And if I'd been there as security, maybe I'd have been more privy to it.'

'But that doesn't explain Peter's death,' Anjli leant back on her chair now, looking around the room. 'Actually, we have something. A clue. And I could do with your help.'

Gates didn't change expression, just nodding as if expecting this.

'Of course,' he said. 'You want someone on the inside who has alibis for the murders.'

'And that's you?'

'I was on stage for the first, and with your DI for the second,' Gates smiled. 'Currently, I'm bulletproof.'

'That's nice, but they're not using bullets,' Anjli said. 'And if Nigel Cummings was right about his theft, they have one more arrow to use.'

'Possibly more,' Gates scratched at his nose as he considered the implication. 'Crockie may have sold Nigel a dozen arrows, as per usual, but he always had a few more in reserve. As I said, he planned for every eventuality.'

He stopped, looking at the floor.

'Apart from the last one,' he whispered.

'Can you think of anyone who might want both Montgomery Pryce and Peter Crock dead?' Anjli asked, lowering her voice again. 'Someone in this room, perhaps?'

'You think one of us did it?' this momentarily surprised Gates, but he then nodded. 'The guest badges. Someone had to use the RFID in them to get out, didn't they?'

'You know about them?'

'They said about it when they gave us them,' Gates nodded. 'Technically, we all know about them. And where they allow us.'

He considered this.

'Nigel may have had an issue with Crockie,' he eventually admitted. 'If he found out what the stupid bugger was doing, that is.'

'And what was he doing?'

Gates sat back, mulling over his next response.

'How much do you know about the arrows?' he eventually asked.

At this, Anjli smiled.

'You mean the fifty quid signed arrows scam?' she replied, nodding across the room. 'Robert Standish told me all about it.'

'Probably not all,' Gates wrinkled his nose. 'So, Nigel has this thing, as you already know, where he keeps arrows with the costume, and then at the end of the weekend he signs them and sells them. He started doing this in Chicago back—'

'Chicago?' Anjli didn't mean to interrupt.

Gates smiled at this.

'You think we're barely known in the UK, and I get that,' he said. 'But in the US, we're rock stars. *Hooded Outlaw* is a BBC show. We're shown on PBS, we had a long run on BBC America, and there's talk of us being put on the Disney Plus network. Yanks love us, have for years. And, for the last twenty years or so, we've attended events in the States. Usually connected to Renaissance Fayres, where people dress up in medieval clothes and pretend to be in "Ye olden times". Probably because the only people who had medieval times in the US weren't who we now call "Americans".'

He picked at the tablecloth.

'Nigel was gifted some arrows, and at the end of the event realised he couldn't take them home, so sold them in the auction. Signed, of course. Made hundreds of dollars for whatever charity they were auctioning for. More, even, than he made in signings. Remember, back then, people weren't paying the stupid amounts for signatures that they are now. Anyway, realising he could make that money for himself, he comes back to the UK, buys up the costumes, and then returns to the US the following year with a full Robin and Sheriff set. Sets them up, gets Crockie to Fed Ex him some cheaply made arrows and makes a killing with photo shoots.'

'So that's why he's all about the props, then?'

'That and he's a collector who needed something to collect,' Gates shrugged. 'Anyway, I digress. Peter makes these in batches, so the cost evens out at a couple of quid for each arrow. He sells packs of twelve to Nigel for a fiver each, so sixty quid in total, keeping the profit for himself, and Nigel sells them for fifty each, thinking he's ripping the poor bugger off. But here's the sneaky bit. The batches Peter made them in were batches of twenty, so every time he made a set for Nigel he'd have eight left over. Every two times he did this, he had sixteen, so one in three of his orders from Nigel was money for nothing, as he charged for arrows he'd already made.'

'So far, I don't see a reason for Nigel to be that angry,' Anjli replied. 'He sells a couple of arrows and makes more than that.'

'Exactly,' Gates nodded. 'But a few years back, people started to pay a *lot* for these things on eBay. Signed arrows are going for thirty, forty quid a pop, and a lot of them are forged. So, Nigel gets Peter to make arrows with special, hidden dates along the shaft. You have to literally see one of these in person to fake it. And now, his fifty-quid arrows are the "official" ones. Any on eBay have to prove they're the same design or they're removed.'

'So only people who buy them at the Con can sell them. I'm guessing that was common?'

'Oh, sure, people tried to flip them, but more often than not they lost out as the internet market was second hand. Thirty quid was the usual price.'

Gates leant in.

'And now, Peter had eight "official" arrows every time he did a batch for Nigel,' he said. 'And more importantly, he could scribble a pretty good facsimile of Nigel's autograph on one and sell it to collectors for twenty-five quid, off books. Now he's making a hundred, two hundred quid off every batch, he's then making his own batches of twenty, selling them to collectors he knows for five hundred quid a batch, and Nigel isn't getting any of this, as his own "double the price" arrows aren't selling, and this is going on for years. Peter made *thousands* in the US from this.'

'Does Nigel know?'

'I think he had his suspicions, but he knew if he called Peter out, he'd lose his arrow supply. And to have these made by someone else? Probably cost double anyway. He'd have all the hassle and still only make the same money.'

Anjli was unconsciously biting at her lip as she considered this. It didn't sound enough to force someone to commit murder, but once more, it was a crack in the community.

'Did Pryce know?' she asked.

'Probably,' Gates looked around the room, and Anjli

noted Malcolm Stoddard enter the Green Room nervously, look across at Gates and Anjli, and then hurriedly leave the room.

'He knows about pretty much everything that makes money.' Gates forced a smile as he half-rose. 'Well, past tense, anyway. Is that all? I need to check on Malcolm. My photoshoot images had some poor prints, so I'm doing new ones over lunch.'

'The convention is on hold.'

'These were taken before that.'

'Then you can wait for one last thing,' Anjli leant closer, forcing Gates to sit back down. 'Tell me about the issues between your wife and Alex Hamilton.'

'That's between them,' Gates said, a little too hurriedly. 'I wouldn't dream of getting into something—'

'And yet you said last night, now what was it ...' Anjli held up a finger as she pulled out and opened her notebook, flicking through it. 'Ah yes, you said to her "If Alex Hamilton says anything, I'll kill his creepy arse myself." That sounds a little more than keeping out of things.'

Ryan Gates stared at Anjli now, and any pretence of familiarity and friendship was gone.

'You're mistaken,' he said.

'We're the police,' Anjli replied. 'We have a witness. And your voice on recording. You also spoke about what we might find in his hotel room.'

'You were following me?' Gates snarled, half-rising from his chair in anger, and his raised voice paused conversations around the room.

In response, Anjli shrugged.

'You spoke outside, in the open, without checking who was already out there,' she lied. 'As it was, one of my officers was leaving a voicemail. When it was listened to, your voice was clear in the background.'

She half-rose now, facing Gates, and her tone was icy as she continued.

'Now how about you sit your arse down and tell me what happened before I forget you've helped us in the past here and arrest you for obstructing an investigation?'

Gates sat down reluctantly.

'You should work in management,' he muttered.

'I'll take that as a compliment.' Anjli gave a humourless smile. 'Now, explain.'

'Luna and Alex don't like each other,' Gates leant back nonchalantly on the chair, and Anjli knew he was now aware half the Green Room was watching him right now. And although they couldn't hear what he was saying, he wanted to make sure he looked like there were no problems here. 'They used to date, back in the day.'

'Oh,' Anjli's eyes widened. 'That must be interesting at conventions.'

'It's more than that,' Gates sighed. 'Luna's father was a Swedish film producer. He financed *Ahab*, mainly so Luna could have a starring role. And, at the time, she was dating Alex, and he was being groomed to play the lead. But then I did an action film, something small budget and in a warehouse, I forget what it was, and anyway, Luna's dad sees it, says I'd be perfect. Alex is a little too "pretty boy" for the role, and he's more well known as a villain, whereas this role was a more anti-hero, more the Captain Ahab from the novel. And, as you probably already know, he had a problem with the pills, and they affected his personality, which concerned the investors. So, the next thing you know, he's out, I'm in, I don't know Luna or any of this, and Alex dumps her by text the first day of filming.'

'Harsh.'

'I get it, as this must have really hurt,' Gates nodded. 'And to be honest, Alex and I were fine about it, as he understood I had no clue what was going on. But something still contracted him to be in it, so he played some mad scientist. Turned up for three days filming, we got pissed and reminisced every night, but then when he left, I learnt what he'd really been up to.'

'Were you seeing Luna at this point?'

Gates nodded.

'For about two months,' he replied. 'I didn't know Alex was the "ex" I'd heard of, and on the second night I mentioned I was seeing Luna. He then explained everything, painting her dad out as a man determined to see him fail. I was mortified. I thought I'd betrayed a friend. But while I was knocking back pints and shots and eventually passed out, he'd been spiking my drinks with Vicodin. And then, when I was out for the count, he visited Luna, telling her I'd been slagging her off, saying how much of a nightmare she was, all that shit.'

'I'm guessing she didn't believe him?'

'Oh, she did,' Gates chuckled. 'She was pissed at me for weeks. I couldn't work out what it was until Nigel turned up as a guest star. He'd seen Alex in London a week after the shoot, and Alex had crowed about it all night long, how he'd got one up on me. All the times Pryce had mocked him for being worse at acting than me? They all came back in spades. He also went to the financiers – not Luna's father but the international ones – and got the funding pulled. That's why we were only one season.'

'Damn.' Anjli shook her head. 'How are you even here, beside him?'

'Years of military training,' Gates shrugged. 'And the fact the next time I saw him, at some convention in Manchester, I dangled him over a hotel balcony and told him if he ever came near me or Luna again outside of work, I'd kill him. And the funny thing was, learning we'd been played made Luna and me stronger than ever.'

'So, what happened two nights ago?'

'We checked in, as all guests were in on Thursday for a dinner. Luna went for a gym session in the afternoon, and Alex was there. He was staring at her, being pretty blatant, and when she went to the pool, he did the same. Unconscious stalking, most likely. But Luna didn't let it lie, she let it fester and when he left, she found he'd left a "love heart" sweet on her towel. She was angry, stormed after him to confront him about this, but barged into the changing rooms to find him naked.'

'Ah.'

'Yeah. He laughed it off, but he knew what he'd done. He knew he'd pressed the right buttons to get her to follow and made sure he was "ready for his close up". And now the visual to anyone learning about this was she was stalking him. She left, almost in tears. And yesterday morning I had a word with him, saying he was out of order.'

'I'm guessing he played the victim?'

'Not at all,' Gates growled. 'He said Luna had forgotten that Little John was always big, and he was always happy to remind her when needed. If he hadn't said it while we were waiting for a photo shoot, I'd have finished the job I started on a balcony.'

This said, Gates rose.

'If we're finished here, can I go find Malcolm?' he asked icily. 'Now you've had all the salacious gossip?'

And before Anjli could answer, Gates stormed out of the Green Room. Leaning back on her plastic chair, Anjli looked around the room, seeing the faces watching her.

'Don't worry,' she smiled as she rose. 'We'll be getting to all of you, too.'

13

STAGED NAMES

FLICK MCCARTHY WAS IN THE BALLROOM, ARGUING WITH A short, black-haired brute of a man, who, from his cauliflower ear had to have played serious rugby at one time, and still had the body of pure stone and muscle to prove it.

Seeing Monroe and Sampson approach, Flick smiled, and the black-haired man, seeing an opportunity to get out of whatever argument had been going on, disappeared quickly out of a side door.

'Well, if it isn't tall, grey and handsome,' she growled. Then glancing at Sampson's ginger locks. 'Bloody hell. Is that real hair or a dye job?'

'Real,' Sampson admitted, unconsciously running a hand through his hair. At this, Flick looked back at Monroe.

'Who's your friend?' she enquired. 'Tell him to go play with the other kids, so us adults can have some grown-up time.'

It was meant to sound seductive, but Monroe couldn't help but shudder.

'You should know DCI Sampson,' he said jovially. 'You quoted him in the press release you sent out last night.'

Monroe expected Flick to deny this, or at least look confused, try to bluff it out, but instead she took a deep breath, blew it out, nodded, and reached a hand out, offering it to Sampson.

'Yeah, sorry about that,' she said. 'All the research in the world doesn't plan for curveballs.'

'So, you admit you sent the piece to the press?' Monroe was surprised at the brazenness in front of him.

'Of course, I did,' Flick snapped back in reply. 'Someone had to control the narrative, and it wasn't going to be the soppy bastards who run this event. The man I just spoke to was John Moss, who co-organises this, and all he's doing is hiding in his bloody room and complaining about his daughter.'

'From what I hear, his daughter had a valid issue with your client,' Monroe replied icily.

'*Had* being the relevant word here,' Flick sniffed. 'Monty's dead now, and all that stuff becomes irrelevant.'

'I think you're trivialising a lot of issues,' Sampson interjected. 'Maybe you should consider that when you do this again?'

'Oh, I probably am, but I'm too old, and too far gone to care,' Flick shrugged. 'Fact of the matter is, Monty pissed a lot of people off, someone had a pop at him and succeeded. The audience weren't expecting it, but several were filming the ceremonies, and suddenly bam! There's an arrow jutting out of the guest. You know this, you've seen the images.'

She was hopping from foot to foot as she spoke and gave the impression of a woman who'd drunk way too much caffeine.

'YouTube is taking the videos down as quickly as they go up, as having live murder on the site doesn't really help them, but papers look for ways to skirt around it. I knew they were going to find out, so I called Milton Keynes up and asked who'd run such a case,' she said, nodding at Sampson. 'I was given your name, and I put it into the piece after Derek refused to close the event and pay us.'

'You wanted fans to keep turning up,' Monroe replied. 'More signings, more money for you.'

'I saw Malcolm was taking photos, so I looked at them, asked to buy one from him. He wouldn't though, but I learnt he'd promised Alex Hamilton one, so I told the soppy sod I'd cover the cost, as it was for a memorial, but I sent it to the papers with the piece. Problem was, I was so busy sorting this out, I didn't realise you City folk came and sniped the case.'

'Which made the story incorrect.'

'I should arrest you for impersonating an officer,' Sampson snapped. 'I'm getting crap from all directions because of you.'

'I was mitigating damage,' Flick folded her arms defiantly, as if daring Sampson to try. 'And I'll do it again.'

'Did Alex Hamilton ever explain why he wanted the photo?' Monroe asked.

'Nope, and I won't ask him either,' Flick replied. 'Not my place to ask my clients why they want trophies of murders. And that's not a line I've said much in my line of work.'

'I noticed we haven't had any new posts from the papers about Peter Crock's death,' Monroe raised an eyebrow. 'I'm guessing he wasn't one of your clients?'

'Never wanted him to be,' Flick said dismissively. 'I deal with talent, not backroom boys.'

'Where were you at nine pm last night?' Monroe asked, tiring of the conversation.

'I was in the hotel, trying to get the show cancelled,' Flick snapped. 'I spoke to you and your Detective Sergeant, remember?'

'I remember talking to you for a matter of moments, and then you walking off.' Monroe faced down Flick, his voice now cold. 'You could easily have gone to kill Peter Crock. Maybe as revenge for him killing Montgomery Pryce? Maybe you killed Pryce as well? I didn't see you in any of the footage showing the stage.'

'That's because I wasn't on it.' Flick shook her head. 'This is pointless. You want to speak to me again, speak to my solicitors. I will not be attacked purely because I did what was best for my client.'

'One last thing, no attack,' Monroe held a hand up. 'Alex Hamilton said you told him to meet in the costume room this morning for a debrief, but Nigel Cummings said he hadn't heard anything about this.'

'That's because it's bollocks and I never said that to Alex,' Flick snapped. 'I don't know what his problem is, but after his attitude towards Luna, his jokes about Monty's death, his constant drug using and his generally shifty behaviour, I won't be working with him again.'

Monroe noted this down.

'But you knew about the drug use,' he said. 'You hired him after his previous manager walked on this very point.'

'Alex promised he was now clean,' Flick replied icily. 'I gave him the benefit of the doubt until I saw him sharing with Peter Crock last night.'

'Alex Hamilton gave Peter Crock painkillers?'

'I don't know what they were, but Crock was definitely blissed out, according to his hangers on.'

Monroe noted this down, taking his time.

'Don't leave the hotel,' he eventually hissed. 'We'll definitely be talking again.'

'I thought you were cute.' Flick stormed past them now. 'Guess I was wrong. We could have had something special.'

'Doubtful, you're not my type,' Monroe replied, looking back at Sampson. 'Well, it looks like we now know for a fact you were used.'

'Tell it to my superiors,' Sampson moaned. 'They're still pissed.'

'I'll get Detective Superintendent Bullman to do it today,' Monroe was already walking towards the side door, and the corridors that led to the hub they'd taken over. 'Look, you're here already, so we could always use an extra pair of hands—'

'I'd better not,' Sampson smiled, offering out his hand to shake. 'I'll be in the Milton Keynes unit if you need anything, but I've had enough theatrics for the day.'

Monroe grinned, shaking the hand.

'Thanks,' he said as Sampson turned and walked off towards the lobby. Then, rotating his neck to loosen it, Monroe walked off towards the hub, and Billy.

BILLY AND JESS WERE WITH DECLAN AND DE'GEER WHEN Monroe entered the room, all gathered around Billy's portable monitor setup.

'This looks interesting,' Monroe said, pouring himself a coffee. 'Is Billy doing a show and tell?'

'Not yet, Guv,' Billy grinned. 'But we might have something. I'm going through Jess's notes, as she's been word crunching for me.'

Monroe nodded as Declan and De'Geer walked over to him.

'So, it was the manager, Flick McCarthy,' Monroe said. 'She sent the papers the press release, trying to sort damage limitation for her dead client. She used Sampson because she didn't expect us to turn up.'

He looked around.

'Where are the others?'

'Anjli and Cooper are checking Pryce and Crock's rooms, sir,' De'Geer replied officiously. 'Bullman and Doctor Marcos are still in the tent area.'

'And you're here because ...?'

'Because I asked him to wait.' Billy looked around from the computer. 'As I said, I might have something, and it's a possible motive.'

'Oh, I like possible motives,' Monroe smiled. 'Show and tell, laddie. Show and tell.'

'Okay,' Billy turned fully now to face Declan, De'Geer and Monroe, while Jess carried on scrolling through a list on an iPad. 'When we started last night, I didn't have much to go on, and we were looking for anything.'

'Aye, I get that.'

'So, I started looking through previous TV shows Montgomery Pryce was in. Seeing if there were any coincidences, or problems with the cast, anything.'

'I'm guessing you found something?'

'Well, Robert Standish was involved with both *Young Robin* and *Hooded Outlaw*, and there were a couple of things here and there, but nothing major,' Billy said. 'But, by that point, I was examining *Young Robin*. We know when *Hooded*

Outlaw was created, it was supposed to be a direct sequel, right? But Pryce didn't want the actors who were with him in the old show to gain success again. There was a different Sheriff, so that was easy, and the only characters they had that would have crossed over were Marian, Tuck and Little John, as the others weren't used in the former.'

'Okay,' Monroe sat down. 'I can see there's motive here, but we're talking over thirty years since they lost their jobs. Why kill him now?'

'Well, to be honest, I don't know if they were the killers, but I wanted to check everything anyway.' Billy turned to the computer, tapping on the keyboard. 'Felicity Marshall played Marian, she was sixteen when she got the part, was a teenage Olympic-hopeful archer when she was cast, and it looks like she acted little afterwards. And Michael Bailey was Little John. He did a few things before and after, mainly one-shots in things like *Doctor Who* or *The Bill*, nothing as big as he had, pardon the pun, as Little John. His last role, in fact, was some small-budget movie with Montgomery Pryce, a couple of years before *Hooded Outlaw*, and directed by Robert Standish.'

'They would have been planning the show then,' Declan commented. 'Bailey might have even lost the role while filming. That could have made him angry enough to kill. Can we find him?'

'That's the fun part,' Billy smiled, and Declan sighed. The worst part of Billy's show and tell sessions was the dramatic build-up he loved so much. 'Michael Bailey doesn't exist.'

Monroe frowned as he looked at Declan but knew better than to interrupt.

'I found an interview with Michael Bailey, transcribed

from a Saturday morning show with Noel Edmonds from 1977—'

'*Swap Shop*,' Monroe smiled. 'Loved that show. I had a crush on Maggie Philbin.'

Billy went to make a snarky comment, but then thought better of it.

'Anyway, in this interview, Noel's talking to Marian and John in their costumes,' he continued.

'No Pryce?'

Billy shook his head.

'And the transcript made it sound like he was supposed to be there but hadn't arrived. Anyway, during it, Michael Bailey points out Little John was his second ever role. He's very excited. Noel asks if Mister and Mrs Bailey, his parents are proud, and Michael says they don't exist, as it's not his real name.'

'A stage name?'

'Exactly,' Billy nodded. 'He uses both David Bowie and Michael Caine as examples of how some people change their name when they become actors or musicians.'

'Otherwise known as David Jones and Maurice Mickle-white,' Declan added. 'Did he give his real name on the show?'

'No, and he said it was a closely guarded secret.' Billy was reading a page of text on his screen now. 'But, in a follow-up story a few years later for a local paper in Kent, where he apparently comes from originally, he said in the interview he'd tried to register his real name with Equity, the Actor's union in 1973, when he started acting professionally, but was told the name was taken the year before. Rather than being a second person with the same name, he changed it.'

Billy nodded over at Jess, who now looked up from the pad.

'But here's the thing,' he continued. 'In this newspaper article, he was asked if he'd seen this actor's work, and Michael was very complimentary, saying they'd bumped into each other while he was filming "down the corridor" during the first season of *Young Robin*, but he was more of a fan of his war show. Jess?'

Jess looked at Monroe and Declan now.

'*Young Robin* was filmed in studios,' she explained. 'The forest was fake trees, taken from an old *Doctor Who* episode. And they filmed it at BBC TV Centre, in White City.'

'So, it makes sense that "down the corridor" means another BBC show,' Declan nodded.

'I started going through the lists of BBC studio shows of the time, to work out what could have been on at the same time as *Young Robin*, and I found a show called *The Brothers*,' Jess continued. 'Was a big hit in the early seventies. And I found an actor's name that was in that show, and also in *Colditz*, which was also filmed by the BBC, a name that didn't appear in anything until 1972.'

'*Colditz* could be the "war show" he mentioned,' De'Geer leant closer, caught up in the mystery.

'Well, come on, lassie, tell us!' Monroe moaned, pointing accusingly at Billy. 'Don't start up a flair for the dramatic like this wee fella!'

'We've held off because we've been waiting for Equity to come back to us,' Billy explained. 'And as it's a Saturday, it took a while for someone to check into it. But I had a call from someone five minutes ago, who knew Michael Bailey well, back in the day, and who confirmed his real name, the same as the actor in *The Brothers* and *Colditz*, was Malcolm Stoddard.'

There was a long moment of silence as the officers in the room took this in.

Eventually, leaping from his chair, Monroe looked over at De'Geer.

'Photo room, now!' he ordered. 'Get that son of a bitch in here immediately!'

DECLAN FOLLOWED DE'GEER AT SPEED TO THE PHOTO OPS room, but found the door closed. Opening it, he found a young man, in the green T-shirt of the volunteers, sitting at the table, his feet up, reading on his phone.

'Where's Stoddard?' Declan hissed.

'Who?'

'The bloody photographer!'

'Oh,' the volunteer sat up now. 'Well, the photos were halted after that guy died. Not the one last night, but the new one. Anyway, he said he needed to take a pee, so asked me to sit in here while he was gone, as there's a lot of expensive stuff in the room.'

'How long ago was this?'

'Only five minutes—' the volunteer looked at the phone, '—oh, more like fifteen minutes. I fell down an Instagram hole.'

He looked back at Declan.

'Were you looking for a photo?' he asked. 'I don't think we're doing them today. There was a guy who died—'

'Do I look like I want a sodding photo?' Declan hissed. 'Does the Police Sergeant behind me look like he wants one?'

He looked around the room.

'Lock the place down,' he said to De'Geer. 'Nobody in or out. He won't have got too far yet, and we still have people at the entrances to the car park. Anywhere he's gone, it's on foot.'

As De'Geer left, Declan looked back at the volunteer, now realising something bad was happening around him, and wishing he was somewhere else.

'Were you here when he left?'

'Yes,' the volunteer nodded. 'He took a call, an old friend, he said. Confused why they called, but I think he'd had someone checking records?'

'Why would you say that?' Declan asked.

'Because he said, "are you sure they asked about my record?" when he spoke,' the volunteer shrugged. 'Disconnected, said he needed a pee, left.'

Declan wanted to punch the wall. The Equity contact probably called Malcolm up to let him know someone was asking about him. Probably thought he was doing a favour for a friend, thinking someone was considering him for a role. But all it did was tip Malcolm Stoddard, the original Little John, that someone was learning his true identity.

And now a potential killer was in the wind, and Declan had let him walk past right under his nose.

'If he comes back, you tell us,' he snapped, leaving the photo room, but he knew it was a weak response.

If Malcolm Stoddard was the killer, he wouldn't be coming back soon.

14

HOODED MANHUNT

ANJLI WAS IN MONTGOMERY PRYCE'S SUITE WITH PC COOPER when the phone call came.

They'd already been through Peter Crock's room and had found nothing of interest as they checked through it; most of his personal items were likely in his bell tent at the back of the hotel, and this genuinely felt like a room that was only used to sleep in. And, added to the fact, housekeeping had already tidied up before they arrived, there wasn't much to see.

Montgomery Pryce's room, however, was different.

For a start, there was a "do not disturb" sign on the door. Anjli had wondered whether this was placed by the police the night before, purely to make sure housekeeping didn't hide any clues, but one step inside the room, using the master key card they'd been provided by the hotel was enough to show this wasn't the case.

The suite was in a state. As they changed their latex gloves for the new location, Anjli could only compare the room itself to the one she'd stayed in the previous night with

Jess, where you entered to a bathroom on the right, and then two beds facing a cabinet, a TV and a small desk table, the wide window at the end looking out over the gardens. On the left as you entered was a closet and in there were a handful of hangers, some shelving, a safe, an ironing board and a hairdryer. Beside the TV was a coffee making machine that took coffee pods, and a fridge underneath that held incredibly expensive minibar items.

Pryce's room was completely different.

For a start, it was a corner room, and as you entered, you found yourself in a magnolia sitting room of sorts, with a more expansive desk next to a sofa and a coffee table that faced a sideboard, with the TV on top. To the side was a marble bathroom that not only held a shower but also a whirlpool bath, and through a door on the right, Anjli faced an ornate, four-poster bed. It was opulent and fabulous, and it looked like a bomb had gone off in it.

On the business desk, there was a room service tray with two plates on it, with the remains of half a porterhouse steak and a salad. Beside it was a bucket with water, most likely once ice, surrounding a half-finished bottle of champagne. There was a robe, hotel branded, scattered across the sofa, and on the floor of the bathroom was a pair of swimming trunks, still damp.

'He must have stormed in, got changed and walked out, after they cut him off,' Cooper commented. 'They said it was early afternoon when he finally turned up, after they had seen him in the pool.'

'And the meal was from the previous night.' Anjli nodded. On the glass coffee table was white dust. Anjli looked at it, before turning to Cooper.

'Do you—' she started, but Cooper had already pulled

out a small phial, opening the top and, with a small, clean Q-Tip from the same baggie scraped up some powder, dropping it into the phial and swirling it around. The reactive agent in the phial turned a very healthy shade of blue, and Cooper sealed it up, placing it into the evidence baggie.

'Cocaine,' she said. 'Quite pure stuff, Sarge.'

'So, he was a coke-head, that figures.' Anjli walked over to the bin beside the desk and upturned it onto the floor. Only torn pieces of paper fell out; a couple of receipts, a post-it note with a phone number and an envelope were there. The envelope had the words *Montgomery Pryce – Per Diem* on it, and Anjli assumed this was his daily stipend for food and drink, given when he arrived.

Apart from the cocaine, the half-eaten and now spoiled meal and the scattered clothes, the room didn't seem to have much else in it, so Anjli walked into the bed area, facing the four-poster bed as she stopped.

The bed was dishevelled and unmade; the duvet tossed to the side. Again, if Pryce had been hurrying to get to the convention, he might not have bothered to make the bed, and to be honest, he wasn't going to have the housekeeping staff come in if there were drugs around.

There was a letter, A4 in size and folded on the duvet, however. Picking it up, and opening it, Anjli called Cooper, showing it to her.

PRYCE
I KNOW WHAT YOU DID. YOU WILL PAY.
SORT YOUR AFFAIRS.

'I don't think that came with the per diem,' Anjli said, as Cooper pulled out another baggie, placing the sheet of paper into it. The message had been printed; the text large. It would have been hard to miss.

'Maybe this was why Pryce didn't do the meal?' Cooper asked. 'He was worried about his safety?'

'Possibly,' Anjli nodded, looking at the side of the bed that hadn't been slept in. The duvet was still tucked into the baseboard, and on it were a variety of scattered items, including a shaver, an iPad, some worn clothing and underwear and a pair of sunglasses.

'He really was a slob,' Anjli said, but stopped as she walked along the bed, pausing and pulling out a pencil, using the end to move a shirt off another item of clothing.

'It's underwear,' she said. 'But not men's underwear.'

It was a pair of deep-red, skimpy panties. Cooper leant closer to examine them.

'*La Perla*. High end Chantilly lace, although they've suffered over the last couple of years.'

'You know your skimpies,' Anjli grinned, and Cooper blushed.

'A girl can dream,' she replied, straightening. 'What these are, Sarge, well, they're a gift for someone special. You don't buy off the rack and hope when you're paying this much.'

'So, we have someone Pryce knows intimately.' Anjli nodded. 'Jenny Moss? The girl from the spa?'

'No,' gently pulling the panties from the floor with her pen, Cooper held them up. 'These are for someone a little larger than Jenny. I saw a photo of her, she's very slim. These are more filled.'

'So now we need a Cinderella for the shoe,' Anjli mused. 'Annoyingly, it could be anyone. We'll need to see if forensics can get any prints, but in a hotel room, it's near on impossible—'

She paused as she moved further around. On the floor beside the bed was a used condom wrapper.

'Mister Pryce may have had issues with Jenny in the spa, but it looks like he got lucky on Thursday,' she said, but paused as she observed Cooper's face. 'What?'

'Are we sure he did what he did?' she asked. 'I mean, I know John Moss said so, but he's the dad. And Luna didn't like him—'

'We have multiple witnesses,' Anjli frowned at the comment.

'True, but there was also one witness who told Linda she didn't see anything happen. I spoke to her – Chantelle – and she said Pryce was as confused as anyone when Luna started shouting at him. And he hadn't even seen Jenny that day for a massage. He'd seen *Chantelle*.'

'Records don't say that.'

'I know, Sarge, that's why I think something dodgy's going on. And now we have someone else in his room the night before ...'

Anjli nodded as she considered this.

'You're right, it's a lot of hearsay, and we need solid facts,' she said. 'We need to find out if anyone saw Pryce on the Thursday, and if so, who he was with, and then check with the spa—'

She looked across at the phone beside the bed as it rang. Picking it up, she held it to her ear.

'DS Kapoor,' she said, pausing as she listened. Then, placing the phone handset back, she looked across the bed at Cooper.

'Malcolm Stoddard is missing,' she explained, already walking towards the door. 'Apparently, he also played the Little John in Pryce's first TV show. Dammit!'

'Sarge? What aren't you saying?'

Anjli stopped at the door.

'When I was talking to Ryan Gates, Stoddard came to the Green Room door,' she said. 'Only half an hour ago. He looked stressed and left the moment he saw me. But then Gates tried to leave as well, claiming he needed to do photo reshoots. I thought nothing of it, but now ...'

'You think Ryan Gates might be connected?'

'We don't know what's going on with Malcolm.' Anjli opened the door, ushering Cooper through. 'It might just be nothing, but the fact he seems to have run is suspicious as hell. Come on, let's go help find an outlaw.'

MALCOLM STODDARD WANTED TO SCREAM, BUT HE KNEW THE moment he did, he'd reveal his location, and they'd find him within minutes.

He knew he shouldn't have stayed after Pryce was killed, but he didn't want to draw attention to himself. He wasn't Michael Bailey anymore. He was simple old Malcolm Stoddard, photographer to the stars.

How the hell did they find him?

He'd been lucky, as a friend of his had been on call in Equity when the request had come through. As the UK's trade union for creative practitioners, they had to be constantly available, as actors could call at any time, with requests that could vary from contract negotiations to unfair dismissals and inappropriate behaviour accusations, either by the member or against the member. The union needed to be there 24/7, and as such, the London number was always manned.

Malcolm had spent a few years as one of the union reps, and the contacts he'd made during that time had just saved his life, as, when his friend had received a call from the London City Police, asking for confirmation that Michael Bailey, a onetime member in the seventies and eighties had been the stage name of Malcolm Stoddard, they'd said they'd check into it, and then immediately called him up to ask what trouble he'd got into this time.

He'd claimed it was just background, explaining he was at the convention where Pryce had just died, and the friend had bought the lie, but they'd also mentioned they were about to let the police know, and because of their friendship, they were suggesting if there was a problem, he should get out quickly.

He knew he didn't have long, so his first call was to find Gates. He'd told the green shirt volunteer to man the table for a moment, citing the cost of the equipment, and had left as calmly as he could, while knowing he was about to become the subject of a manhunt. He'd quickly walked to the Green Room, knowing most of the guests had been placed there, but stopped at the entrance when he saw Gates and the copper, Kapoor, talking.

The bastard's sold me out, he thought, catching Gates's eye, but as the copper looked around, Malcolm kept moving. After all, he didn't know if they already *knew* who he was.

The hotel was open for business now, as all the attendees details had been logged for the police, and now people could come and go, although they were still checked at the gate by local officers with lists, so Malcolm decided his best chance would be to grab his car, explain to the police that he needed more photo paper, and as soon as he was away, he could find a place to lie low and hide. But, as he exited the hotel, he saw the large police sergeant, De'Geer, running across the lobby of the hotel. Malcolm had backed against the wall beside the main entrance, hiding from the giant, in case he glanced outside, but one look at the gates to the entrance of the hotel showed the police officers on duty there were watching him in confusion, the sight of a man leaving the hotel and immediately hiding to the side not normally the type of thing innocent people did.

As one of them spoke into his radio, Malcolm quickly walked into the car park, breaking into a sprint the moment he was out of sight. The car park didn't go anywhere, but there was a chance he could get into the medieval part of the grounds, sneak through the tents and enter back into the hotel through the guest door. They'd all be looking for him out the front and, now in the building, he could find an empty room to bed down in and hide—

'*Hey!*' The police officer that'd been watching him now moved back into view. '*Stay where you are!*'

There was no more time for subtlety, so Malcolm sprinted across the car park, heading for the wooden-slatted wall that blocked the car park from the hotel grounds. Using the slats as a ladder, he quickly shimmied up the wall, throwing himself over and landing in a painful heap on the grass bank on the other side.

Winded for a moment, he tried to catch his breath, but then rose, limp-running through the tents, past Rory and the other confused hippies that always followed Peter when he was alive, aiming for the far end of the hotel and hoping his appearance was surprising enough to pause them from shouting, or even understanding what was happening here right now.

He didn't expect the quarterstaff that spun out from

behind one of the bell tents, the blow catching him in the chest and sending him stumbling backwards, clutching at his ribs. The wielder of the quarterstaff, a white-haired woman in a business suit moved into view, and Malcolm groaned. He'd met her earlier and knew she was the boss of all the bloody police.

'Stop,' she said. 'Don't make me play Robin Hood and best you with a quarterstaff, Little John.'

Malcolm desperately grabbed at a piece of timber on the floor beside him, holding it up. It was the centre pole for a yet un-erected bell tent, and it was weighted wrong, but it was a weapon and it evened the odds up as he spun it in his hands.

'You're making a mistake,' he said. 'I can't be taken in. You need to let me pass.'

'I thought the rule was Robin wanted to pass and John wanted to stop him?' Bullman – yes, that was her name, *Bullman* – settled into a balanced stance, holding her staff up. 'If you're going to play the part, get the sodding story right!'

Malcolm didn't reply, instead swinging his makeshift staff hard at the detective, who only just managed to block it as she brought both arms up. He would have whipped the staff around and taken out her legs, but the end was too heavy. As he tried to do this, it scraped along the grass, slowing the momentum, and he had to bring it up himself to stop a vicious downward swing from her quarterstaff, the impact knocking them both backwards. Malcolm could see people noticing the fight, and others were coming out of the bar, onto the patio. He cursed his own stupidity; *of course, the police would still examine the crime scene.* He now needed to find another way—

He stumbled as something hard and wooden slammed into the back of his legs, taking him down at the back of the knees, and he staggered forward as Bullman slammed down with the staff, knocking his makeshift weapon out of his fingers and onto the grass. As he rose again, he felt another wooden weapon against his neck, and turned to see another woman, in a grey PPE uniform, holding an unstrung longbow as a sword, the wood against his throat.

'Stand down,' she said, as Bullman pulled out handcuffs, walking over to him, spinning him around and cuffing him from behind.

'You don't understand!' he cried out. 'I need to get out of here!'

'Why?' the PPE woman asked, lowering the bow. 'So, you can kill again?'

'Kill?' Malcolm stammered; his eyes wide in shock. 'I'm not the killer!'

He pointed at the tent where, hours earlier, Peter Crock had been found.

'I didn't kill Peter!' he exclaimed. 'And I didn't kill Monty Pryce!'

'Then why run?'

Malcolm fell to his knees, sobbing in fear.

'Because I'm the next bloody victim!' he cried.

15

CUPBOARD INTERVIEW

'WE FOUND THE LETTER,' COOPER PLACED AN A4 SHEET ON THE table. 'It was where he said it was,'

Declan picked it up, currently in a clear evidence bag, holding it up so he could read it properly.

'Stoddard,' he read aloud. 'I know what you did. You will pay. Sort out your affairs.'

'It's exactly the same as the one we found in Pryce's room, except for the name on it,' Anjli nodded at the second piece of paper, found earlier, currently being held by Billy, latex gloves on, as he placed it into a scanner. 'But we haven't found one anywhere Peter Crock could have been. No note in his tent, nothing in his hotel room.'

'He could have tossed it away,' Monroe suggested. 'Thought it was a joke.'

'Do me a favour,' Declan looked at Cooper. 'Check the fire pit where the re-enactors are. There's every chance Peter got the letter and burned it. We might find it in there.'

'We might only find the ashes of it in there,' Monroe added.

'Worth a try, though,' Declan shrugged. 'No stone unturned and all that.'

There was a machine noise that echoed through the room, and everyone looked at Billy, who reddened.

'It's a portable scanner,' he explained, taking the sheet out once it had been scanned and passing it back to Anjli, placing it into the baggie she was holding out. 'It's louder than the one in the office.'

'So, what magic are you using here?' Monroe pointed at the scan of the letter sent to Pryce. 'Zooming in for fingerprints?'

'Zooming in, but not for that.' Billy was already on his computer, magnifying the image, and scrolling across the top of it. 'I'm looking for machine identification code, or MIC. You can tell by the ink on the paper that it was printed by a LaserJet, or something similar.'

'So, a laser printer, not a more common inkjet?' Declan asked. 'What do we have in the office?'

'We have laser printers,' Billy replied. 'That's the problem. Unless you actively buy the printer, you don't really know what you have, and most people don't really care, unless they're printing promotional literature that needs a particular quality. These days, laser printers can almost be as cheap as inkjets. And that's where the fun starts. You see, a few years back, printer companies made agreements with US law enforcement that allowed their printers to be forensically traceable. Some inkjets have this, but all lasers do.'

On the screen, he played with filters, enhancing the blue levels on the screen as he zoomed in even deeper.

'I'm looking for tracking dots,' he explained. 'They're effectively invisible to the naked eye, a matrix of yellow markings, a tenth of a millimetre in diameter, and placed in an eight by sixteen format.'

He zoomed across the page again.

'In total, they cover only four-square centimetres, and encode any page that comes out of a printer with a serial number, date and time, all of which can be interpreted using a simple cipher.'

'This sounds like a needle in a haystack,' Anjli muttered, peering at the screen.

'It is, but imagine the needle is a tenth of the size of the needle and doesn't look like a needle,' Billy smiled. 'But, once I find it, I'll have the binary matrix, and once it's deciphered, we'll know when the documents were printed, and where.'

'I'm guessing this isn't an immediate art?' Monroe asked. Billy shook his head, not replying as he scanned the image, and Monroe sighed, looking over at Declan.

'Right then,' he said. 'Let's go and talk to our Little John.'

———

THEY HAD PLACED MALCOLM STODDARD IN A SMALL OFFICE AT the back of the reception area, with De'Geer standing guard. It was a basic room, one desk beside a door, and two chairs had been positioned, one on either side of it to create the semblance of an interview room. Monroe had considered taking Malcolm to the Milton Keynes Command Unit, but Declan had pointed out that currently they didn't have anything on the man, except for the fact he'd lied about his identity. And even then, it was more a case of not mentioning he used to be an actor, so not exactly *lying*.

'Right then,' Monroe said as they entered the room, Malcolm sitting at the table. 'This isn't an official interview, as we don't have the equipment here, but with your permission, I'd like to record it with my phone.'

Malcolm nodded, and Declan stood to the side of the now-sitting Monroe, currently turning on the voice recorder app and placing the device between them.

'You do not have to say anything,' Declan added, stating the police caution Bullman had already given the man when she arrested him. 'But it may harm your defence if you do not mention when questioned, something which you later rely on in court. Anything you do say may be given in evidence.'

'Do I need a solicitor?' Malcolm asked.

'Your call,' Monroe replied. 'Do you think you need one?'

'I attacked your boss with a plank of wood.'

'From what we hear, you were in fear for your life, and people do stupid things, irrational things when they feel this way.' Monroe leant closer, resting his elbows on the table. 'However, I think that's not the problem you should be worrying about right now, laddie.'

Malcolm swallowed.

'I think I'm okay,' he said. 'I'll answer what you need.'

'Did you kill Montgomery Pryce?'

'No!' Malcolm exclaimed. 'I was taking photos out the front! Five hundred odd people could see me!'

'Did you kill Peter Crock?'

Again, Malcolm shook his head.

'I've known him for forty years,' he said. 'Do you think I'd wait until now to kill him? I could have done it in his house, I could have ...'

He stopped.

'No,' Declan smiled. 'Please, keep telling us about the many ways you'd kill our murder victim.'

Malcolm stared across the table, but Declan felt that

rather than being stared at, he was being stared through, as if Malcolm was mentally miles away.

'Why did you run?' Monroe asked. 'You were told we were on to you, weren't you?'

'A friend let me know, and I knew you'd put two and two together and make five,' Malcolm muttered. 'That I killed Pryce because he replaced me with Alex Hamilton.'

'Did you?'

'No!' Malcolm protested. 'Pryce knew who I was. It's not a secret. I just knew you'd take me, arrest me, place me somewhere ...'

He looked around the room again.

'Somewhere I could be got to.'

'You think someone could kill you while we're here?'

'Why not?' Malcolm looked up defiantly. 'Someone got to Peter.'

'Last night, around nine in the evening,' Declan said, noticing Malcolm's surprised expression. 'You didn't know?'

'I assumed it was this morning,' Malcolm replied. 'I didn't see Peter after the ... well, after.'

'Tell us about the letter,' Monroe changed tactics. 'When did you get it?'

'Thursday night,' Malcolm whispered. 'It was slipped under my door.'

'Did you see who posted it?'

'No, I wasn't there when they did it,' Malcolm shook his head. 'There was a crew dinner. I was in a Toby Carvery half a mile away when it happened.'

'Do you have any idea who could have sent it?'

Malcolm didn't reply.

'Malcolm, we're trying to help you,' Declan said. 'We

know Pryce had the same message. Peter didn't have one, but you think he would have, don't you?'

Malcolm nodded.

'So why don't you tell us what this message to you means?' Monroe asked. 'Show us why we should protect you and not arrest you?'

Malcolm rubbed at his chin, pursing his lips as he worked out how to answer this.

'We were in an incident,' he said. 'Years ago.'

'Tell me about it.' Monroe tapped the table, reminding Malcolm of the phone recording the conversation. 'And speak clearly.'

'It was thirty, forty years ago,' Malcolm eventually spoke. 'Middle of the eighties, and we were in Prague, Eastern Europe, doing a film. It's now the Czech Republic, but back then, it was just Czechoslovakia.'

'Define "we" for us.'

'Me, Monty Pryce, Robert Standish, Peter Crock,' Malcolm replied.

'The director?' Declan asked, and Malcolm nodded.

'Yeah, he'd got a gig doing a small-budget film, and we'd all kept in touch after *Young Robin* was cancelled,' he explained. 'It wasn't much, but neither of us had done that well. Monty had done a couple of *Coronation Street* episodes; I'd been in *Juliet Bravo*. Robert needed safe hands, as we all knew it was a nightmare.'

'Why a nightmare?'

'Czechoslovakia before the fall of the Iron Curtain was a logistical problem,' Malcolm explained. 'It was a war story, and financed by both Western and Eastern Europe, but while we were there, we needed military protection and everything.'

'Why was Peter there?'

'Props,' Malcolm replied. 'He was an explosives expert. We were doing a war story. Anyway, it was a quick shoot, and pretty painless.'

'Doesn't sound so bad,' Monroe mused.

'While we're shooting, Robert got a fax from the UK,' Malcolm continued. 'He'd been talking to the BBC about revamping Robin. We'd heard rumours, but when the ITV show started, we assumed it was off the table, because who'd do conflicting Robin Hoods at the same time? It was insane. But we'd also heard that there was a chance the current ITV season was the last – they'd even replaced the lead actor, so that never bodes well unless you were James Bond or Doctor Who – so if we took our time, we could have it out in eighty-seven, a year or two after the show on the other channel ended. And, we had the opportunity of creating a show that was a direct sequel to *Young Robin*, establishing a lineage ITV didn't have.'

'And you were going to be Little John?'

'Robert wanted us all back,' Malcolm nodded. 'He had stories already worked out, he thought Peter would be a good addition as he'd helped with props on the last season of *Young Robin*. Everything looked great, and the fax was effectively the BBC green-lighting the show, and saying they wanted him to work on a pilot.'

'Still doesn't sound so bad,' Declan commented.

'Yeah, well, that was when everything turned to shit,' Malcolm muttered, kicking out at the chair leg as he spoke. 'We were so convinced we were about to become stars, we started partying. We took our eye off the movie we were making, because in our minds we were two years down the road and playing Saturday nights in the *Doctor Who* spot.

Monty's role in the film was minuscule, and so he started demanding rewrites. The lead actors in the film, the older ones, avoided us, and that made us more ballsy. We felt we were the new wave, and they were the establishment. We were punks to their Tories.'

He stopped, looking away.

'And then she died.'

'Who died?' Declan frowned.

Malcolm looked up, and his eyes were misty, filling with tears.

'I don't remember her name,' he said. 'She had an accident while we were in a house party ... no, wait, I think it was a cast party, actually. Pretty woman, no older than mid-thirties, she'd been working as an extra on the film, and was married to one of the film's financiers. Both me and Monty fancied the pants off her, probably because she was an older "Mrs Robinson" character and all that, but she was married, and not interested. I moved on, but Monty didn't. Couldn't believe she wouldn't be interested in him.'

'So, he was a keeper, even back then?' Monroe wasn't impressed. Malcolm made an apologetic shrug at this.

'Anyway, he kept plying her with drink throughout the night, and at some point gave her something, maybe a hallucinogenic? I'm not sure. All I know is one minute I'm downing shots with the British soldier they'd sent with us to keep us safe while we were there, and the next minute Peter's pulling at me, saying we need to go, that Pryce has gone too far, that the woman climbed onto the roof and jumped off, breaking her neck.'

He stopped, his eyes vacant, reliving the moment.

'We were taken back to the hotel we were staying at, and Robert was furious,' he said. 'We weren't supposed to be out of our rooms. But Monty spoke to him, cleared it all up, and the army consultants we had made sure everything was sorted, kept us out of the picture so the press couldn't put two and two together. We'd finished our scenes, so we were shipped back to the UK, and told to keep our heads down, and get on with things.'

'Harsh.'

'We were young, and we were being told this by experienced people,' Malcolm shrugged. 'Anyway, Robert stayed behind, made sure everything was sorted, and in the end it was pinned on an East German agent trying to gain information on the Westerners. There were a couple at the party anyway, there usually were, so the military people just worked their magic.'

'Okay, so we have a party where you, Peter and Montgomery pretty much shit the bed, but two years later they're on the show and you're replaced.' Monroe stroked at his chin. 'What happened during the intermediate time?'

'I started drinking,' Malcolm replied. 'Like, more than I did usually. I couldn't cope. I was useless without a couple of shots in me. And then that turned into a small bottle of scotch. I was let go from a couple of roles because I couldn't be relied on, and when they started casting for the Robin Hood sequel, I'd met with Monty and Robert, and they saw me in a terrible mess. Utter state, completely un-castable.'

He sniffed, wiping at an eye.

'I don't blame them,' he whispered. 'I'd have fired my arse too. They took one look at me and realised I was a liability. They went another way and recast everyone. BBC were pissed, because they wanted a sequel series, but in the end *Hooded Outlaw* came out of my inability to walk past a bottle.'

'What happened after that?'

'Ryan Gates sorted me out.' Malcolm wiped his eyes and looked up. 'He saw how bad I was. He was working with Robert by this point, just after he got the role as Will, and put me in a clinic, got me clean. Showed me what was wrong with my life.'

'And what was that?'

'Anything connected to Michael bloody Bailey,' Malcolm forced a smile. 'I realised I needed to stop being him. I needed to be Malcolm Stoddard again. And so, I started taking my hobby, photography, more seriously. I stopped talking to anyone "Michael" knew, and I began a new life. Lots of crime scene stuff, local press shots, village fairs, everything. Then, about ten years back, Ryan contacted me, asking if I did conventions. He'd had someone pull out of a Con he was doing in Glasgow, asked if I could step in. I was worried, because I knew Monty would be there, but I'd dyed my hair black as I was going grey, and I used to be a dirty blond, so it was a change anyway, and he didn't recognise me. He never knew me as Malcolm. None of them did, I'd asked Ryan to keep quiet on it, and I'd lost half my body weight once I stopped with the drink. Completely unrecognisable.'

'So, you carried on doing it?'

Malcolm nodded.

'Not just the Robin Hood shows, I did a lot of other pop culture ones. Anything with a guest having a photo taken was in my wheelhouse. And there's a show every weekend in the UK, so there's work going if you're known.'

'And the letter?'

'Came out of nowhere,' Malcolm admitted. 'But I knew I wasn't alone. Ryan told me he'd been approached by Monty to be his bodyguard a few months back, and he thought it was Monty trying to get one-up on him, but I think he had a message as well, and he was scared. Needed security, but someone he could trust. Heard nothing more, and on Thursday I came into my room to find the letter and heard Monty hadn't even shown in public. Next day – yesterday – when he's having photos, I can see he's shaken, watching everyone who came in for photos carefully. Mentions "bloody fan mail" and I know he's had the same. Fliss McCarthy confirmed it later.'

'Fliss?'

'Sorry,' Malcolm smiled. '*Flick*. Fliss is a nickname. But going back to Monty Pryce, the entire issue about not being around? He was trying not to be too visible.'

'I heard he was quite visible,' Declan muttered. 'According to Jenny Moss.'

'Yeah, I heard that too, the useless bastard,' Malcolm sighed. 'But the fact of the matter is, I know this is the first time in three years me, Peter and Monty have been in the same place.'

'So, you think someone knows about the death, almost forty years ago, and they're looking for revenge?'

'What else could it be?' Malcolm shrugged. 'And they're doing a bloody good job of it, too.'

'One last question,' Monroe asked, looking up at Declan as he spoke. 'Ryan Gates. How much of this does he know?'

'All of it, I reckon,' Declan replied, looking back at Malcolm. 'DS Kapoor saw you looking for him earlier today. Not casually, but more a "I'm in trouble and need your help" way, and this was shortly before we started looking for you.'

Holding a hand up to stop Malcolm's reply, Declan was suddenly reminded of his first conversation with Gates.

'When I got out, I was still in my twenties. Started working on

sets as an advisor, which was in a way similar to what I'd been doing before I left, although militarily.'

'Ryan Gates was the military advisor who sorted things out for you on that shoot, wasn't he?' Declan asked. 'He helped you out, fixed the problem for Robert Standish, and as a favour, when he was out of the military, Standish gave him a job on set.'

Malcolm nodded, and Declan slammed his fist on the table.

'You've kept this from us deliberately,' he hissed. 'Explain to us right now why we don't just lock you up and throw away the key?'

Malcolm didn't reply, just staring at the table.

'Do you know if he had a letter too?' Declan asked, forcing himself to calm down and continue.

'No,' Malcolm replied. 'That is, no, I don't know.'

'Ryan Gates went looking for Malcolm after Anjli spoke to him,' Monroe said, considering this. 'He hasn't been seen since.'

'Well, I think we should have another chat with the man,' Declan replied. 'Because currently, I'm thinking everything he's said so far has been a lie.'

16

THE POINTY END

'I'M NOT SURE WE SHOULD BE OUT HERE,' JESS MUTTERED AS she looked at Billy. 'We're being watched.'

'We're always being watched,' Billy replied, taking a mouthful of his cheese and ham toastie. 'But while everyone else runs about the hotel playing cops and robbers, we're stuck in a room with no air con, no windows, no natural light and no vitamin D.'

He waved around the half-empty patio, squinting up at the blue sky.

'Of course, I also wish I'd brought my sunglasses,' he moaned.

Jess smiled as she sipped at her coke, watching around the patio as she did so, taking in the other attendees.

'Why don't they just go home?' she whispered conspiratorially. 'They're not going to restart the convention now, surely?'

'You'd be surprised.' Billy dabbed at his mouth with a napkin. 'The organisers still can't pay out, and if anyone leaves, they're forfeiting their ticket cost. It's a weird and stubborn stalemate.'

He waved out at the medieval village with the remains of his toastie.

'They're finishing up the forensics right now, so I reckon they'll close up the village and the archery, and just focus on signings and photos. I saw more security arriving, so they're obviously taking it seriously.'

'Just not serious enough to cancel.'

Billy smiled.

'See?' he mocked slightly. 'You're getting it.'

'Do you think Mister Stoddard did it?' Jess sipped at her drink. 'It doesn't sound like it. Sounds more like he's the next victim.'

'Be pretty difficult with him under our protection.' Billy stretched his arms, letting the afternoon sun fall on his face. 'But yeah, I think he's innocent. Well, of this, at least.'

'Have they found Gates yet?'

'No,' Billy finished his food, speaking through half-filled mouthfuls. 'They think he went back to his room. His wife's rather worried.'

'She's not with him?'

Billy shook his head.

'And going on what Malcolm said, there's every chance he could be in a backroom corridor with the third arrow in his chest by now. Cooper said they've found the note left for Peter Crock. It was almost burned to a crisp in the fire pit. He probably read it and then tossed it straight in.'

Jess shuddered.

'We really need to find that arrow,' she said, finishing her drink.

It was Nigel Cummings who first brought the theft to light.

After being held in the Green Room for much of the morning, after lunch, the lockdown had been lessened, and guests and crew were allowed to return to whatever they wanted, as long as it was within the confines of the convention hotel. Which of course was fine for the organisers, as they could now demand, once more, that the guests return to the convention as if nothing bad had happened, while the guests themselves just wanted to hunker down in their rooms until the psycho killing everyone with a bow and arrow was caught.

Annoyingly, the sodding attendees were still there too; none of the soppy sods had the brains to understand the whole thing was over, and they should just leave, piss off, go about their lives. Nigel didn't even care that he hadn't sold his arrows, as getting home alive was better than being murdered.

If you were even going to be murdered, that was.

Nigel knew he was safe. Pryce and Crock had deserved what they got, for various reasons. Both had been liars, fakes and utter bastards, as far as he was concerned. If anyone else was to be offed, Nigel hoped it'd be Alex Hamilton or that fat ex-friar Terry Leighton.

Nigel knew people were just waiting for the moment Terry and Nigel started a fight again, as even though they'd done the whole public "kiss and make up", it was all for the cameras, and their hatred for each other in the nineties was pretty well known. They'd both fallen for the same man while at a celebrity event in *Heaven* Nightclub, in London. It'd been run by an acquaintance of Nigel's, who now lived in LA, living the high life as a drag club DJ. But back then, he'd been a sycophantic little shit, always taking Terry's side on things, and never resisting a moment to rub Nigel's nose in it.

No, that wasn't true. Nigel just liked that story better, as he got to be the victim. The truth was, he'd been just as bad as the others, more so even. And, when that little twink Richard Garcia went off with Carlos, the bloody barman of all people over both the aged queens trying for him, Nigel decided it was Terry's fault, and vice versa.

They played nice for the crowds, in the same way people who hated each other acted with each other. It was called acting for a reason, and their friendship was all part of an act. And Terry, knowing that Pryce loved to upstage people, would goad him into upstaging Nigel at every moment; partly to wind Nigel up, but more likely because if Montgomery Pryce was winding up Nigel, then he wasn't winding up Terry.

But then Richard had died a few years back in America, and the arguments they'd had back in the nineties seemed petty, as Nigel attended his funeral, brought back to the UK by his grieving aunt. A beautiful young man, brought down by a drug-dealing *vampire*.

That third arrow should be for that bastard.

The problem was, Nigel knew who had possession of the third arrow now. He'd been watching the others in the Green Room, he'd seen the problems between Luna and Alex over the last few years at events, and he'd spoken to Luna many times over the years, learning about her unknown history with Alex Hamilton. And, as far as the Green Room guests were concerned, it was the Wild West out there. *Maybe Luna was the one who had the arrow, and was intending to kill him for what he did? Maybe Alex had the arrow, and was going to shoot Luna for the hatred they seemed to have for each other?* All Nigel knew was Luna had recently found a solution to her Alex problem, and Nigel had offered to help, as long as he wasn't found out to be involved.

Because all Nigel cared about was *revenge.*

So, while the organisers now took the afternoon and following day's schedules, ripped them up and started working out what to do with the remaining guests, Nigel wandered into the costume room, checking to make sure nobody had been playing in there while he was away.

As expected, there were several blank mannequins now; when the actors from the other shows went, the people who'd brought their costumes left as well. Now, there was only one tabard and armour from the Ridley Scott movie, the Herne The Hunter from Nottingham Council, and his own collections, including the weapons. Nigel had removed the arrows earlier in the day, just in case someone needed more ammunition, but now he brought them out from behind a wooden chest and, with a sharpie taken from the desk beside it, he started to sign the arrows. With the three lost arrows counted, there were only nine now, as he'd been sold twelve by Peter at the start of the event and, being honest, that wasn't going to change soon, but Nigel had another eight in his bow bag, extras that could be used now if the interest was high.

And Nigel expected the interest to be high now. The arrows were the murder weapons; it had pretty much been shouted out to the world when it was published that morning, the closeup of one of Nigel's arrows, speckled with blood. Usually, he'd sell the arrows for fifty quid, but already he'd been offered five hundred for one, and he could see why the interest was there, as the arrows now had a story.

An arrow from the quiver that once held the shaft that killed Robin Hood himself.

Sort of.

It was still one of the set that killed Monty Pryce and Peter Crock, although Peter *Crook* was a better title for that man. And the killer's hands could have stroked past these as they picked their murderous messengers of death. He'd seen how much Nazi memorabilia went for. There was a definite market for death curios. He'd sell a few here, make a couple of grand from the big-time investors, and he would sell the rest under the counter, so to speak. Which was even better for Nigel, as with nobody knowing who'd bought what, there was no way of knowing that instead of seven arrows from that fatal quiver of ten, he'd sold a dozen, even more. Maybe he'd leave them with the costume, as he could make ten times what he paid for it now. It annoyed him he'd sold one before he'd realised their worth, but he could still make a killing, if people pardoned the pun.

Nigel couldn't help but grin at this. For years Pryce had been a prick of the highest degree, deliberately holding Nigel back, but in one selfless act of dying, he'd probably paid off Nigel Cummings' mortgage.

It was around now that Nigel realised something was missing.

The table opposite was strangely bare, and Nigel realised with a shiver down his spine that the Nemrod Corbeta speargun wasn't there anymore.

Had Ryan Gates taken it? Had someone else taken it to use on Ryan Gates? Nigel looked around nervously. *Was someone else now deciding to end old rivalries, using a speargun rather than a bow?*

No. He was being silly and overly dramatic. Peter and

Montgomery had been killed for valid reasons. Someone had most likely taken the opportunity of the lockdown to come into the room and steal an unguarded item.

Then why not Excalibur? Why not anything else?

It was true; the speargun was the only prop here that wasn't connected to Robin Hood and was only at the bloody convention because Ryan had asked for it. Nigel wondered if this was something to do with Ryan's past as a soldier coming out; there were many convention stories of old lady American actresses who carried claw hammers in their handbags when doing signings in the UK, as they weren't allowed to bring their guns, and Nigel had received a nasty shock the last time he was at a small convention in Florida, when he realised just how many guests were armed, and more importantly, how many attendees were as well.

Nigel straightened and headed towards the main door. The fact of the matter was, no matter whether or not it was Ryan Gates, that someone had taken an item from the room, an item that, although broken and unable to be used, was only so based on the word of the man who brought it. A man who, right now, could walk around the hotel with it, as although he'd been in the room when they locked it down, he'd disappeared early in the wait, after speaking to the female detective.

'Hello?' he called out from the room. 'Um, I was wondering if someone could call the police for me?'

―――――――

BILLY HAD RETURNED TO THE HUB AND WAS ONCE MORE scanning through algorithms when the news came out that the convention had restarted, as PC Cooper popped her head around the door and let Billy and Jess know. Then, realising she had a chance for a cheeky coffee, Cooper came in and poured herself a drink, sighing as she sipped.

'Ahh,' she smiled. 'I need this. I'm exhausted. Didn't get a wink's sleep last night.'

'Oh yes?' Billy asked with mock innocence. Cooper scowled at him.

'We were going through options,' she said. 'Work stuff. And then he had a shower, and I couldn't be there, so I took a long walk to calm myself down.'

'Why did you need to calm yourself—' Jess started, before stopping herself. '—Oh.'

'You've been away,' Billy said to her. 'Things moved on after Davey went.'

'You're seeing De'Geer now?' Jess asked Cooper, but it was Billy who answered.

'Let's just say she'd like to,' he smiled. He was going to continue when his machine made a strange tinkling sound.

'I think a fairy's trapped in your computer,' Cooper suggested, sipping at the coffee.

'It's the software.' Billy opened a screen on his monitor. 'It's worked out the decryption of the binary matrix.'

'You know the printer?'

Billy nodded, opening up a message window.

'It was printed on Thursday, six in the evening,' he said. 'On a Hewlett Packard M430.'

Cooper pulled out her notebook, flicking through the pages.

'Is that the same as a LaserJet Enterprise M430?' she asked as she read the page. 'Because I can tell you now, if it is, then I know where the printer is.'

Billy rose from the chair.

'It's the same thing,' he said. 'Is it here?'

"In the Business Suite,' Cooper nodded. 'There's two of them in there, and an inkjet. The woman on the front desk said they're mainly used to print out boarding passes.'

Billy looked at Jess.

'Hold the fort,' he said. 'If anyone comes in, tell them what happened.'

With that said, he read from the screen, writing a number down on a post-it note and tearing it off the others as he opened the door to the room, motioning for Cooper to lead the way. Taking a last, reluctant gulp of coffee and placing the cup down, Cooper led Billy out into the corridor, and down to the main lobby area.

There, to the right of the reception area, was a glass door with BUSINESS written on it in gold letters.

Walking to the door, he saw it, like all the others, needed a room key pass to open. Using his own, he unlocked the door, walking into the suite.

It was large, with five desktop computers, all Windows-based, with small monitors and cheap keyboards. They were all linked, it seemed, to a bank of printers on the back wall, a window to the outside above it.

Looking around, Billy smiled.

'If they used the printers here, I could check the serial number,' he said, walking to the first one. 'Look on the back, and see if it ends in—'

He stopped, pulling out the folded post-it note.

'—ends in four-five-capital D-seven,' he finished. 'That's the serial the paper was printed on.'

Cooper was already turning the second LaserJet around, examining the base with a pen torch.

'Four, five, D, seven,' she said triumphantly. 'This was the printer?'

'Yes,' Billy looked up at the corner of the Business Suite, directly at the small security camera in there. 'And at six pm Thursday, on that camera, we'll see who printed off the warning letters.'

17

PRINTER ERRORS

'HELLO THERE, LASSIE, WE'D LIKE TO SEE YOUR SECURITY footage.'

Monroe smiled at the receptionist behind the counter, nodding at the clock behind her.

'In particular, we'd like to have a look at Thursday, six pm in your Business Suite,' he finished.

The receptionist, having already helped several times with the case over the last twenty-four hours nodded, waving them towards a side door, which brought them into the back of the reception area, before leading them through to the back room where, rising from his chair, a young man in a suit, a duty manager badge on his lapel, nervously rubbed his hands together.

'Have you found the killer?' he asked hopefully.

'Doing our best, laddie, doing our best,' Monroe smiled warmly, even if he wasn't feeling it at the moment. 'We need to check some of your footage, as we might have something.'

'Of course, whatever we can do to help,' the duty manager replied as he looked back at his monitor. 'We only have one camera in the Business Suite, though. You might not get what you want.'

'We just need to see who was in at a particular time,' Monroe nodded with his head for the duty manager to continue. 'And, with a little luck, it'll lead us to a potential solution to this mess.'

Declan, having arrived with Monroe after being informed of the printer revelation by Jess and Billy ten minutes earlier, leant against the table.

'Has the organiser told you what they intend to do yet?' he enquired. 'I'm guessing they have to run everything past you?'

The duty manager gave a small shrug as he turned on the camera system.

'They were all for carrying on, until you found the body in the tent,' he said. 'Now the attendees are cancelling their Saturday nights, and more than half the guests are gone. I think they're making a statement in the ballroom this afternoon.'

Declan glanced at his watch and wondered whether John Moss and Derek McAfee were hoping they'd catch the killer before their talk, allowing the convention to continue.

It was possible, especially as by now the news that Malcolm Stoddard was in custody – and was also "Michael Bailey", the onetime Little John – would have leaked out, which in turn would have started the rumour mill going.

'I'll look forward to seeing that,' he said as Monroe and the manager scrolled through the previous day's footage, moving backwards through the Business Suite's CCTV recordings.

There was a sudden rush of frantic movement on the

screen as the scrolling, currently moving back at a minute per second, had a burst of seven seconds of activity.

'Stop there,' Monroe waved. 'It's just after five-fifty, something happened.'

On the screen, they watched an empty room. The duty manager was about to speak when on the screen the door opened and a woman walked into the room, sitting down at one of the terminals that lined the far wall.

Her face couldn't be seen, but from her clothes and hair, it was obvious who she was.

'Luna Hedlun-Gates,' Declan said, leaning closer. 'Could Luna be the killer? She would have known Montgomery Pryce and Peter Crock from the years she was with Gates, I suppose, but what was her reason? The only person we know she has a problem with is Alex Hamilton.'

'She wasn't on stage when Pryce was shot with an arrow,' Monroe mused, but before he could continue, on the screen they saw the door open once more and another figure walk into the room.

There was no sound through the cameras, but Declan could see that Luna and the new arrival were talking heatedly, the new arrival waving their hands.

'That's Alex Hamilton,' he said. 'And as I said, they've had problems.'

'Aye, I recall something about him exposing himself to her,' Monroe raised an eyebrow as he looked back. 'But perhaps there's more than it seems here?'

Declan watched as the man sat at a terminal three computers down from Luna, typing on his keyboard.

'Two minutes to six,' he said, tapping the digital clock on the tape. 'They made the prints at six, so it could be either of them.'

'At the moment, all they're doing is typing,' Monroe leant back. 'We need to see who prints something, and if they use the printer. Can anyone wirelessly use it?'

'You mean the laserjets?' the duty manager looked surprised as he realised Monroe was asking him the question. 'We have another at the back of reception. We do all reception prints on that. We don't allow anyone to connect to these by Wi-Fi as it'll make them vulnerable to attack. Anything those printers print, it's only from those computers, or if someone has a USB stick.'

'Come on, come on, print something you bampot,' Monroe muttered, watching the screen as, in the bottom corner, the LaserJet printer with the same serial as the prints spat out papers. 'Yes. Now, pick them up.'

On the screen, Luna stood up, and everyone in the back office leant forward, watching the screen intently as she started speaking to Alex, waving her hands angrily and eventually spun on her heels, storming out of the room.

'That's interesting,' Declan commented. 'Did she forget the prints, or did Alex—'

He wasn't able to finish his comment though, as seconds after Luna left the Business Suite, Alex closed his browser, got up out of his chair, grabbed the printouts from the top of the printer and left the business room.

'Alex Hamilton printed the letters,' Monroe said with a mild amount of surprise. 'I should hang my badge up because I never saw that one coming.'

'I think we've learnt the hard way that things are never what they seem,' Declan straightened. 'But we should definitely have a chat with him.'

'Where is Alex now?' Monroe muttered, but this was

more to himself as he checked a printed schedule for the day. 'I don't think the convention's running to this anymore.'

'One thing,' Declan frowned. 'Alex was on stage when Pryce was killed. Which means he's not working alone here.'

'Aye, I'd considered that,' Monroe led Declan out of the door, nodding thanks to the duty manager as he stared out into the lobby. 'He's working with someone, to be sure, and might not even have been the killer. But with luck, he'll give us what we need when we speak to him.'

'We should be careful when we find him,' Declan was already texting Anjli the news. 'Let's not make it too visible we want him, as if he *is* the killer, he's not going to come in gently. And, considering the fact that the last person we captured, who wasn't even the killer, managed to almost take out Bullman with a large stick, I'd hate to see what happens this time.'

As they exited the back office and walked into the lobby of the hotel, Declan noted Anjli walking towards them, checking the message on her phone.

'You know, you could have just told me,' she said, waving it at Declan. 'It's not like I'm miles away.'

'I didn't know,' Declan shrugged. 'And I wanted you to know immediately.'

'Ah, that's love,' Monroe mocked, as Anjli turned her attention towards him now.

'So, do we have a killer, Guv?'

'Well, I think Alex Hamilton is the man who wrote the notes, but we need to check, as so far nothing's been commonplace,' Monroe scratched at his beard. 'Young Declan here is going to ask Doctor Marcos if they found any fingerprints on the sheets, and if any of them match Alex Hamilton's prints—'

'Do we have Hamilton's fingerprints?' Declan asked.

'That's a question to ask Doctor Marcos,' Monroe smiled.

'Only because you called me young,' Declan replied. 'But, so I know, is there a particular reason why you're not asking her?'

'Things are a little tense,' Monroe looked across the lobby as he spoke, as if looking for someone, or, more likely, avoiding someone. 'She seems to think I have a crush on Flick McCarthy.'

'And why would she think that?'

'Because you might have suggested it to her,' Monroe sighed, looking at Anjli. 'What can I do? I'm just too good looking.'

Declan paused from replying to this, turning back to Anjli.

'You looked stressed when you were walking towards us,' he said. 'What have we missed?'

Anjli let out a long, drawn-out sigh.

'I've just been speaking to Nigel Cummings,' she said, pointing back down the corridor, towards the back rooms being used for the convention. 'He said a speargun has been taken from the prop department area.'

'Is that the room with the mannequins?'

'Yes.'

'And you mean speargun as in the one that Jess talked about?'

'Yes,' Anjli repeated. 'Nigel thinks that Ryan Gates has it.'

Monroe and Declan glanced at each other.

'Why would Ryan Gates have a speargun?' Monroe asked, immediately frowning. 'No, don't answer. It's for protection, isn't it?'

He started walking across the lobby as he continued.

'If he had a letter like the others, and he knows someone's after him, he's a soldier, so he'll think like one. Declan?'

'He'll look for a weapon,' Declan agreed. 'Even if it's to scare the killer away. And a big scary speargun would do that.'

'I thought it didn't work?' Monroe glanced now at Anjli.

'The impression I was given was it's only Ryan who knows how to make it work,' she said, miming a speargun in her hand. 'So, if we go with the possibility he knows how to arm it, now we have a crazy man wandering around with an active speargun, looking for a killer who's attacking people with a bow and arrow.'

She actually chuckled at this.

'When do we get the normal cases again, boss? I just want a nice, simple murder with a blood-stained man with a knife in his hand, a sign in his hand saying, "I did it, it was me". Is that too much to ask for?'

'Be careful what you wish for, lassie,' Monroe smiled darkly. 'Grab Cooper and go check out Hamilton's room, will you? Maybe he'll have a T-shirt just like that.'

'Remember, though, Hamilton was on stage,' Declan muttered. 'So be careful, as somewhere out there, we could have an accomplice.'

As Anjli and Cooper went hunting through Alex Hamilton's personal effects, Monroe and Declan started the hunt for the man himself.

Bullman and De'Geer had already begun this the moment Monroe had sent a message out to everyone, but nobody seemed to have seen the man for the last hour, which was either bad for them, or bad for Alex Hamilton, as the last guest missing for a while turned out to have an arrow through their chest.

Declan was about to suggest checking the ballroom, where in the next hour the organisers were about to make some kind of announcement, when he heard a commotion outside the photos room.

Knowing that no photos were being taken right now – partly because of the convention once more being on pause, and also because Malcolm Stoddard, the photographer, was in a room down the corridor with Billy and Jess, hiding from a killer – Declan knew that any noise coming from the room was probably not normal.

It wasn't.

The room was half full of attendees, staring in shock at Ryan Gates, standing by the window, speargun in his hands as his wife tried fruitlessly to get them to stop taking photos on their phone, and leave the room. Seeing her distress, Declan spun to face the crowd and held up his handcuffs.

'Right,' he snarled, 'who wants to be arrested first?'

This did the job, and immediately the room emptied until there was only Monroe, Declan, Luna and Ryan Gates left, the last of these shifting his grip on the speargun as he glared at the detectives.

'I'm not putting this down,' he said. 'You can do what you want and you can say what you want, but someone out there wants to kill me, and if they're gonna try, they're gonna have to fight me.'

'Baby, what's going on?' Luna asked, confused, her eyes darting from husband to the police and back. 'Are you in trouble?'

'I fought for Queen and Country and I didn't give a

second thought to who I went up against while in the Service, so why would I let some random loon kill me with a bow?' Gates was half-shouting this now, staring wild-eyed around the room. 'You get that, right, DI Walsh? You were military!'

'What's going on?' Luna shouted. 'Tell me!'

'I'm not letting anyone kill me or you!' Gates shouted back.

'Why would they kill us?' Luna replied, now calming slightly. 'Why are you connected to this?'

Declan stared at Luna for a long moment before realisation kicked in.

'She doesn't know, does she?' he said, looking back at Gates, who refused to match his gaze.

'What don't I know?' Luna asked, walking up to her husband now, placing a hand on his wrist. 'Whatever it is, we can work through it together.'

With tears now in his eyes, Ryan Gates opened and shut his mouth several times, unable to speak.

Instead, Declan spoke for him.

'It looks like the reason Montgomery Pryce and Peter Crock were killed this weekend was because they were connected to a death during filming of a movie in the mid-eighties,' he explained. 'Malcolm Stoddard was also connected to the death and all three, we believe, were sent an anonymous letter on the Thursday night.'

'Written by who?' Luna stopped Declan. 'And don't repeat the word anonymous. I could literally hear your air quotes around the word.'

'We don't know for sure, but we think perhaps they were written by Alex Hamilton,' Declan explained. 'In the letters, they were told to get their affairs into order, because they would be dead soon.'

'But we didn't get a letter!' Luna said, confused. 'And why is their mistake landing on us?'

'Just because we didn't get the letter doesn't mean somebody didn't want to write it,' Gates finally spoke, lowering the speargun. 'Maybe Alex changed his mind or found some other way of killing me.'

'Luna, when you spoke to Alex Hamilton on Thursday night, how was he, mentally?' Declan asked.

'What, in the changing rooms?' Luna frowned. 'He—'

'No, in the Business Suite,' Monroe added. 'The CCTV shows you talking to Alex Hamilton around six pm on the Thursday evening, and we believe Alex Hamilton wrote three notes on the computer, sending them to one of the suite's printers.'

'I don't know,' Luna struggled to think back. 'He was typing something, and he was hissing, mumbling to himself as he did so. I assumed he was working through lines for a panel, or his opening event speech. I was checking the schedule on my email.'

'You don't get a printout?'

'Ryan does, but I'm just a plus one.' Luna made a mocking smile. 'I print my own. But I still don't understand why you're worried about Alex and these notes. Do you think Alex is using the stolen arrows to kill people?'

Declan and Monroe kept quiet at this, but their silence spoke volumes.

'Christ, you *do* think this!' she exclaimed, looking at her husband. 'And you're making a fool of yourself, walking around with a speargun! But I still don't understand why you think you're connected to this?'

'Because Ryan was involved in the cover-up of the death,'

Declan replied, looking over at Gates. 'Tell your wife what happened, Mister Gates. You owe it to her.'

Ryan Gates stared off into the distance for a moment before replying.

'I was a soldier then, one who was working as a military liaison to Robert Standish when the woman at the party ... she committed suicide, or jumped from the roof, or whatever you want to call it,' he began. 'She died, end of. It was horrific, and more importantly, this could cause genuine problems with the British film industry, if it came out she was on drugs, ones given to her by the stars of the film.'

'Malcolm Stoddard said Pryce kept plying her with drink throughout the night, and at some point gave her something, maybe a hallucinogenic. Later on, the girl climbed onto the roof and jumped off, breaking her neck,' Declan said. 'Does that match what you knew?'

Gates nodded.

'I was tasked with cleaning everything up, making sure that nobody could blame Montgomery, Malcolm, or Peter,' he admitted. 'I never learned her name, or who her husband was, as it wasn't information I needed to know. And a couple of years later, when I left the military, Robert Standish remembered this act, and that's what gained me my advisor role in *Hooded Outlaw*.'

'You were involved in the death?' Luna's tone was ice cold now.

'I've been involved in a lot of deaths, darling,' Gates sighed. 'I was a soldier. This was one of many and it wasn't even one I was directly connected to. I was just a clean-up squad, nothing more.'

He looked over at the door, pointing at it with the tip of the speargun.

'But someone out there has decided to take offence at this, and I'll be damned if I'm gonna be killed by them,' he hissed, glancing back at Declan and Monroe. 'And you can both stop wondering if you can take this from me, because as far as everyone's concerned, this is nothing but a prop, and I can walk around any convention with it.'

'If you fire that weapon at anyone, and you cause injury or death, we'll be arresting you,' Declan hissed.

'DI Walsh, if I fire this weapon at anyone, it'll be in self-defence, and because they tried to kill me,' Gates replied. 'Now, if you'll excuse me? My wife and I need some time alone.'

Declan stared after them as they left the room.

'He's right,' Monroe said. 'It's a TV show prop as far as we know.'

'It's going to kill someone by the end of the day,' Declan prophesied. 'The question is, however, *who*?'

ALEX HAMILTON'S HOTEL ROOM WAS A STANDARD ONE, WITH twin beds, although one had been covered with a variety of items and a duffel bag and looked untouched.

'One man, two beds,' Anjli said as she checked it. 'Probably stuck him in the first room they had. It's exactly the same as a double room.'

'I don't get it though, Sarge,' Cooper said, looking around the room. 'He had the housekeeping sign on, so he wasn't worried about anyone finding something. Which to me says there's nothing here.'

'Or it means he's hidden something incredibly well,' Anjli smiled, pulling on a pair of latex gloves, opening the sideboard. At the back was a leather bag, and she pulled it out, opening it up.

'Pills,' she said, pulling out silver blister packs, the word *Oxycodone* written across the top. 'Lots of them, it looks like. But this isn't enough to prove anything. We need to find a place he knew nobody would ...'

She trailed off, looking at the second bed.

'One man, two beds,' she said. 'Housekeeping won't alter it because it's not been used.'

'Which means it could hide things,' Cooper walked to the bed, patting down the sides, and checking under it. 'What are we looking for, exactly?'

'We'll know when we see it,' Anjli said, performing a similar patting motion on the top of the bed now, moving up before stopping. 'Cooper.'

Cooper rose, seeing that Anjli had paused at the fold of the duvet, where the sheet came over and was folded down.

'Feel here,' Anjli said, running a finger along the fold. Cooper did so and stepped back.

'All yours,' she said as Anjli pulled the sheet up, pulling it from its secured tucks, and revealing, stretched out along the fold of the bed and at the top of the duvet, a single, white-feathered longbow arrow.

'Oh shit,' Cooper whispered. 'I mean, oh, wow, Sarge.'

'Shit indeed,' Anjli leant closer, examining the red line and white fletchings. There was a rattling at the hotel room door, and it opened to reveal a shocked Alex Hamilton, standing in the doorway, his hand still outstretched, a hotel room card in it.

'What the hell's going on?' he said in both shock and anger.

In response, Anjli held up the recently discovered arrow in her latex fingers, a blister pack of Oxycodone in the other.

'We could ask you the same thing, Mister Hamilton,' she said sadly.

18

BIG JOHN, LITTLE JOHN

ONCE ALEX HAMILTON HAD BEEN ARRESTED AND PLACED IN handcuffs, Anjli had brought him to Monroe who, unsure whether or not to remove him from the premises, had eventually placed him in the same reception back room he'd had Malcolm in earlier that day. But now, almost two hours later, Monroe had decided to finally sit down and talk with him.

He hadn't waited out of spite, though. First, he'd wanted to take time to check the hotel room, to see if a bow could be found, but no weapon had appeared. Second, he'd wanted Doctor Marcos to return with information on the sheets of paper, and whether Alex Hamilton's fingerprints were on them, but again, there were no fingerprints to be seen, which had niggled at Monroe, as he'd seen Alex Hamilton pick them up on the CCTV footage.

Was he wearing gloves? Maybe he'd printed pages before and after to make sure he wasn't holding the pages he'd be passing later?

Whatever the answer was, the one person who could give

it was sitting in an empty storeroom now, in the same chair Malcolm Stoddard had been in only a few hours earlier.

Christ, had that only been this morning?

Bullman had asked to go in with him, and, before they entered, De'Geer had made sure there were four chairs, as Alex had demanded a strange legal representative.

'Mister Hamilton,' Monroe said as he and Bullman entered the room. 'Ms McCarthy.'

Flick McCarthy nodded silently, sitting beside Alex as he glared balefully at the detectives. Bullman placed her phone on the table, setting it to record.

'In the room are Flick McCarthy, Alex Hamilton, Detective Chief Inspector Monroe and Detective Superintendent Bullman,' she said. 'The time is two-twenty-three. We are conducting the interview in a small office within the Milton Keynes Hilton Hotel, where Mister Hamilton has asked Ms McCarthy to be his legal representative.'

She looked over at Flick.

'Ms McCarthy, are you a practicing lawyer?' she asked.

'I have been,' Flick nodded.

'In that case, I'll expect copies of your papers to be sent to DC Fitzwarren,' Bullman replied. 'But for now, we'll continue as if we've checked through and accepted your accreditations.'

Flick nodded approval at this, and then, realising, leant close to the phone.

'I agree with this.'

Monroe watched Alex, who sullenly stared at the table during this.

'You seem a little twitchy,' he said, then looked over at Bullman. 'Maybe he needs a pick me up?'

'I'm fine,' Alex muttered.

'Okay then,' Monroe straightened, turning back to him.
'Did you kill Montgomery Pryce?'

'No.'

'Did you kill Peter Crock?'

'No.'

'Did you *want* to kill either Montgomery Pryce or Peter
Crock?' Monroe continued.

At this, Alex looked up at him.

'Did I want to kill Peter? Of course not. Everyone loved
him. The guy was a blissed-out hippy who preferred to play
dress up in a tent than play politics. Did I want to kill Montgomery Pryce?'

He considered this, looking at Flick.

'I don't think there's anyone here who knew him that
didn't want to kill him,' he eventually replied. 'Would you say
that was a fair comment?'

'For the record, Ms McCarthy is here as your legal counsel, and not as a witness,' Monroe added quickly. 'Anything
she suggests or says is classed purely as hearsay.'

'Okay,' Alex nodded, leaning back. 'I get that.'

'So, we've discovered that you, like many others, in your
opinion wanted Montgomery Pryce dead.'

'No, you asked if I wanted to kill him, not if I wanted him
dead.' Alex shook his head. 'In my opinion, that's two
completely different things.'

'Oh aye?'

'Well, wishing someone dead shows harm against someone, but wanting to kill someone is visceral, emotional,
yeah?' Alex tried to explain. 'He was a self-centred, obnox-
ious wanker, and he could wind anyone up. So yeah, there
were times I wanted to kill him, but that didn't mean I'd actually do it, you see?'

Monroe nodded.

'So, you allowed someone else to do it then,' he said, more as a statement than a question. 'Tell us about the letters.'

'I told your detective,' Alex snapped. 'I don't know what you're talking about.'

Monroe nodded, leaning back on his chair as Bullman rose, walking to the door and opening it. PC Cooper was standing on the other side, a folder in her hands.

'Why were you in the Business Centre on the Thursday evening?' Monroe asked.

'I have a flight tomorrow,' Alex replied, looking nervously at the folder. 'I was checking in.'

'You can't usually check into a flight until twenty-four hours before,' Monroe said as Bullman sat down.

'I ... yeah, I realised that when I started,' Alex forced a small, thin smile. 'So, I checked my schedule.'

'You weren't given a physical copy?'

'I was, but not at that point.' Alex was getting angry. 'I'd only checked in a few hours earlier.'

'Tell us about the check in,' Bullman said, placing the folder down. She'd intended to show it, but watching Alex nervously stare at it made her want to hold off, see if anything else came out as the tension built. 'You arrived at lunchtime?'

'Around one-thirty,' Alex relaxed a little. 'I checked in but was told by the front desk my room wouldn't be ready until three, as a lot of others were checking in too. A lot of attendees were already in the lobby and the bar, so I used the other facilities.'

'The gym and the pool?'

'Yeah, exactly.'

'And how did you get into these?' Monroe asked, frowning. 'I thought you needed a room key?'

'I had a room,' Alex replied irritably, looking at Flick as he continued. 'I just couldn't go into it until housekeeping had finished.'

'And how many room keys did you have?'

'I don't know,' Alex shrugged. 'They gave me one, maybe two?'

'Was it one or two?' Bullman leant in.

'Why does it matter?'

'Hypothetical,' Bullman replied. 'If you have the only hotel room key to your room, then you can't blame anyone else for entering without your knowledge and hiding, oh, I don't know, a longbow arrow in your spare bed.'

'I don't know.' Alex looked daggers at the detectives. 'I think there was one. Yes, one, as I opened the room to go in and I tossed the cardboard sleeve thing away, and there wasn't another card in it.'

'There,' Bullman smiled. 'That wasn't so difficult.'

'Can we move on now?' Flick sighed, checking her watch. 'As exciting as learning about room keys is.'

'Let's go back to the Fitness Suite,' Monroe looked back at Alex now. 'Do you go to the gym much?'

'Sure.' Alex was confused where the conversation was going. 'I'm on TV. You have to look good.'

'You have a routine?'

'Cardio, weights, then if there's a pool, I'll swim,' Alex replied, relaxing as he spoke about a topic he was more familiar with. 'I had my gym kit with me, so as soon as they said I was checked in, they took my suitcase for safekeeping after I'd taken the kit out, and when I was in the spa, I was given a towel to use.'

'You left your personal items with them?'

'Sure.'

'You left your drugs with them?'

Alex's eyes narrowed.

'I have a prescription for those,' he said.

'Oh, I'm sure you do,' Monroe smiled. 'But I'll pretty much guarantee it was from a more dubious source than, say, my local doctor or chemist.'

'I don't know your chemist,' Alex replied, his tone a little more conversational now, more challenging. 'But it looks like they're shit out of *Just For Men*.'

'As fun as it is watching you snark at my colleague, let's get back to the Fitness Suite,' Bullman continued casually. 'Were you alone in there? Or were there others?'

'There were a couple in the pool,' Alex considered this for a moment. 'But I'd planned to do three miles on the running machine first.'

'The treadmill.'

Alex looked quizzically at Monroe.

'Do you run on a treadmill?' he asked.

'Well, aye—'

'Then it's a running machine, isn't it?'

Monroe let the comment slide.

'So, after your run, you did weights?'

'Free weights,' Alex replied. 'It's a hotel gym, you're not going to get CrossFit or anything. So, I did some dumbbell exercises, and then, seeing the pool was empty for the moment, I went in and did some lengths. Again, not much, because—'

'It was a hotel gym,' Bullman finished for him. 'We get the point. And, talking of points, at which *point* did Luna Hedlun-Gates appear?'

At this, Alex paused, and Monroe saw for the first time the slightest hint of fear in his eyes.

'I'm sorry, but what does that—'

'Oh, aye, we hadn't really got into that, had we?' Monroe smiled. 'We have a witness that claims while you were in the gym, running on the tread – on your *running* machine – Mrs Hedlun-Gates was in there as well. And when she went to the pool, you followed her.'

'I did nothing of the sort,' Alex insisted. 'Yes, she was in the gym. I remember seeing her there. But I wasn't stalking her.'

'I don't recall using the word stalking, Mister Hamilton, just that you followed her. Yet you claimed the pool was empty.'

'I ...' Alex looked helplessly at Flick.

'What Alex meant was that the pool was empty of civilians,' Flick offered. 'Paying punters, attendees, muggles, call them what you will. Alex couldn't swim while they were there, as he would have been hassled. However, Luna Hedlun-Gates is the wife of an old friend, so Alex most likely misspoke.'

'That's exactly it,' Alex nodded.

'So, she was there? She swam?'

'I think so, yes,' Alex wasn't sure now. 'Wait, what else did this witness of yours say?'

'Tell us about the arrow,' Bullman deliberately changed the subject to keep Alex off kilter. 'The one we found in your bedroom.'

'I've never seen it in my life.'

'Never? You've never seen an arrow like that?'

'No!' Alex exclaimed angrily, but then his eyes widened. 'Wait. You deliberately led me down that path. I've seen arrows like that, we have them in the show. *Had* them.'

'Do you still think you're in the show?' Monroe asked, his

voice soft and curious. 'Is that why you killed Peter Crock with an arrow?'

'I didn't kill him!'

'But you admit to knowing the arrows?'

'Nigel has them!' Alex almost pleaded. 'He sells them at conventions. I've even signed a couple.'

'And you took three on Thursday, didn't you?'

'No!' Alex shook his head. 'And I don't know how someone put one in the bed.'

'It's a good place to hide,' Bullman mused. 'You can hide anything in a made bed, as the housekeeping staff won't touch it.'

'I didn't hide it!'

'Someone else did?'

'Yes!'

'But how?' Monroe steepled his fingers together, his elbows resting on the table. 'If nobody else had a key?'

'We checked with reception,' Bullman added. 'At no point in the weekend was a replacement key asked for.'

'I even asked for the spare hotel key from him, just in case,' Flick noted. 'Alex wouldn't let me have one, which is strange, as he's allowed this at every other Con.'

'I usually get two room keys at every other Con,' Alex hissed. 'And you're my counsel, not a bloody witness.'

'We also checked with reception about that,' Bullman smiled now, but the humour was lacking in it. 'They say it's hotel policy to give two room keys.'

'And I told you, there was only one in the cardboard sleeve.'

'So, who's lying, you or the hotel receptionist?' Bullman waited. 'Because one of you is.'

'Where were you this morning?' Monroe asked, changing

the subject, keeping Alex off balance again. 'Nobody saw you at breakfast.'

'I wasn't feeling well.'

'What about nine in the evening yesterday?' Bullman asked. 'We spoke to a few people, and many of them said the moment the opening ceremonies were over, you disappeared.'

'Damn right I disappeared,' Alex replied angrily. 'I was terrified. Someone tried to kill us. I decided to hide in my room, pack and then get the hell out of here.'

He once more looked at Flick.

'But my manager here wasn't able to get my fee sorted, so I had to stay.'

'That's not completely true,' Flick frowned, looking at the detectives. 'Sorry, I know you said as I'm his counsel I can't be a witness, but I have something here that might be important as a witness. Can I speak?'

She glanced at Alex as he glared daggers at her.

'Sure,' Monroe shrugged. 'It's not exactly the most by the books interview we've done, anyway.'

'It was while you were all looking for the bowman, which was around eight, nine, maybe, I was beside the back door, the one that leads to the archery field,' Flick explained, staring at Alex as she did so. 'And you came in through it. You looked wired.'

'I did no such thing!' Alex half-rose from his chair in horror at this. 'That was earlier, around seven, right after it happened!'

'Oh,' Flick frowned, back-tracking. 'Apologies, detectives. I'm old, my memory isn't what it was.'

'You were told you were staying at the convention before

nine pm, though,' Monroe looked at Alex. 'I'm guessing you stayed in your room all night?'

'Yes.'

'Alone?'

'Unfortunately, yes,' Alex sniffed. 'So no, I don't have a witness for a bloody alibi.'

'In fear for your life?'

'How many times do I have to say this?' Alex wailed out. 'Yes! Yes! A hundred times yes! I was in fear for my life, following the death of my friend!'

'Your friend?'

'You know damn well what I mean.'

Monroe paused, leaning back on his chair as he watched the now sweating Alex Hamilton.

'Were you in fear for your life because of an attack from a mad fan, someone you'd given drugs to, or from Ryan Gates?'

Interestingly, the concern and worry immediately disappeared at this, replaced with a sneering, angry expression.

'That prick might think he's *Who Dares Wins* and all that, but he's all talk, no walk.'

'I heard he dangled you over a balcony once.'

'I slipped. He caught me.'

'I heard you had a conversation on Friday about his wife.'

Alex pursed his lips.

'This your mysterious witness, again?' he half-mocked, and Monroe noticed that now, in *this* conversation, he seemed more assured. 'You should interview them, not me. I reckon they'd solve the entire case.'

'Tell me about the love heart.'

'The bloody what?' Alex rose fully from the chair now, staring down at Flick. 'This is bullshit! Why are you letting them talk to me like this? Bloody rumours about sweets on towels now?'

Monroe rose now, slow and steady, facing Alex, losing a little of his intimidation with lack of height, but regaining it within the intensity of his gaze.

'I never mentioned sweets and towels,' he said. 'But interestingly, you're right on the nose there. So, sit the hell down and answer my question.'

19

PAYMENT IN KIND

'TELL ME WHAT YOU WERE TOLD THEN,' ALEX RELUCTANTLY complied, sitting back down on his chair. 'I'll tell you how far down "utter bollocks" street we've travelled.'

Monroe considered this, and then nodded.

'Luna Hedlun-Gates was in the gym, but felt self-conscious of you watching her,' he started. 'She went swimming, but you followed her. And, when you left, you couldn't help yourself, and left a little love heart sweet on her towel. She was angry, and you'd pushed all the right buttons, and she followed you into the men's changing room. Where you were naked and waiting, knowing this would shock her.'

Alex stared at Monroe for a long moment, glancing at Bullman, as if to confirm she too was behind this belief.

And then he laughed.

'That's what she told you?' he asked. 'Or was that what her husband told you?'

'Is there a difference?'

Alex nodded at this, looking around the room, working out what next to say.

'Yes, I was naked,' he said. 'But she didn't come into the room to shout at me, she came in to screw me. We've been having an affair for three years, on and off.'

Monroe didn't answer this, looking over at the now-frowning Bullman.

'So, the gym, the pool, the love heart, these were all courting?'

'Courting's a bit old school for what it was, but the sweet said "I want you" and it was a message. I made sure the changing rooms were empty, she came in and we shagged against the lockers.'

He looked to the wall, his mind back in the changing rooms.

'She was a six out of ten, but she was worried we'd be interrupted and not at her best, so I'll let that slide. Anyway, we shagged, rolled around all over the place, and then she left as I dressed. I didn't see her until we bumped into each other in the Business Suite.'

'And what happened there?'

'She said someone saw her leaving the changing rooms, so she had to explain she'd had a go at me. I was sick of always playing the bad guy though, so told her to tell Ryan about us, or we were over. She stormed out.'

'Followed by you, and the printed paper.'

'I didn't print anything,' Alex insisted again. 'Luna did. I picked it up, meaning to give it to her. And I did, in the lobby.'

'Where conveniently there's no camera aimed at you to show this,' Monroe smiled. 'We looked.'

'Well, look at the papers!' Alex hissed. 'Go speak to Luna and get them off her! She'll show you!'

'We asked Mrs Hedlun-Gates about the papers, and she said you never came after her,' Bullman replied. 'Which means we can't show you the ones you picked up from the printer.'

'There you go then,' Flick smiled. 'No proof. And I'm sure Alex has a reason why he hid the arrow.'

'I *didn't hide the bloody arrow!*' Alex exploded at his manager. 'Are you trying to help me or hang me here?'

'Do you know much about printers, Mister Hamilton?' Bullman picked up the folder again, opening it and pulling out a handful of A4 papers. 'Laser jets really are incredible things. And in case of printer jamming or other errors, they always keep the last things printed in their memories.'

She held up the papers.

'The Business Suite printers keep the last ten jobs in the network, placed by time and date. And, at six pm on the Thursday night, it held in its memory this print job.'

She threw the papers onto the table.

'Which meant we could reprint it,' she smiled humourlessly. 'And, as you can see, I'm not exactly sure why Luna Hedlun-Gates would print these pages?'

There were six sheets of A4 paper. The front two were cut and pasted schedule times for a convention guest. The top of the pages read:

ALEX HAMILTON – LITTLE JOHN (HOODED OUTLAW)

'Please,' Bullman tapped at the page. 'Explain to me why Mrs Hedlun-Gates was printing out your schedule?'

The pages were moved now, and there were three sheets, almost identical to each other, to follow.

'*I know what you did. You will pay. Sort out your affairs,*' Bullman read from the first. 'This one was to Montgomery Pryce. The next one was to Peter Crock, and the third to

Malcolm Stoddard. I'm guessing you were making Ryan Gates pay a different way?'

'I didn't print those,' Alex looked at Flick, his eyes wide and horrified. 'I didn't print those!'

'And then we end with this,' Monroe slid the pages out of the way, showing a last sheet. 'Montgomery Pryce's schedule for the Friday. All collated together, and all printed by you, and picked up by you.'

He leant back on the chair.

'Look at it like this,' he said. 'You play a guy who works with a coroner on TV, right? Light-hearted daytime crimes and all that? How would your character see this? First, we have you printing pages on camera, pages at least one victim was proven to have in their possession before they died. Second, you have one of three stolen arrows in your possession, hidden, of which two have already found their marks. And third, your own manager has contested your own alibi, saying you were seen by the exit to the field tents around the time Peter was killed.'

'I said I might have been wrong there,' Flick admitted.

'Who's helping you?' Bullman asked. 'You couldn't have killed Pryce, as you were behind him on stage, so who was your accomplice?'

Alex opened and shut his mouth a couple of times, but it was Flick who spoke.

'Oh, you bastard,' she said angrily, looking at Alex now. 'You used a fan, didn't you?'

'Ms McCarthy?'

'There was a man yesterday,' Flick hissed, rising from the chair and staring at the horrified Alex. 'The photo shoot.'

'Care to explain?' Monroe gave a small, hopeful smile.

'You've seen the photos, right?' Flick asked. 'One guy

there had a replica of the bow in the show. But it wasn't exact because they made it for foam arrows and all that shit. So, Alex calls Nigel, asks if they can swap the bow for the photo, because Alex knew Sam.'

'You knew he was Montgomery's son?' Monroe asked Alex, but the expression on Flick's face as he spoke this made him look back at her.

'You didn't know,' he said, in realisation.

Flick shook her head.

'Margot mentioned his name this morning, but I hadn't a clue who he was,' she replied. 'I guessed he was the son of Carol Hardy because of the surname, but it was a guess, nothing more, and I never knew about the dad.'

'But *you* did, didn't you?' Monroe said, looking back at Alex.

'Yes, but it wasn't my idea to swap the bows!' Alex insisted. 'And they swapped it back!'

'Or did they?' Flick glared at Alex. 'Nigel said you were in the costume room this morning, when he realised the arrows were missing. He said you were fiddling with the bow.'

'I did no such thing!' Alex hissed. 'And you told us to meet in there!'

'I said the other room,' Flick insisted, looking back at Monroe and Bullman. 'I pulled in all my talent for a council of war. When Alex didn't turn up, I assumed he'd taken a handful of magic pills and gone to spend the day in Disney's Sherwood. Instead, Nigel found him. Ask your DI Walsh and DS Kapoor, they saw him there—'

She pointed an accusatory finger at Alex.

'—replacing the murder weapon.'

'Now, let's not get carried away,' Monroe looked at Bullman, already texting, likely telling everyone to keep an eye out for Sam Hardy. 'But I'm afraid things aren't looking good, Mister Hamilton. We've got you printing death threats, swapping bows with a potential killer, being around the area of the second death without reason, and being in possession of the third arrow. Ms McCarthy, we'll need your accreditations sooner than we thought, if you're—'

'I won't be sending you anything,' Flick rose, glaring balefully at Alex Hamilton. 'I won't be representing this murderous piece of druggie shit in any manner. And that includes personal management.'

With this statement made, Flick pushed past Monroe, opening the door to the outside world and leaving, slamming it behind her.

There was a moment of awkward silence before Monroe pulled out his handcuffs, suggesting Alex Hamilton turn around.

'We'll be moving you to Milton Keynes police cells,' he said. 'I'm sorry, Mister Hamilton, but currently, you won't be catching that plane tomorrow.'

DE'GEER STOOD TO THE SIDE, WATCHING FROM THE WINGS AS John Moss walked up beside Derek McAfee on the stage, as they faced the remaining attendees of the Robin Hood convention. Whereas on the Friday this had been filled to capacity, now it was barely a third filled, as many of the attendees, like the guests, had left after the second murder.

'Thank you for taking the time to come here and listen to us,' Derek spoke into a radio microphone, even though he probably could have just spoken loudly and been heard. 'We have some things we'd like to say.'

'Obviously, we weren't expecting this,' John said, taking the microphone and now speaking into it. 'We thought this would be a fun weekend for all involved, but when Montgomery Pryce passed away on the Friday night—'

'Pass away?' someone shouted from the audience. 'Someone shot him with an arrow!'

'When Montgomery Pryce was sadly taken from us on the Friday night,' John carried on without breaking his stride, 'we decided it was in the best interest of the convention to carry on, and on Saturday more people turned up because they'd heard about the convention, no matter how this was learnt.'

Derek took the microphone.

'We knew we could possibly find a way to build something good from such a tragedy,' he said sadly, 'however with the death of prop master extraordinaire Peter Crock, and with the reveal that Malcolm Stoddard, our photographer, was once a Little John, and of the current Little John, Alex Hamilton's arrest for multiple murders ... this is proving untenable.'

'And with the disappearance or exit of many of our guests and crew, we feel that we have to step up and cancel this event,' John leant in, speaking into the microphone as Derek now held it out. 'We understand all of you here will be disappointed about this. The guests have been wonderful and have stepped up and stayed, even when they should've been getting home to safety. But right now, we are officially saying that this convention is over.'

'We will provide vouchers, redeemable for our future shows, to anybody who wishes one,' Derek took control once more. 'However, anyone who has left of their own decision will not be receiving these, as they left before it was closed. We're able to offer these vouchers, though, because the management of the actors have kindly waived their fees, so that down the line our conventions can happen again.'

There was a small smattering of applause at this, mainly from people glad there would be another chance to see their TV idols, as Derek took a deep breath.

'And,' he finished. 'We hope we will see you at some point—'

'*This is bullshit!*' someone shouted from the back of the room. 'I didn't even want to see Robin Hood or some props guy. I wanted to see the movie people who ran away! And now, what, we're being kicked out? We should be allowed to do what we want!'

'And you will be,' Derek added. 'The hotel isn't closing; you can stay the weekend – no one will stop you. But be aware that the convention is now over.'

'Sounds like you're just passing the blame,' another voice said. 'I didn't get my photo with Pryce on Friday! You gonna give me a voucher for that? I ain't seen a refund!'

'*For Christ's sake!*' De'Geer couldn't stop himself and stormed out onto the stage. 'You didn't get a photo because he died! A man died and you're bitching about a photo!'

There was a sullen silence as De'Geer faced the audience.

'Do you think I wanted to spend the weekend working?' he snapped. 'I was cosplaying Little John yesterday, and I've bloody *arrested* two of them today! This convention should have ended the moment the arrow struck Montgomery Pryce!'

'Maybe Peter Crock would have survived if they had done,' a voice spoke out, and De'Geer saw Sam Hardy, pointing at both John and Derek. 'Their love for money killed him!'

'That's unfair!' John shouted back. 'We couldn't cancel because the managers wanted money we couldn't give!'

'You didn't care because you wanted Montgomery Pryce dead!' Sam, on a roll now, shouted at the organiser. 'You wanted him dead the moment he slept with your daughter! Did you kill him? We'll never know, will we? Did you kill the messenger?'

'*That's enough!*' De'Geer grabbed the microphone before John could speak. 'This convention is done. If any of the guests want to sign anything or take photos? It's done between you and them. If you've booked until tomorrow, I suggest you keep out of my way, if you're going to act like vultures.'

There was an unhappy rumbling amongst the remaining attendees, and De'Geer tossed the microphone at Derek.

'He's right,' he muttered, low enough for the audience not to hear. 'If you'd cancelled after they killed Pryce, Peter Crock might still be alive.'

'If you guys did your jobs quicker, we might have caught Alex Hamilton before he did it,' John Moss snapped back.

'We don't know if Alex is the killer,' De'Geer replied, looking back into the audience at Sam Hardy, defiantly staring at the men on the stage. 'He must have had help for the first death. In fact, we'd like to speak to someone in particular about that once more.'

And, as Sam Hardy turned to leave, finding Thames Valley Police officers standing either side of him, De'Geer stormed off the stage and out of the ballroom through the back entrance before he started arresting people for getting on his nerves.

Cooper was standing there, watching him.

'Don't,' he hissed.

'Don't what?'

'Don't tell me how unprofessional I was just then,' De'Geer looked at her, angry tears starting to build. 'I've loved this legend, this folklore, these shows since I was a kid, and I'm seeing everything destroyed around me.'

'It seems to be the norm for us, Morten,' Cooper replied, patting him on the arm. 'I heard about DI Walsh's case with the *Magpies*, and how he worshipped them as a kid, and Bullman's love for the eighties group *Alternator*, and how she left that case cynical. We seem very good at finding what we love and investigating the crap out of it.'

'And what do *you* love, Esme Cooper?' De'Geer shook his head, shaking himself out of his melancholy.

At the question, Cooper blushed.

'I—I haven't worked that out yet, Sarge,' she stammered.

'Well,' De'Geer smiled. 'When you work it out, tell me. I'd love to know. In the meantime, I'm off to arrest Sam Hardy. Again.'

And, this said, De'Geer, clueless as to what he'd started within her soul with his question, walked off, leaving a flushed PC Cooper able only to watch after him.

'Dammit,' she muttered, before walking off in the other direction. 'If the convention was still on, you might have worn the costume again.'

20

REVELATIONS

SAM HARDY SAT, IRRITATED, IN THE ROOM ONCE USED AS THE photo ops room, as Declan sat opposite him.

'Sorry for the location,' he said. 'But all the other rooms seem to have Little Johns in them.'

Sam glowered at Declan.

'Why am I here again?' he asked, and Declan could tell he was holding back an anger that threatened to spill out.

Maybe he could use that.

'It was hinted strongly by an unnamed source, that the bow you used on the Friday night was the original bow, while the one you used on our test later that evening was a different one,' he explained. 'That you had it swapped when you were in here, having your photo taken.'

Sam frowned as he took this in but stayed silent.

'It's also been hinted strongly that Alex Hamilton checked the bow was back in place on the mannequin, first thing on Saturday morning,' Declan continued, leaning closely. 'Basically, it was hinted pretty bloody strongly that you killed your father, and then had Alex Hamilton swap the bow for you.'

'I didn't do that,' Sam shook his head. 'I didn't even want to be here.'

'I know, you told us all this before,' Declan replied. 'You also said you weren't a fan of the show, and as you *didn't* have a tearful reunion with your father this weekend, and you're known to us as Samantha Hardly, how about you cut the shit and just tell me what's going on.'

He waved around the room.

'No cameras, no recording. Just two men trying to work out who killed two people.'

Nothing.

Declan sighed, stretching out on the rather uncomfortable chair as he watched Sam.

'My Sergeant said you shouted out "*did you kill the messenger?*" at the organisers,' he continued. 'What did you mean by that?'

'Kill a killer,' Sam muttered.

Declan leant forwards now.

'Start from the beginning,' he said. 'Because we checked your hotel booking, and guess what? You're not paying it. Alex Hamilton is. Which makes me wonder, why did Alex Hamilton want Monty Pryce's bastard son here?'

Sam considered this, and then nodded.

'I had an email from Hamilton,' he said. 'He said he wanted to reunite us together at this convention. Said he'd known about me through mum for years, but thought dad should know me, too.'

'Why this one?'

Sam looked to the floor.

'Because he said he was dying. Alex Hamilton had seen Pryce while visiting a friend at a chemotherapy centre or something. Complete surprise, and he wasn't visiting anyone, if you know what I mean. Dad played it down, but eventually explained he was terminal. A matter of years, even with chemo, and then *boom*, no more Montgomery Pryce. Alex knew I was the bastard son, as I've already said, and then this convention happened, and it looked like it was our last chance to reunite, as Alex said dad was considering stopping conventions, because he didn't want people seeing him get visibly ill.'

'Understandable,' Declan replied. 'You spend your life in the spotlight, and you're constantly reminded of what you looked like thirty years ago ...'

'Sure, I get it,' Sam nodded. 'Alex even got me to beg mum to contact him, to make peace. And she did. They met up, just to talk, a couple of weeks back, and they even got together here for dinner on Thursday, but she didn't want to stay for the weekend, as she still had problems with Margot from the years on the show, so left late Thursday night.'

'Problems with Margot?'

'She was Marian's replacement,' Sam shrugged. 'Margot left, but she didn't expect to be replaced.'

'So, let me get this right, your biological parents met up on Thursday?' Declan raised an eyebrow at this. 'I thought they hated each other?'

'I suppose being shown your own mortality changes someone,' Sam said, and Declan sensed a hint of bitterness in the reply. 'But yeah. They hadn't really spoken in decades until the coffee chat, but this was a longer conversation.'

'And how did it go?'

'I don't know,' Sam replied. 'I arrived Friday morning, couldn't get through to her during the day, but she was working and they don't let them have phones on the shop floor.'

'What does she do?'

Sam blushed a little.

'Lingerie saleswoman,' he said. 'Big store on Oxford Street.'

Declan held a hand up.

'Did you just blush?' he asked. 'I've seen your stuff as Samantha Hardly now, so how do sexy panties make you blush?'

'It's my mum, dude.' Sam looked horrified at Declan.

'Okay, sure, I get that. Carry on.'

'So, I just left a message, said I hoped it was all okay.' Sam straightened as he replied. 'But in the evening, when I called mum to let her know dad had been murdered, she was utterly stunned, even broken by it, so I guess they mended their friendship. My stepdad is looking after her.'

'Your stepdad was okay with this?'

'Why wouldn't he be?' Sam frowned. 'It was just dinner.'

Declan decided that, for the moment, it was best *not* to mention the dinner was held in Pryce's suite, followed by what looked to be a more *sexual* outcome than Sam realised, complete with sexy knickers being left behind, next to a used condom wrapper. If Sam wanted to believe his mum had been an angel, then it wasn't up to Declan to say anything.

'So, you arrived in costume—'

'That wasn't my idea.' Sam shook his head. 'The whole plan was for me to arrive in costume, or cosplay, as they call it, and Alex sent the costume to me, as he had friends who made things like this. He sent me an email on Thursday evening with all the details.'

'What time Thursday?' Declan felt a pit open in his stomach. 'Around six?'

'No idea.' Sam shrugged apologetically. 'I didn't see it

until almost midnight. Basically, I was going to enter the cosplay competition, and they'd have me do a skit. Apparently we can use the guests in them if there's enough advance planning, and Alex had got dad to agree to do one, just one. *My* one. And, in it, I was going to out myself.'

'As his son?'

'No, he already knew that. He just didn't care. I was going to out myself as Samantha Hardly. As part of the skit. Alex and Flick reckoned the fans would go wild.'

'This doesn't seem well thought out,' Declan frowned. 'Why would he do this?'

'Yeah, well, it wasn't thought out,' Sam muttered. 'Alex had suggested that although Dad didn't give a shit I was his son, he might give a shit if he realised I was *famous* and his son. Samantha's a big thing in certain circles. Dad might have realised I was someone he could get something from, and even though it was still self-serving for him, I could be on stage with him, even establish my own relationship.'

He looked at the carpet, his face darkening.

'But that's not what happened, is it?' Declan asked gently.

'No,' Sam replied sadly. 'I learnt when I arrived yesterday morning, that Alex had done all this to get one over on dad, because he'd learnt dad was the one who grassed him up to his US agents and they'd had him removed from the States. During the skit, he was going to out me as his bastard son in front of everyone, and he had something else, something I don't know, that he was going to do. He'd used me to humiliate dad.'

Declan wondered if the other thing was connected to the private dinner Pryce and Carol Hardy had on the Thursday, one pushed for by Alex Hamilton. *Did he have photos? Could he have been prepared to post them on the screen? Show everyone Sam Hardy's mum, Lady Eleanor herself, in an affair with Pryce?*

'So why have the photo with him?' he asked, shelving that concern for the moment. 'In the photo shoot?'

'I didn't know then.' Sam looked like he was about to break into tears, and Declan understood. 'It was after the photo in the afternoon when I saw Margot. Even though mum had replaced her, they'd kept close, because Margot had chosen to leave the show. And when we talked, I said how sad it was about dad's cancer, assuming she knew. But Margot was mortified I even thought this. Apparently, dad wasn't dying. Alex had lied to everyone just to get mum and me here. All to screw with our heads like some sick joke.'

'You didn't shoot the arrow?'

'No, and if I had, I'd have been shooting at Alex,' Sam muttered, wiping a tear as he replied. 'The bow wasn't swapped, either. The photographer tried his best, but—'

'Wait, it was the *photographer* who wanted this?' Declan rose from the chair. 'In here?'

'Sure, why?'

'Not Alex Hamilton?'

'That wanker ignored me the moment the photo was taken,' Sam hissed. 'Literally ghosted me. I'd heard he had issues with Ryan Gates, or he was zoned on ketamine or something and so I left it, deciding to confront him later, but now? Now I know he did everything he was accused of.'

'Except he couldn't have killed Pryce without help,' Declan said, pacing. 'Help we're hearing from witnesses was given by you.'

He stopped.

'*Did you kill the messenger?*' he repeated softly. '*Kill a killer.*'

Sam looked up at Declan as he sat down, facing the younger man.

'You believe you know who killed your father, don't you?'

Sam nodded slowly.

'I know who killed dad,' he replied. 'That is, I think I do, but it's pointless. Nothing can be done. I said nothing last night because I thought it was stupid.'

'You think it was Peter Crock,' Declan continued, putting the pieces together. 'Kill a killer, kill the messenger, they're both about killing the person who does the task. Was that why Peter died? Because he killed your father?'

Sam shrugged.

'Peter Crock was at the back of the hall, to the left of where I was, and he had his bow with him,' he said.

'Did you kill him?' Declan couldn't help himself.

At this, Sam barked out a laugh.

'How could I?' he asked mockingly. 'Apparently, when he was killed, I was under arrest.'

'Stay here,' Declan said, already moving towards the door. 'If you try to leave, I'll arrest you again.'

'Wait, I'm not *already* arrested again?' Sam looked even more bewildered.

'Let's just say you've had a stay of execution,' Declan replied as he left the room at a run, heading for Billy's Batcave.

'I THOUGHT YOU WERE WITH THE BOY?' MONROE ASKED AS Declan barged through the doors to the hub.

'Do we have anyone showing where Peter Crock was on

the night of the murder?' he asked. 'Sam Hardy is convinced he was at the back of the hall.'

'Well, maybe Mister Hardy should tell us this while sitting in a cell?' Monroe raised an eyebrow.

'He didn't do it,' Declan said, shaking his head. 'And the killer's been one step ahead of us all the time.'

He looked at Anjli.

'Oh, the underwear in Pryce's room? I think that was from Carol Hardy. They met for "dinner" on the Thursday, and if you speak to Sam Hardy about this and his mum's relationship with Pryce, I'd suggest never mentioning this.'

'I think I just threw up a little in my mouth,' Anjli replied.

'Okay, stop, think this through,' Monroe said. 'What do we know right now?'

'I've been thinking about that,' Declan replied. 'Putting aside the whole Sam Hardy and Alex Hamilton scenario, Flick McCarthy's been in the middle of everything, and wasn't around when Montgomery Pryce was murdered.'

'You think Pryce's manager killed Pryce?'

'I think his manager also repped Alex Hamilton, and if Hamilton was sending death threats, there's a chance she could have known about it,' Declan replied, pacing the room as he spoke. 'She worked with Montgomery three years ago, after his previous manager quit, right?'

'Billy would know—' Monroe went to ask Billy but halted as he stared at the empty space.

'Where is Billy?' he said, looking around. Only Anjli, De'Geer, Declan, and Monroe were in the room. Even Malcolm Stoddard had left at some point, likely after Hamilton's arrest.

'He said he had something to check,' De'Geer replied. 'Left with Jess about half an hour back.'

'Something he couldn't check by computer?' Monroe frowned at this. 'What is the world coming to?'

'You're just annoyed that you're the great DCI who didn't notice your computer guy wasn't at the computer the entire time you've been here,' Declan grinned.

'I've had a lot on my mind,' Monroe muttered. 'And Billy's often skulking around—'

As if appearing at the call of his name, though, the door to the room smashed open, and Billy came in at a run, Jess immediately behind him.

'Will you please stop running around the bloody place?' Monroe exclaimed. 'This is a police scene!'

'True, boss, but maybe not ours for much longer,' Billy replied, already moving to his computer. 'Thames Valley Police are coming to take it over.'

'What?' Declan looked at Billy as he typed on the screen. 'How do you know this?'

'There was a complaint made about how we've handled this,' Jess said, and Declan noted how she'd included herself on the team. 'John Moss, the organiser, went to Milton Keynes' nick after they picked up Alex Hamilton. He's demanded a new team take over.'

'Let me guess ... DCI Sampson,' Monroe muttered. 'And there I was, thinking he was a good guy.'

'He might still be, boss,' Declan replied. 'He's just doing his job.'

'I have a contact there,' Billy replied. 'Well, someone I'd been working on data capture with, and they said they couldn't send me any more responses from HOLMES2 on the case until the new DCI agreed on it.'

'Fine, let's give him everything and let him get on with it,'

Monroe sighed, stretching. 'Why's he coming, anyway? We've sent him the killer.'

'One of them,' Billy typed on the keyboard, watching the screen as he replied. 'They're charging Sam Hardy with the other murder.'

'It's not Sam,' Declan said. 'There's a chance it could have been Peter Crock.'

'From the back of the hall?' De'Geer paused at this. 'Guv, he had a separated shoulder.'

'Which I'd like Doctor Marcos to confirm,' Declan shook his head. 'We don't know—'

'That's the problem, Guv,' Billy replied, looking back. '*We don't know.* That's what we're being accused of. I reckon we have an hour tops before we lose access to the case. And I think that's what Flick McCarthy wants.'

Declan moved closer to the screen as he heard the name.

'And why do you think this?' he asked. 'And where exactly were you, for the last half an hour?'

'On the phone, away from Malcolm Stoddard,' Jess replied. 'When we left, he was still here, listening to everything we did while hiding from his secret killers. We wanted to check something he said.'

'Which was?'

'When you interviewed him, he called Flick McCarthy "Fliss",' Billy leant back in the chair. 'When I heard the recording made, it made me think. You see, I'd seen that before. Couldn't think where, though. It was Jess that pointed it out.'

'Fliss is a nickname for "Felicity",' Jess explained proudly. 'And another nickname for Felicity is "Flick". Michael Bailey used "Fliss" in the *Swap Shop* interview when he talked about Felicity Marshall, the Maid Marian of *Young Robin*.'

'You think Flick McCarthy is Felicity Marshall?'

'I don't think it, I know it, Guv,' Billy replied, opening up an email. 'I had the British Sports Council reply to my question. After *Young Robin*, Felicity Marshall went back into archery, and eventually coaching. Her mother, divorced, married again, and Felicity took her new name.'

'McCarthy.'

Billy nodded, pulling up a photo of a young woman, a bow in her hand. It was a stretch, and the image was over forty years old, but the eyes were the same.

'Flick McCarthy never lied to us about her name because we never asked her,' Billy said. 'She is a manager, she trained as a lawyer, and she was an Olympic hopeful in archery. And she was at the back of the ballroom during the opening ceremony.'

'How do you know that?' Declan frowned. 'No witnesses saw her—'

Billy pulled up a folder.

'Malcolm Stoddard didn't give you all the photos of the opening ceremony,' he said. 'When he went on the run, we gained his other images. And, in another folder, he has photos of the audience coming in before anything even started.'

He opened an image; the picture was aimed at the chairs in the middle of the hall, the audience entering in lines, but at the very back, and unmistakable, were three very recognisable people.

'Peter Crock, Luna Hedlun-Gates and Flick McCarthy,' Declan said. 'They were all there.'

'A couple of minutes after this, he takes another picture and Luna's gone, but it kills her alibi of spending the whole day in the spa, sorting out issues.'

'Why did you let Malcolm leave?' Declan asked.

'He wasn't a suspect,' Billy replied. 'He was only here for security. But as we realised something was going on, we also realised that Malcolm Stoddard was sitting in the back of our ops room, listening to everything. And we've had that before.'

Declan nodded at this. On his first case with the Last Chance Saloon he'd learned, halfway through the case, that the intern, Trix Preston, had actually bugged the briefing room and was reporting to her superiors outside of the office.

'So, you left the room, allowing him a chance to walk out?'

Billy shrugged.

'I felt we'd do better without the only person who seemed to know Flick was Felicity being in the room,' he said. 'Now we have to wait to see if he goes to her.'

'And how do we do that?'

Billy opened a window on his screen, and a little dot was seen on a map of the hotel.

'Because I placed a tracker on him,' he said. 'For his own safety, of course. He is, after all, a potential victim still.'

'Good man,' Monroe nodded, turning to Declan. 'Get everyone in and let them know, we have until Milton Keynes nick turn up to solve this case. And *someone find me that bloody woman!*'

21

AGAINST THE CLOCK

MALCOLM STODDARD WAS MOVING QUICKLY AS HE WALKED through the hotel back corridors; he didn't know what was still open, and he didn't want to cause any panic by suddenly appearing out of nowhere. After all, many of the attendees of the convention had seen him run from the police earlier that day, and now, with the Saturday drawing to a close, many of them were still in the bar, aware the convention was over, but not wanting to leave, and be charged for an extra night they didn't use.

There was a term Malcolm had heard in US conventions over the years, something called "Lobby Con". This was where the fans didn't care that much about the convention itself, but wanted to spend more time in the bar, or lobby, meeting new fans of the shows they loved, and catching up with old friends, socialising over a drink, often brought from home, as well as eating cookies, which were basically home-cooked biscuits, and small cakes. It was effectively a mini-convention within the convention, and although everyone there paid to attend the original convention, and actually enjoyed a lot of the programming, there was a point, every day, when "Lobby Con" took over.

And here, right now, with the hotel closing the ballroom and con-related rooms, the volunteers signed off and the convention officially stopped; the lobby continued the convention. People showed off costumes they hadn't had a chance to wear, all for a cosplay contest that would now not happen. The bar had agreed to show old episodes of *Hooded Outlaw* on the screens around the lobby, and fans sat and watched, cheered, criticised and cried, mainly every time Montgomery Pryce appeared on screen.

There were also those that sat and drank, that grieved, and those that held small, candlelit vigils, with the candles in this case being tea lights, flickering on tables as grieving fans told stories of their meetings with Pryce, all most likely embellished.

Malcolm laughed a little at that. The prick was probably watching down at this with Errol Flynn, telling him "see, they love me more than you." Maybe even the real Robin Hood was watching, confused at how the fans could mourn such a piece of shit.

If you ever find out, Robin, Malcolm looked up at the ceiling as he thought this, *please tell me how. Because I don't have a bloody clue either.*

He'd left the back room he'd been sitting in for the last few hours, not because he felt safe, but because he realised things were changing, and not in a good way. The pretty-boy copper in the three-piece suit had picked up on a mistake Malcolm had made, calling Flick "Fliss". It hadn't been deliberate, and he was pissed he'd done it. Somehow, he needed to fix this.

He stopped in the corridor, taking a deep breath.

No. He needed to delay this.

That was all he needed to do, keep the clock running until the investigation was taken over by the Milton Keynes Police. They were the ones who were supposed to have taken this from the start; they were the ones who would have knee-jerked to the immediate and obvious answers on the Saturday morning, that Alex Hamilton and another, yet unnamed person had not only killed Montgomery Pryce but also Peter Crock. The unnamed person was likely to be the blond man, Sam Hardy, who'd been a slam-dunk for the role since Pryce had scuppered all the plans on the Thursday, thanks to Alex having his own stupid bloody machinations to run during the weekend. Then, once they realised that Hardy and his bow at the back of the hall had been the answer to their prayers, they'd made sure he'd do what they'd wanted him to do, and grass up Peter Crock as being there in the back of the room.

But then Flick learned that morning he was the son of Montgomery Pryce.

Malcolm admitted he hadn't expected *that* twist. When Alex had paid for Sam's room and ticket, they thought he could have been Alex's son, not Monty's. Still, it fitted the narrative, even with the last-minute changes, and this created a very nice bow on the case. Sam Hardy would go free, Peter Crock would be too dead to counter the statement, and Alex would be damned.

Alex Hamilton brought Peter Crock into his scheme to kill Montgomery Pryce, promising not to kill Peter for what he did in Prague, all those years ago.

Peter Crock then killed Montgomery Pryce with an arrow Alex gave him.

Alex then killed Peter with another of the stolen arrows, after drugging him earlier in the night.

Alex was then found with the third of the arrows, no alibi for the deaths, and a printout of the letters "he" had sent.

There was no way Milton Keynes wouldn't be locking up Alex Hamilton, especially with DCI Sampson running the case.

Malcolm had felt bad at the start, as Alex technically hadn't deserved this, but he had enough skeletons in his closet. Malcolm knew this for a fact. That Alex Hamilton would go down for a crime he didn't commit while being guilty of so many others was actually Karma playing out for the cheap seats.

But the show only continued if the City Police *couldn't* finish their investigation. And, as he left, he realised they'd moved one step closer to doing that, when they found images from before the opening ceremonies had started, showing Flick at the back of the ballroom. They'd quickly work out she could have been the one that shot Montgomery Pryce, but even then, they wouldn't have the *truth*.

Malcolm needed to get hold of Flick now. They needed to change the narrative.

There was a creak, and a door opened, a member of the bar staff staring in confusion at the man in the back corridors of the hotel.

'Don't worry, I'm supposed to be here,' Malcolm smiled, waving the pass, hoping the man hadn't heard the news about the convention being stopped. Apparently he hadn't, as he shrugged, walking off into the kitchen area. Taking a deep breath and letting it out, calming his still-rising nerves, Malcolm gathered his bearings and opened the door to his left, expecting to emerge into the back of the onetime Green Room—

Only to stare at the tip of a harpoon spear, currently within a Nemrod Corbeta speargun.

'Hello, Malcolm,' Ryan Gates said, looking past him, checking both ways down the corridor before waving him into the empty room. 'Why don't you come in and have a chat?'

'RIGHT THEN, PEOPLE, TELL ME WHAT WE HAVE.' MONROE stood at the end of the boardroom table, looking around the room. At the computer station were Billy and Jess, beside them were Bullman, Declan and Anjli, then Cooper, and finally De'Geer and Doctor Marcos stood the other side. 'Rosanna, could you give an update?'

Doctor Marcos nodded.

'Montgomery Pryce, sixty-three years of age, killed when an arrow pierced his chest,' Doctor Marcos started. 'An arrow causes a wound that is both punctured and incised, and this wound often allows the outward flow of discharges because of its structure, high velocity, and that an arrow wounds tissue continuously. The arrowhead didn't impact bone, and without X-ray and computed tomographic scanning facilities available, I performed a twisting action on the arrow to confirm it was free of bone. The arrow itself pierced the left ventricle and clipped the lung, and death was almost instantaneous, mainly due to shock.'

She stopped as Monroe held up a hand.

'Rosanna, as much as I love hearing you talk like a doctor,

we're on the clock here,' he said. 'We're about to lose this case.'

'Fair point,' Doctor Marcos nodded. 'Arrow was a longbow arrow, identical to the ones made by Peter Crock. It was, however, not shot by a longbow.'

'How do you know?' Anjli asked.

'Because it would have punched right through him,' Doctor Marcos looked at Billy. 'Did your weird 3D thing work out?'

'Yes.' Billy looked back at her. 'It would have killed Margot Trayner.'

'We have photos showing Peter Crock, Sam Hardy and your girlfriend at the back.' Doctor Marcos now turned her attention to Monroe. 'I'm sorry, did I say your girlfriend? I meant Flick McCarthy.'

'Tell us about her,' Monroe waved at Billy. 'And just the facts, not paranoid conjecture like my fiancée here.'

Billy went to speak, but then stopped.

'Wait, what?' he asked, looking at the shocked Anjli. 'Did I miss something?'

'Lots of things,' Monroe smiled. 'But now's not the time to go into it. Please?'

Billy swallowed, nodding.

'Flick McCarthy, of McCarthy Premier Management,' he started. 'Began managing people around seven years ago, primarily as a favour for Nigel Cummings, who was having issues with his then management.'

'So there has to be a link between them,' Declan said. 'How did Nigel know to call her?'

'Malcolm Stoddard suggested her,' Cooper read from her notes. 'She was overheard having a row with Traynor at breakfast, and during this she said Malcolm was an old friend who, when he saw Nigel was being screwed around by his then manager, he called Flick in, knowing she was looking for a challenge, or something.'

'Or something?'

'It's not verbatim, boss,' Cooper reddened. 'I didn't hear it in person.'

'Okay, so Malcolm and Flick know each other since before she was a manager,' Billy carried on. 'Which, considering she was Felicity Marshall, and was Marian to his Little John for a while in the seventies, it makes sense.'

'She's also an ex-Olympic archer,' Anjli added. 'Came seventeenth in the Women's Individual Event during the 1980 Moscow Olympics, and eleventh in the 1984 one in Los Angeles.'

'And after that?' Bullman pursed her lips, curious.

'She disappeared for the 1988 ones,' Billy read. 'But then if she was expecting to return to Sherwood Forest for the show, she might have stopped training. And in two Olympics, she didn't even hit the top ten.'

'Of the best people in the world,' Jess added.

'Oh, I'm not knocking her, but back then, they didn't have the licensing deals we have now. It would have been expensive to carry on. As it is, we next see her in 1990, where she takes on a coaching role prior to the Barcelona Olympics in 1992. She did well, working for the Grand National Archery Society, and we had our first archer in the top ten, possibly because of her help. But she stepped down from coaching after Rio, in 2016.'

'Which would fit with her taking a new challenge in 2017, when she took on Nigel Cummings,' Declan counted back on his fingers.

'Apparently there was a death in the family, and she

started caring for her sister,' Billy read from the screen. 'Was off grid for a year before returning.'

'Archer like that, though, she'd kill both of them,' Monroe mused. 'What about Peter Crock? He was at the back?'

'He had a separated shoulder, found it impossible to draw a bowstring back,' De'Geer shook his head. 'Wasn't faking, either. He really wanted to be able to shoot in the contests.'

He stopped.

'He would have been able to if he was on strong pain medication,' he said. 'Like, for example, Oxycodone.'

Doctor Marcos pulled up her notes on her iPad.

'We don't have the toxicology report yet, but preliminary reports on Peter Crock showed there were opiates in his system, maybe enough to mask excruciating pain like pulling a bow with a separated shoulder, but it's unlikely.'

'We thought he didn't defend himself because he knew the killer,' Monroe clicked the top of his mouth with his tongue. 'Not only did he know him, he was possibly too baked to rise, let alone stop his killer.'

'So, Felicity Marshall takes on Montgomery Pryce and Alex Hamilton as clients,' Monroe frowned. 'Wouldn't Pryce recognise her?'

'The impression I got from people was Pryce didn't pay much attention to women who wouldn't sleep with him, so maybe he just didn't click who she was?'

'Or didn't care to,' Monroe mused. 'But why take them on? Everyone hates Pryce, And Hamilton doesn't seem to be loved.'

'Or *do* they hate Pryce?' Bullman leant against the back of a chair, stretching her back as she spoke. 'We know they all think he's a prick, but so far, the only person Flick McCarthy seems to hate is Margot Trayner.'

'Who she believes took her job, maybe even owes her Oscar win to Flick,' Declan considered the options. 'Maybe she was trying to kill Margot, and Pryce got in the way?'

'Okay, we're in circles,' Monroe frowned. 'Talk to me about Pryce.'

'Came here Thursday, is a bit of a dick according to everyone,' Anjli read from her notes. 'Last Robin Hood convention was three years ago, where he slept with Jenny Moss, the organiser's eighteen-year-old daughter. It was claimed to be consensual, so even if we think it's icky, it's not illegal.'

'Although there's a rumour she'd taken pills from Alex Hamilton, which muddies the water slightly.'

'True, but they're rumours and nobody's confirming them, so we have to work around that. Anyway, after this there were issues. John said he'd never run a convention with Pryce invited again. Pryce's manager dropped him and Alex, and Flick took them both on.'

'She didn't get him any appearances in the next couple of years, so maybe this was her plan?' Declan asked.

'No, something else happened,' Anjli replied. 'He started getting death threats, but they were glossed over.'

'In hindsight, maybe he shouldn't have.'

'He apparently tried to hire Ryan Gates, because of his ex-military training, to work as his bodyguard, but it was a case of the boy who cried wolf, or in this case, the man who was a prick to his co-stars so many times before, they naturally assumed he was trying to screw them over again.'

'Gates, who cleaned up his mess in the mid-eighties,' Monroe asked.

'Yes, but Gates didn't know it was connected to them, or who the victim was,' Declan replied. 'It was just a job for him. Only reason he's still around was because Robert Standish remembered him and made sure he was looked after when he came out of the military a couple of years later.'

Monroe nodded.

'The underwear?'

'Sam Hardy's mum, it seems,' Declan replied. 'Although Sam Hardy doesn't know it was more intimate than a simple chat. And, with Pryce being dead, I think we might want to keep a lid on that.'

'And Hardy isn't your pick for this?'

'I don't think so,' Declan considered this. 'I think he's there purely to lead us down a path. He was led to believe Peter Crock killed Pryce, and then Alex Hamilton killed Crock, giving us a simple case to wrap up.'

'Which he could have done, still,' Monroe mused. 'Tell me about Pryce and the spa.'

'Luna, John, Jenny, all claim Pryce was coming on strong to Jenny and had to be pulled out,' Cooper read from her notes. 'But the other masseuse on call yesterday, Chantelle Waters, said she was the one who massaged Pryce, not Jenny, and that when he left, he was fine. Never even stared at her funny.'

'Maybe he did this after?'

'Had a second massage?' Declan frowned. 'Maybe. Or, rather, he's being set up, giving people a reason to hate him before they judge him.'

'But why that?' Bullman frowned. 'Who else would get angry at this, and how could it affect his case?'

'Someone look into that,' Monroe looked around the room. 'Running out of time. Alex and Luna.'

'If you speak to Luna, he's been stalking her, wouldn't

take a hint and exposed himself to her in a changing room on Thursday,' Anjli replied.

'If you speak to Alex, he was having an affair with Luna. Ryan didn't know, and they met in the changing rooms to have sex,' Declan added.

Monroe nodded.

'And he sent the letters?'

'Looks like it,' Declan nodded. 'And also had the arrow in his bed, although he claims he was set up.'

'Only way that happens is if someone stole his second card, but he said he didn't have it when he got to his room,' Anjli said, before pausing. 'What if he lost it before he went to his room? While he was in the gym?'

'The lockers were padlocked. They would have stopped someone.'

'Not if they had a key, maybe a master key?'

'Or if they were with him while the locker was open,' Declan added.

'You think Luna took the room key while she was shagging him?' Doctor Marcos looked appalled.

'Maybe he gave her the key, told her to visit him later?' Declan suggested. 'She said nothing because her husband might overhear.'

'We need to speak with Luna too,' Monroe nodded. 'Preferably before her husband shoots someone with his speargun. Do we have anything on their location?'

Billy grinned, bringing up the hotel plan, pointing at the flashing blue button.

'If Malcolm Stoddard found him, then he's in the Green Room,' he smiled.

'Let's go see who Malcolm's talking to,' Monroe went to carry on, but was interrupted as the door to the room opened, and three Thames Valley Police officers walked in, followed by a tall, Asian woman in a suit, and finally DCI Sampson.

'Sorry, DCI Monroe, but this is now a Thames Valley investigation,' he said. 'I've been ordered by my Divisional Chief to take over, and you've been ordered to pass all information over to me, while my team works out what really happened here.'

'We're close to solving the case—' Monroe replied calmly but stopped as Sampson held up a hand.

'With all due respect, and no offence meant, but I don't really care how close anyone believes they are,' he said. 'We have a killer in our custody, thanks to you. And I believe you have the second killer in the photo room?'

'Sam Hardy isn't the killer,' Declan shook his head. 'You need to—'

'You need to remember how to speak to a superior officer,' Sampson snapped back, 'DI Walsh. Now, it's getting on, I'm sure you all want to get home, so why don't you all go check out of the hotel? DC Fitzwarren can get my cyber expert DS Temer up to speed, Monroe and I can have a little chat, and then we'll bring this case home for you before your dinner's cold.'

'Now listen here—' Bullman started, but DCI Sampson held up a hand to stop her.

'Ma'am, I know you're a superior rank, but you're City Police and this is Thames Valley jurisdiction,' he said. 'So, unless you're going to help me stop a killer, I suggest you stand down before my superiors talk to yours. As far as my orders go, and my orders *do* go here, if I see you performing any police duties on hotel grounds, I'll have to take this higher.'

'Hotel grounds,' Monroe sneered. 'Nice touch.'

'Sir,' Cooper pulled gently at Monroe's arm. 'Can I have a word?'

'Now is probably not the time, lassie,' Monroe hadn't taken his eyes off Sampson.

'Sir, it's important,' Cooper replied. 'I can't check out, as I have a problem with my card. I need to speak to you now.'

Monroe glared at Sampson, who nodded at him. 'We're not enemies,' he said. 'No matter how you spoke to me when we first met. Speak to your officer. We'll be right here, as you dismantle all this.'

Furious, Monroe walked out of the room and down the hall with Cooper.

'This had better be bloody important, lassie,' he hissed. 'You know your card wasn't used to book the—'

'Sir, I've seen that man before,' Cooper whispered.

'Of course, you have,' Monroe sighed. 'You came and told me he was here, remember?'

'No sir, I never met or saw DCI Sampson.' Cooper shook her head. 'I had Thames Valley officers deal with him if you recall?'

Monroe was about to reply but stared back at the room.

'Where did you see him then?' he hissed.

'In the spa,' Cooper replied quietly. 'In a photo with Jenny Moss. The woman with me at the time, Linda, said he was her boyfriend.'

Monroe nodded slowly.

'Aye, that sounds about right,' he said. 'So, the boyfriend of the woman molested by Pryce is taking over his case, after her father went straight to him. That's the piece of the jigsaw missing. Pryce had to be molesting Jenny to anger Sampson, so Chantelle's story has to be correct.'

He stroked his beard for a moment.

'I'm wondering if Flick McCarthy was as innocent as she claimed when she quoted DCI Sampson in that article.'

'What do we do, though, sir?' Cooper looked nervously at the door, expecting Sampson to emerge at any moment. 'We're off the case.'

'Oh, we're still on the case, lassie,' Monroe set his jaw as he spoke. 'Our friend in there? He just doesn't know it yet.'

———————

22

OUTLAWS

'So, what's the plan?' Declan stared across the lobby at the Thames Valley officers at the patio doors, as the forensics officers who had been working for Doctor Marcos until fifteen minutes earlier, left with their equipment.

'Currently, my boy, we don't have one,' he said. 'Cooper went down to the spa, but it's closed. And until we can gain that photo, we can only place our word against his that Sampson's connected to this somehow.'

He straightened as, across the lobby, and as if appearing at the sound of his name like a rather officious devil, DCI Sampson appeared, walking with DS Temer, deep in conversation.

'The problem I have, is we've dealt with our fair share of corrupt coppers over the last year, and I didn't get any vibes from Sampson when he was here earlier, that he was in any way shady,' Monroe finished, lowering his voice.

'Don't be too worried,' Declan smiled. 'He might not be. Dating someone doesn't make them implicit. It just makes them one-sided sometimes.'

Starting away from Monroe now, Declan walked towards DCI Sampson.

'Sir,' he said, nodding as Sampson looked over at him. 'We've had a chat, and we'd like to help. After all, your officers have been helping us all weekend, and we'd like to return the favour.'

'It's appreciated ... Declan, isn't it?' Sampson nodded. 'But honestly? We'll probably be out of here in an hour.'

'Really?' Declan was surprised by the abruptness of this.

Sampson shrugged, looking around.

'Alex Hamilton is caught on CCTV printing death threats, he has one of the murder weapons in his room, he's not exactly showered himself with praise with Mrs Hedlun-Gates, he's a known prescription drug dealer who's spiked hotel staff's drinks in the past, and Sam Hardy claims he was groomed into killing Pryce when Alex convinced him he was going to be reunited with his father, after Pryce dismissed him.'

'Wait, Sam has admitted to killing Pryce?' Declan looked back at Monroe who, on hearing this had subtly pulled out his phone.

'Well, no, not yet, but it's only a matter of time, and Flick McCarthy spoke to him about this.'

'And how the hell did she do that?' Declan snapped. 'She didn't even know who he was until about an hour ago.'

'Well, she knows him now,' Sampson replied with a slight smile. 'He's guilty as hell, and the whole porn writing thing shows a deviant personality. And we have a witness claiming they saw him hold the bow up while at the back of the room.'

'Let me guess,' Declan's voice was flat now. 'Flick McCarthy.'

'Actually no, Ryan Gates,' Sampson frowned, leaning in, a

move that was supposed to be comradely, but felt threatening.

'I saw you arrested Hardy last night, but let him go,' he whispered. 'When this goes to trial, that will be commented on. Why did you do it?'

'Because he's innocent,' Declan replied calmly. 'As you'll find out soon, *Guv*.'

'Well, whatever we find out, we'll let you know,' Sampson leant back now, all smiles for the public. 'Safe journey home. All of you. We'll let you know by email what happens.'

'Oh, we'll be here until tomorrow,' a familiar voice spoke, as Bullman walked over. 'I just spoke to reception. They'd already taken the money for our rooms, and as we can't claim it back, we'll be staying for the night. As civilians, of course. We might even use the spa.'

'Spa's closed,' Sampson replied, a little too quickly. 'Shuts at six on a Saturday.'

'Well, that's good to know,' Bullman smiled. 'But we've asked them to open up especially for us. And the gym and pool are open until ten.'

Declan could see Sampson struggling to find a reply that worked here, but instead he chose better, nodded and shook Bullman's outstretched hand.

'Just stay out of our way and we'll be fine,' he said.

'You won't even realise we're here,' Bullman's smile stayed on, but Declan knew her too well; she was forcing it, playing nice. 'Oh, one thing, where did you hear he'd spiked drinks? I missed that part.'

Sampson froze at the question, the mask slipping slightly. But then he smiled, returning to the moment.

'Someone mentioned to one of my officers,' he said. 'They

didn't tell you? You obviously spent your time talking to the wrong people.'

Nodding to his DS, Sampson walked off, with DS Temet following him. And, now they were alone, Declan noted Cooper appearing from the other side of reception, no longer wearing her full uniform.

'Did you get in?' Declan asked softly, glancing around to make sure Sampson hadn't stopped, or found a way to eavesdrop.

'I did,' however, Cooper's face gave the answer to the question before her words did. 'But someone already removed the photo.'

Bullman's face tightened, and Monroe had to look away so as not to swear loudly.

'Dammit,' he hissed. 'That was our leverage. Has Billy found anything on Instagram?'

'No,' Cooper admitted. 'I got Jenny Moss's mobile phone number, but she's probably been told to lie low right now if she's part of whatever's going on.'

'Aye, and I'd really love to know what's really going on,' Monroe muttered. 'The line Sampson said there about hotel staff's drinks being spiked. That has to have been Jenny Moss, three years ago. And as she's not here right now, what's the chances she told him that while off the clock, so to speak?'

'It'd also explain why he wants Hamilton charged for this.' Declan nodded. 'But unless we can prove he knows her—'

'Hold that thought,' Monroe smiled. 'I think I might have an idea. How did you get here?'

'Me sir? I drove,' Cooper replied. 'I brought one of the squad cars. Was that okay?'

'More than that, it was excellent planning,' Monroe

nodded. 'Get De'Geer, put some uniforms back on and go for a drive.'

'Where to, sir?'

'I'll come back to you on that one,' Monroe winked. 'All you need to do is *not* be police on the hotel grounds.'

Cooper went to reply to this, but then slowly smiled as realisation dawned.

'I think we'd be thrilled about being police officers *outside* of hotel grounds,' she said, already turning. 'I'll let De'Geer know he needs to change back.'

'She's remarkably eager.' Declan frowned.

'Of course, she is, laddie,' Monroe grinned, tapping on his phone. 'She's hoping to catch our Acting Sergeant in a state of undress. I've just texted Billy. Hopefully, he's still got a connection to HOLMES2, and we can find Jenny Moss's current address.'

Declan waited a moment, working out the correct words for what he was about to say.

'So, are we going to talk about it?' he asked.

'The case?'

'No, boss. The "fiancée" comment you made.' Declan looked at his mentor, raising an eyebrow. 'Was it on one knee? Did she propose to you?'

'Can we do this after we fix this case and make sure an innocent man isn't taken down?' Monroe asked.

'Sam Hardy?'

'Well, it sure as hell isn't Alex Hamilton,' Monroe smiled. 'So, I now have a plan. Delay the police from leaving until we have what we need.'

'And how do we do that?' Declan asked.

The Scot looked around, leaning in conspiratorially to Declan.

'We arrange a hostage situation,' he whispered.

'Great idea,' Declan grinned. 'And I know exactly how to do that.'

RYAN GATES HAD BEEN SITTING IN THE GREEN ROOM FOR QUITE a while after Malcolm Stoddard had left, heading to the costume room and the others.

Gates had never been a tactical genius, but he had been a soldier in some of the worst places in the world, both on and off the books, and he knew when an Op was going pear-shaped. And whatever this was, it was distinctly going that way.

Pryce was dead, and he didn't particularly care about that. The son of a bitch had been running from Karma for years now, and his death wasn't really a massive loss to the world. But as for Peter Crock, though, that *had* been a shock. If anyone was going to be the second dead body, it would have been Hamilton, but for some reason someone had wanted the blissed-out hippy to be offed.

This was something Ryan Gates didn't get. *Peter Crock didn't have enemies.* The only person he'd ever pissed off was Nigel Cummings, and that was because he was ripping him off. Everyone knew it. So, what the hell was going on?

Could Peter have been Pryce's killer?

Gates sat back on his Green Room chair, sipping at his soda as he considered this. Peter hadn't shot an arrow in years, claiming injury, but that didn't mean he couldn't. And if he had, then it was a good chance that someone had killed him afterwards, purely to tie up loose ends. In fact, Gates felt this was a more likely answer than Sam Hardy, because he was a story that could eventually be proven to be innocent, and it was always a plan to "focus in on other areas", when setting someone else up.

Could that have been the reason for him being involved?

Gates nodded to himself. If he'd been asked to arrange this Op, and he'd not cared about anyone involved, then using someone to kill your enemy and then remove them would be his first plan of attack. However, he'd heard Peter had been murdered only a couple of hours after Pryce, and that meant someone had to have planned this out in advance.

But, whatever the planning, the fact of the matter was someone wanted Pryce dead so badly, they'd kill another just to ensure he was dead. And that brought Gates to his primary concern. Was this murder, or rather were these murders connected to the death in Prague?

Gates leant back in the chair as he considered this. The police had pointed out that Alex Hamilton had printed death threat letters to Malcolm, Peter and Montgomery, and they believed these to be connected to the death of a woman in the eighties, at a party during the filming. Malcolm had gone on the run and not been murdered, but the other two had, which made no sense. Alex Hamilton had no connection to the event, but at the same time Alex was out of his head half the time on painkillers, so who knew what was going through the druggie's head.

But having Alex write threatening letters was a great way to kill your enemies and have an unknowing patsy, though.

Gates thought back to the night in question; he'd never known who the woman was, or even what had happened, just that Robert Standish, the director of the film, needed a reason for this to not be connected to anyone involved. And filming in the Eastern Bloc in the eighties, the last thing you wanted was to be British, and accused of murder.

Gates hadn't even needed to know the name of the victim, as he'd been brought across in his connection with the Special Reconnaissance Unit. They'd realised having someone on the other side of the Iron Curtain was a bonus, and Gates was young and eager to put himself over. He'd spent the two weeks he'd been in Prague as film crew, but at the same time had clocked several of the locals as intelligence agents for the other side. And, when the police were called, Gates could make it look as if one agent had killed her, possibly because her husband was involved in the financing of this British movie.

It hadn't taken more than an hour to fix the problem for Standish, but now Gates wondered whether he'd painted a target on his back by doing this, a target that had appeared this weekend.

But why was bloody Alex Hamilton involved?

The answer to that was obvious.

He wasn't.

Someone was setting Alex Hamilton up, making sure he was completely unable to prove his innocence. If it wasn't connected to Gates in any way, he'd actually be impressed at this. He couldn't have done better if he'd done it himself.

So, someone wanted Pryce dead, and they wanted Hamilton blamed for it.

Gates couldn't help himself; he unconsciously grabbed at the speargun, bringing it close once more. The police had arrested Hamilton, but the killer was still out there. Gates knew that for sure.

But here was the problem. He could write a list on who'd want Pryce dead, but there was a smaller list of people who wanted to see Hamilton destroyed. Gates knew that because he was on the smaller list.

As was Luna.

Gates rose from the chair as he heard movement from outside. Nobody else knew he was here, and the convention was over, so if someone was trying to enter the Green Room, there was every chance they were looking to hide, like Malcolm had. Or it was Luna returning; they'd had a brief conversation after he'd spoken to the detectives, and in it she'd told him she needed space and had walked away. Gates didn't blame her, to learn her husband had held this secret from her for so many years was likely to be something that could change her entire worldview. Gates just hoped she could forgive him—

Could Luna have been the one behind this? She'd been in the Business Suite with Alex, had she known he was writing these letters? *Could she have helped him? But why kill Pryce? She barely knew the man.* No, there was something more here, but Ryan simply couldn't work it out.

The door to the Green Room rattled, and, holding his speargun up, Ryan Gates walked to the door, steadying himself. He opened it; the gun aimed outwards ...

Only to find DI Walsh facing him.

'Hi, Ryan,' Declan gently moved the spear away from his chest with his finger. 'We were looking for Malcolm, but guessed you'd be here.'

'You shouldn't be here,' Gates shook his head. 'They're coming for me.'

'Yeah, but that's the problem, isn't it?' Declan said as he pushed past Gates, walking into the Green Room. 'Is the coffee still hot? We got kicked out of our room, so we have to buy it now. Do you mind?'

'What's the problem?' Gates frowned as Declan walked to the coffee urn, pouring out a black coffee, grimacing as he sipped.

'Urgh, cold,' he said, finishing it anyway. 'The problem is, you don't know who's killing everyone, but you damn well know it isn't Alex. He's being set up, isn't he?'

Gates stared at Declan.

'You seem to know more about this than me,' he said, and unconsciously the speargun turned to face Declan, who was looking around.

'You didn't kill Malcolm, did you?' Declan asked innocently. 'Just curious.'

'He came here but didn't stay long,' Gates explained. 'He told me Alex had been arrested, that a new DCI had arrived, and you'd been kicked off the case.'

'There are reasons for that,' Declan smiled, placing the cup back on the sideboard beside the coffee urn. 'And if you have a couple of minutes, I'd like to tell you about it.'

'And why would I want to know about it?'

'Malcolm left because he needed to speak to Flick McCarthy, didn't he?' Declan replied. 'Do you know where she is?'

'Helping Nigel take down his costumes, I think.' Gates narrowed his eyes. 'What's Flick got to do with this?'

Walking to a chair, sitting down and placing his feet up onto the table beside it with a grateful sigh, Declan looked back at him.

'Please put that gun down,' he said. 'You're going to be needing it in a moment. Let me explain what's really going on.'

23

HOSTAGE TAKING

MONROE HAD BEEN WATCHING SAMPSON FROM ACROSS THE BAR when Billy walked over to him, a bundle of nervous energy with an iPad in his hand.

'Try to look like you're enjoying your time off, not secretly working, laddie,' he said, pushing over a glass of coke. 'Here. It might have gone flat, though. You've been gone a while.'

'I have something else on Flick McCarthy, and I think it explains everything,' Billy said, pausing as a shadow crossed the table. But it was only Anjli, sitting down beside Monroe.

'De'Geer and Cooper are almost back with the squad car, Bullman and Doctor Marcos are in the gym as far as anyone's concerned, and Declan's missing.'

'Declan's been arranging our surprise guest,' Monroe smiled. 'Jess?'

'Following Sampson,' Anjli explained. 'She's not police or officially part of our team, so if she's stopped she can just claim she's super excited and wants to learn.'

'Good,' Monroe looked at Billy. 'Go on, tell us what you learnt about that bloody woman.'

'She has a sister,' Billy said. 'Rebecca Garcia. Older sister by five years, had a son, named Richard. Apparently, in the nineties, he was young and pretty, and both Nigel Cummings and Terry Leighton had crushes on him. Nothing happened, and he ended up, years later, working in LA in the club scene.'

'Okay.' Anjli looked at Monroe. 'That's around the same time Hamilton was there.'

'It's exactly the same time,' Billy replied. 'Richard died of a drug overdose in 2016, after a party, which Alex held, went wrong. The police couldn't charge Alex with murder, or prove he gave the drugs, but he'd done enough to get kicked out, especially after Pryce, hearing about this in the UK, passed a character assassination of Hamilton to his US agents via some friends, which sealed the expulsion.'

'You said there was a death in Flick's family around then.' Monroe nodded. 'This gives Flick McCarthy a reason to really hate Hamilton.'

'And having him arrested for Pryce's murder works well,' Anjli said, typing a text and sending. 'What's the plan?'

'I think we're going to need nothing less than a confession,' Monroe looked up as he saw Sampson enter the room, marching a grinning Jess back towards them. 'Luckily, I know how we're going to manage it.'

'I believe this is yours,' DCI Sampson said irritably, showing the smiling Jess. 'I'm assuming you sent her to spy on us?'

'She's a kid, Sampson,' Monroe shrugged. 'She wants to be a copper. What can I do? She realised we were off the case, so followed you. They're so fickle when they're at that age.'

'Well, you can have her back,' Sampson muttered. 'If you'll excuse me—'

'Actually, laddie, I wanted to have a chat,' Monroe said, rising and walking over to Sampson, keeping his voice low. 'Got a bit of a problem.'

'And what's that?' Sampson frowned, unhappy with the closeness of the rival DCI.

'Well, you know we're now civilians, right?' Monroe leant in. 'Not police and all that? It seems that young Declan, this wee bairn's father, has got himself in a little snit when he was taken as a hostage, not ten minutes back.'

Sampson stared at Monroe for a long moment, his eyes narrowing as he tried to recall if he had actually heard the old man correctly.

'A *what?*'

'Aye, we thought that too,' Monroe puffed out his cheeks, shaking his head sadly. 'But there's some mad ex-soldier actor fellow running around with a speargun that you need to sort out, and currently, he's demanding answers.'

'Oh, for Christ's—' Sampson held his tongue, glaring out across the lobby. 'No matter. We'll deal with him once we get the Hardy lad out.'

'You'd rather remove evidence than help a police officer?' Monroe looked at Sampson in disgust. 'You know, I'd hoped you weren't corrupt, that you were just misguided, or stupid. Looks like you're all three.'

'*What did you call me?*' Sampson hissed.

'Corrupt and stupid,' Monroe repeated. 'As in easily led.'

'That's it,' Sampson snapped. 'I'm done with you, old man. You're out of here. I'm having you arrested for obstructing justice.'

'You know, that's a grand idea,' Monroe grinned, nodding at the entrance to the hotel, where, flanked by De'Geer and Cooper, a nervous Jenny Moss entered, looking around. 'You do me, and I'll do *you* for obstructing justice.'

Jenny ran over to Sampson, pausing as she realised who he was standing with.

'The police officers said you were in danger,' she said, confused, aiming her statement at her boyfriend.

'Oh, sorry, no, I asked them to tell you a "certain DCI" was in danger.' Monroe looked at De'Geer and Cooper accusingly. 'Did you get the message wrong?'

'No sir,' Cooper smiled. 'I'm afraid Miss Moss took the wrong implication from the message. She seemed to think DCI Sampson was in trouble when we knocked on her door. Or, as she called him, *Craig*.'

'Now, your name wouldn't be Craig, would it?' Monroe said in mock shock to the now reddening Sampson. 'That's a hell of a coincidence, isn't it? How would that lassie know this?'

'Okay,' Sampson skipped the formalities. 'You obviously know Jenny's my girlfriend.'

'No, DCI *Craig* Sampson,' Monroe seemed to rise in stature as his voice rose. 'What I *obviously* know is that a man dating a victim of the murdered actor I'm investigating, a victim who was also fed drugs by the man currently *accused* of the murder, has taken this case over on the orders of his girlfriend's father, and seems to be doing his best to make sure justice – justice for *her*, that is – will be swiftly and wrongly dealt with.'

Sampson glared at Monroe.

'You don't know the entire story,' he stated sullenly.

'Aye, I don't, and you know what, I don't particularly care to know,' Monroe smiled now. 'So, you have a choice, *Craig*.

You can continue with this facade of investigation, and my boss will let yours know about these little irregularities in great detail, or you can stop following orders given to you by Flick McCarthy, Luna Hedlun-Gates, John Moss or whomever the merry hell is doing this, *and let us actually solve this case.*'

Monroe looked at his phone as it beeped, reading the message.

'Because believe me, it's about to come out one way or the other, right now,' he said, turning it around to show Sampson. 'Wouldn't you say?'

———

Flick McCarthy was in the costume room, helping Nigel and Luna put the carefully curated costumes away into their labelled boxes. She didn't have to help, and neither did Luna, but after Malcolm had arrived, telling everyone the case was being taken over by DCI Sampson, and that Ryan Gates was getting very trigger-happy with a spear gun, she'd decided that staying in a crowd was a far better idea. Not because she wanted company, but by simple maths.

The speargun only had one shot, and here there were multiple targets.

One of these was Luna, Ryan's wife, who right now didn't even want to hear her husband's name. Flick understood this, as Luna had only just learnt of her husband's involvement in the coverup of a murder, and Flick knew exactly why she'd kept away from him, as there was a very strong chance that, left alone, she'd take the speargun from him by force and end him there and then.

Love could be like that, apparently.

Pulling the Little John tunic off the mannequin, Flick looked over at Nigel.

'You sure you want this packed?' she asked with a wry smile. 'People won't want their photos taken with it once the news gets out.'

'Yeah, it's still part of the show, no matter how bad it gets for Alex,' Nigel said, ignoring the soft comment of "not bad enough" from Luna across the room. 'I'll stick it in a special exhibition with the Robin costume. I'll make some banners up, talking about the friendship of Little John and Robin, and how it led to murder.' He smiled. 'I'll make a mint from it,' he said, looking over at Malcolm, staring at him in disgust. 'What?'

'A man died,' Malcolm hissed. 'Two men. And we shouldn't make jokes.'

'I wasn't making a joke,' Nigel watched the photographer for a long moment. 'I was stating a fact. These costumes, and the events of this weekend, will pay my mortgage, tenfold.'

'As long as they carry on with the plan,' Flick muttered. 'And I'm not sure our pet copper will be able to stick the landing.'

'We've primed Hardy,' Malcolm replied. 'He's pointed them at Peter Crock, and the circle will close. We can go on with our—'

He didn't get to finish the comment, as the door to the costume room, currently closed, slammed open with incredible force, and Declan was pushed through it, stumbling to the floor as a furious Ryan Gates entered behind him, pushing the door shut, speargun still in his hands.

'What in God's name are you doing?' Luna exclaimed as Nigel helped Declan to his feet. 'Ryan, he's a policeman!'

'One who's working with the killer!' Ryan waved the

speargun at Declan, who quickly and wisely stepped back. 'He thought I'd help him, that I'd turn against you, but he was wrong!'

'I didn't do anything like that,' Declan protested. 'I said DCI Sampson was wrong, and I think Alex Hamilton was framed!'

Declan gave a moment for the words to sink in, watching the body language of the people in the room change imperceptibly, confirming his suspicions, before continuing.

'And not only did Sampson think I was mad, but my team said it too!' he moaned, leaning against the mannequin. 'They don't think you're in danger anymore because they caught the killer.'

'And you think they haven't?' Flick looked concerned, and Declan saw her move slowly towards the weapons, still in their places on the table.

'No, and you're all in danger!' Declan replied. 'Because she's coming for you, I'm sure of it.'

'She?' Flick paused as she went to grab a sword. 'Who are you talking about?'

'Margot Trayner!' Declan frowned. 'How have you not worked this out?'

'Margot? How's she involved?' Flick looked immediately at Luna as she spoke, her body language relaxing now. She knew she wasn't in the immediate firing line and Declan quietly noted this, turning to Ryan Gates as he continued.

'Tell them!' he shouted. 'Go on!'

'She told the police who killed Peter Crock,' he said. 'Said she'd seen the murderer walking in from the garden.'

He turned now, aiming the speargun at Nigel.

'She said she saw you with a bow in your hand. The one from the Robin costume.'

'That's insane!' Nigel replied. 'The bow was with Malcolm! We'd swapped it for the photo shoot!'

'I know it's insane, as we'd already spoken to you!' Declan waved his hands at Nigel, holding them up to show he was no threat. 'Margot said Alex had confided in her, said you and Peter were trying to kill him to keep him quiet.'

'Quiet? About what?' Nigel looked around. 'This is bullshit!'

'You were at his party the night someone called Richard died?' Declan said. 'I don't know who Richard was, or why you were fighting Richard, I don't care, but Alex said you'd killed his career—'

'Richard Garcia?' Flick's voice was ice cold now as she spoke.

'I don't know,' Declan shrugged. 'Before we could learn more, DCI Sampson took us from the case.'

'Nigel, were you in LA when Richard died?' Flick looked around, confused.

'No, I swear,' Nigel was sweating now as he moved away from Flick. As he did this, Gates placed the speargun down, walking over to his wife.

'We need to get out of here,' he said. 'She told the police we were involved too.'

It was only for a moment, but it was long enough for Flick McCarthy to grab the speargun, aiming it at Nigel.

'*Were you in LA when Richard died?*' she repeated, more insistently, her trigger finger twitching.

'I told you, no!' Nigel grabbed a sword from the table, the one his Sheriff had used back in the day, as if a metal sword could stop a harpoon spear.

'Yeah, he's right,' Declan, smiling, spoke calmly now,

walking to the door. 'He wasn't. I just wanted you agitated and holding that gun.'

Turning, he banged on the door twice.

'You can come in now!' he shouted. 'She won't listen to sense!'

The double doors to the costume room opened, and De'Geer and Cooper walked in, extendable batons in their hands. Beside them were Derek McAfee and John Moss, looking confused why they were there, and they were followed by Monroe, Sampson and Anjli.

'She won't put the weapon down,' Declan said, pointing at Flick. 'She's very agitated and I don't know what to do.'

Luna looked at her husband now, who walked backwards, away from her.

'I needed to keep you safe,' he said. 'It was the only way.'

Flick frowned, speargun still in her hand as, at the back of the room and through the other entrance, Robert Standish entered, flanked by Billy, Doctor Marcos and Bullman, Jess half hidden behind them.

'Oh, well played,' Flick smiled at Declan. 'Manage the manager. But all you did was make me look unstable after a suitably harrowing weekend, where one of my clients died, and you arrested another for his murder. And unfortunately for you, Mister Walsh, the *actual* DCI on the case, DCI Sampson, has a completely different opinion on how things went down than you seem to have.'

'I'm sure he has,' Declan looked over at Monroe and Sampson, the latter looking a little sick to be in the room. 'But I think there's a little bit of movie magic here, and things aren't quite what they appear.'

'Look, I'm sure there's something important going on here,' Flick forced a smile. 'But Alex obviously did this, you have him dead to rights. And if Sam wasn't the killer, then his comments about Peter Crock killing Pryce are enough to damn him ...'

She stopped.

'Yeah, I'd keep quiet, lassie, unless you'd like to tell me how you know what happened in a police interview you weren't privy to?' Monroe asked. 'Maybe because you told him to say it?'

'Now, wait a moment!' Gates was furious now, spinning to face the people at the door. 'I said I'd help, but only to keep my wife safe. And because he said he'd explain who really killed Peter and Monty.'

The "he" was aimed at Declan, and as everyone turned to face him, he smiled.

'I'll be honest, I didn't really know when I asked for your help,' he said, looking around the room. 'But being in here, seeing your reactions? I think I know exactly who killed who, why they did it, and who told them to do it.'

24

TALES OF FOLK

Monroe looked at Sampson as Declan stood in the centre of the room.

'Well, I don't know about you, but I'd love to know who really did it, wouldn't you?' he asked. 'I mean, with all respect, you being the detective that's taking the credit for this and all that.'

'We have our suspects,' Sampson replied stiffly.

'You do,' Declan replied. 'But you also know you're completely wrong, and for some reason you don't seem to care. I wonder why that is?'

Sampson glared at Declan for a long, dangerous moment, before looking back at Monroe.

'If one of my DIs spoke to me like that, I'd have them written up on report,' he snarled.

'Well, then it's a good thing he's not one of your DIs,' Monroe smiled disarmingly. 'Because I prefer my officers to tell me when I'm wrong.'

'You think I'm wrong?'

'I think if Declan here says you are, then there's a bloody

solid case for that being true,' Monroe shrugged. 'I've seen him solve cases nobody else could before, and I suggest you give the lad the benefit of the doubt.'

Sampson nodded, still staring at Declan.

'Go on then,' he finished. 'Wow us.'

Declan shrugged, looking over at Flick, now holding the speargun.

'The story you've told us all weekend is good,' he said. 'Believable. Has all the beats needed to keep us following the breadcrumbs. But if I've learned one thing all weekend, it's not to believe the folk tales. You spin a good yarn; how Alex wanted people dead, and how he did it, but you're leaving out a lot of subplots. The letters, for example.'

'What about the letters?' John asked, frowning. 'I thought we all agreed that these were printed by Alex on the Thursday night?'

'The man's right,' Flick replied calmly. 'Alex did it all. And any second-rate detective would see that.'

'Yes, but any *first*-rate one would note how it doesn't gel,' Declan carried on, looking around the room at the guests. 'So, let me tell you all another story. One that doesn't just involve one wronged man, fighting for a revenge he's not owed, but a whole cabal of people, looking to gain justice.'

'A cabal?' Ryan Gates looked around. 'Out of this lot?'

'Absolutely,' Declan nodded. 'But to start this, we need to go back a few years, all the way to the end of *Young Robin*, and right before the sequel is green lit. Felicity Marshall and Michael Bailey, aka Flick McCarthy and Malcolm Stoddard, are released from the upcoming show. Felicity doesn't realise for years it's because of a death that happened while on a foreign shoot, and she's left in the dark. But life goes on. She carries on with her archery. Does quite good in a couple of Olympics, but never really gets anywhere near the medals.'

He watched Flick as he said this.

'That must have really bitten, not getting close. And you'd always wonder, if you hadn't screwed around being Marian, maybe your training would have pushed you that extra step.'

'It's not about the medals,' Flick muttered, admitting she was Felicity Marshall in the process. 'It's the taking part. How did you know?'

Declan pointed across the room at Malcolm.

'He used an old nickname for you, and we're very good at our jobs,' he smiled.

'So how does that equate to deaths this weekend?' Sampson asked. 'We would have learned her true identity at some point.'

'I'm sure you would have,' Declan nodded. 'But there's more to this. Felicity leaves competitive archery and becomes a coach. But, before this, she has a moment where she looks to be returning to the BBC as Marian, and then ... nothing.'

'I'd moved away from acting.'

'And probably for the best, judging from what happened,' Declan nodded. 'She coached until 2016, when tragedy hit her family. Her nephew, Richard Garcia, died of an overdose at a party in LA. He was brought back for the funeral, and she spent the next year looking after her sister. During the funeral, however, she links back up with Nigel Cummings, who also had a history with Richard.'

'I had no such thing!' Nigel exclaimed, and Declan held a hand up.

'Apologies,' he said. 'I meant *wanted* a history. Because in the nineties, you met Richard in London, and both you and Terry Leighton fell for him. Neither of you ended up with

Richard, but you fell out over it anyway, and it was only after his death that you reconnected.'

Nigel looked away.

'He was best off without us,' he muttered. 'But if he'd ended up with either of us, he wouldn't have died there.'

'That's very possible,' Declan nodded, leaving a moment of silence before continuing. 'But now it's five years ago, and Flick and Nigel have both decided Alex Hamilton needs to pay for the death. At this point, Alex isn't directly accused of the murder by the LA police, but shown to be responsible for the party, and the now classed as "accidental" overdose. His conduct, the drugs they find at his house and a letter damning him, sent by Pryce to Hamilton's US agent, gets him kicked out of the US, and now he's back in the UK.'

'He never paid his penance,' Monroe muttered. 'He got away with literal murder.'

'He should have been gassed for what he did!' Flick hissed.

'Possibly, but that's not for anyone here to decide,' Declan replied.

At this, Flick shifted her grip on the speargun.

'Go on,' she said. 'Continue your fascinating story.'

'Well, now you're with Nigel, the two of you follow Alex,' Declan continued, turning from Flick as he continued. 'She claims she's Nigel's appearance manager, and they attend events where Alex Hamilton is signing for the next two years, looking for something they can use. And then, three years ago, she meets Malcolm at one of these conventions. Now, he's lost a lot of weight and they're both under unfamiliar names, but she recognises him when nobody else would.'

'You're reaching.' Flick shook her head.

'In fact, it was a convention run by John Moss, wasn't it?'

Declan ignored her, looking across at the promoter now. 'Two classic characters beside you at the time, and you didn't know. You could have made a fortune from them.'

John didn't reply, instead choosing to stare at the floor.

'It was here, maybe in a bar during a catchup, that Malcolm finally comes clean and tells Flick why they'd been fired from *Hooded Outlaw* all those years back,' Anjli now explained, stepping forward. 'How Montgomery Pryce had drugged a financier's wife in a wrap party, trying to "roofie" her to sleep with him, resulting in her death by falling.'

Declan looked over at Robert Standish. 'And how the creators of the new show did whatever they could to keep him happy, while keeping the news out of the papers.'

'You have nothing,' Robert hissed. 'And don't look at me. I'm nothing to do with all this.'

'In that respect, you're quite correct,' Declan smiled. 'Because now, things move quickly. At the same convention, Pryce has groomed John's daughter, Jenny working as his assistant for the weekend, into sleeping with him, possibly by using Alex's prescription painkillers, always on hand, to make her more suggestible. John's furious when he finds out. Pryce's management walks away from the situation, sickened by what happened, leaving both Hamilton and Pryce in the lurch. But here's where the revenge plan starts, as Flick is suggested, by Nigel or Malcolm, maybe even both, as a replacement. After all, she's been repping Nigel for years. And she takes both Hamilton and Pryce on.'

Declan spun to face the photographer.

'You hated Pryce for what he did, but you were more than happy for Alex to take the fall. You'd hated him ever since he replaced you, ever since you watched him on panels take the piss out of his predecessor, unaware he was in the same room. So, you were quite happy to help, weren't you?'

'So far you have a grieving woman taking on new clients,' Sampson threw his arms up in frustration, glancing back at Monroe. 'Is he always like this?'

'It's a process,' Monroe grinned. 'Give the laddie space. He's coming to the good bit.'

'You're right, I am,' Declan nodded. 'Because it's around now, at the same convention Flick takes on Pryce, that she talks for the first time to Luna Hedlun-Gates, wife of another guest, Ryan Gates, learning the history between her and Alex, but also learning the story of her mother's tragic death, at a wrap party, thirty years earlier.'

There was a stunned moment of silence here, broken by Sampson as he looked at Luna.

'Is this true?'

Luna nodded.

'My father financed the movie they were in, and his wife, my mother, died when slipping from the roof,' she said. 'I never knew the true story until Flick told me. And, to prove it, she had Malcolm confirm it, begging for my forgiveness.'

'You never told me!' Ryan Gates stared at his wife. 'I fixed that mess up!'

'And I only learnt *that* this weekend,' Luna replied icily. 'If I'd known sooner, you would be long in the ground, you *bastard*.'

Gates stared at his wife, tears filling his eyes.

'If I'd known how much I'd hurt you, my darling, you wouldn't have had to do it,' he said. 'I'd have pulled the trigger myself.'

Luna glared at Gates, but the anger was softening, as Declan took back the attention in the room.

'So now Luna, Malcolm, John and Flick are all working together,' he continued. 'The list has gone up, too. Now Peter Crock needs to die, as he provided Pryce with the drugs that killed Metté Hedlun. And although he's been around from the start, they finally brought in Nigel Cummings.'

'Oh, this is insane!' Nigel snapped. 'Why am I involved now?'

'Because you had just learnt how Peter was ripping you off.' Declan replied. 'Selling you arrows while making hundreds on the side.'

Nigel went to reply but paused before saying, 'I saw first-hand how Flick had been destroyed by them all. And when I saw Luna, heard her story, heard Malcolm's ... it wasn't hard to pick a side. I dare you to have done differently.'

Declan also paused, forcing himself to keep focused. Nigel was right. He'd almost quit the force to investigate his father's death, and when he faced the killer of his parents, he'd chosen an option that wasn't the law.

No, you didn't kill the Red Reaper. These people aren't the same as you.

'Now you have the team, and the plan,' Declan continued, shaking the thought away. 'John convinces Derek to have the convention at this hotel, as Jenny works in the spa, and it's within the remit of Thames Valley Police and DCI Sampson here.'

'Unfortunately, you're a bit "by the book", mate,' Bullman made an apologetic face as she spoke to Sampson. 'They trusted you to see the "facts" they provided and jump to the wrong conclusion.'

'And of course, there's the other reason,' Monroe smiled. 'Your relationship with Johnny's wee girl.'

Sampson screwed his face up, pinching his nose, feeling the tension rise, knowing he was trapped.

'Go on,' he hissed.

'It's why Flick used you in her PR piece,' Declan continued. 'She didn't expect anyone else to turn up. And John knew with his daughter working here, Pryce wouldn't be able to help himself, and would cause trouble, making him an unlikable victim. And, when this happened, you, the gallant boyfriend, who knew all about Pryce's history through conversations with Jenny, would leap to her defence, and take down the people who hurt her. In this case, Pryce and Hamilton.'

'Once they set this, they booked the convention in the normal way, with Flick making sure Alex, Montgomery, Robert and Nigel all attended,' Monroe added. 'Which brings us to Thursday.'

'This is where the plan took shape, but also fell apart.' Anjli took over now. 'Alex Hamilton checked in early but couldn't go to his room. When he did, he had one room key, while the front desk insisted he had two. Which meant that someone took one of the keys. The only time this could have happened was when Luna and Alex were together in the men's changing room.'

'They didn't do anything,' Gates insisted. 'It was a fight.'

'No, it was sex.' Anjli shook her head. 'Luna and Alex had been having an on-off affair for close to three years. But if it makes you feel better, the clue's in the length of time.'

'You were screwing Alex for three years?' Gates was stunned at this, staring at Luna.

'He hated you,' she replied by explanation. 'He wanted you destroyed. I did this for us.'

'You did it for your own damn needs,' Gates hissed. 'You hate me for what I did, but you did this? You did ... *him?*'

'Now Alex's spare key is taken, Flick has a way to get into the room,' Declan pressed on, to avoid the next awkward silence. 'But they're not finished. Luna knows Alex is going to the Business Suite, so arranges her arrival for the same time. Maybe she even suggests he can check in early. Who knows? What she does know is that the camera in the room will catch them. So, she prints a selection of sheets, making it look like Alex printed them before leaving.'

'It was a nice touch,' Monroe smiled. 'Adding his printed schedule in. It also meant he didn't read the messages as he brought them to you, so didn't realise what you were really doing.'

'This done, you pass one to Malcolm, one to Peter, and one to Pryce, passed under his door. But this wasn't his first death threat, was it?'

'No,' Flick grinned darkly. 'I've sent him a few over the last year. Really tuning him up for this.'

'Malcolm places his letter in his hotel room, ready to be found, and I'm assuming Peter's was in his tent,' Declan continued. 'We found part of it, charred in the fire pit. And, while there, whoever dropped the note also took three of Peter's spare arrows.'

'I thought they were taken from Nigel Cummings' collection?' Gates asked, confused.

'They were supposed to be.' Anjli nodded. 'But the bar staff came in and were playing silly bastards with the props on the Thursday night, so John Moss had to lock everything down. Which meant you couldn't use the bow and arrow on Pryce, as planned, on the Thursday.'

'Thursday?' This time, it was Sampson who looked confused. 'Pryce was killed on Friday.'

'He was, but that wasn't the plan,' Declan replied. 'Originally, it was going to be done on the Thursday, as the organisers had a "guest dinner" that ended with a campfire party out back. Lots of noise, music, dark corners and a big fire. At some point, Pryce would be killed by an arrow, nice and silent, and the body wouldn't be found until the following morning.'

'But unfortunately, there was one person who wasn't privy to this plan.' Bullman smiled darkly. 'Alex Hamilton.'

'Alex had his own plans for the weekend,' Declan replied. 'He was embarrassing Pryce on stage by revealing his secret son, Sam Hardy, and his affair with Sam's mother. And, to seal the deal, after arranging a small coffee meet up where they could reunite, Alex then invited Carol to the guest dinner on the Thursday.'

'But the meeting had gone a little too well.' Anjli looked over at Flick. 'And your letters had shaken Pryce. So much that Pryce asked Carol to have dinner in his room that night, and they never left it, if you know what I mean.'

'And here's problem two,' Declan shook his head. 'Pryce realised he actually loved Carol, or at least wanted to make a go of it. She was married, but not happily, going on what happened, and over time something might have changed. But now your plans are seriously going awry. Pryce is still nervous, so hides in the spa, convinced he's going to die. And, by chance, he sees Jenny.'

'But he doesn't do what was expected.' Anjli shook her head. 'He'd had a revelation the night before. And, rather than groping Jenny Moss, he avoids her, going to Chantelle

Waters instead. But Jenny's been told by her dad he needs to be removed from the spa, so her boyfriend—'

She looked at the now shocked DCI Sampson.

'—that'll be you, DCI Sampson, will believe she was in danger, and he'll be biased in his investigation. Luna arrives on schedule, and the two of them make up a story where Pryce groped Jenny. When, in fact, and possibly for the first time ever, he was a perfect gentleman. Isn't that right?'

At this, Anjli looked at Jenny Moss, who had her head in her hands.

'Yes,' she whispered.

'You told me he molested you!' Sampson hissed at her. 'You *used* me!'

'*Everyone* used you,' Monroe said. 'Even after the murder, they believed you'd turn up and fail in your duties.'

'But now Alex adds more problems to the story,' Declan said. 'We found that while Luna was setting him up on the Thursday night in the Business Suite, Alex was actually sending Sam Hardy an email, explaining he'd provided him with a costume. Which was lucky for you, as you needed a scapegoat for your improvised new plan, and Sam appearing during the Friday, dressed like Pryce during his *Hooded Outlaw* days in the photo shoot, was a gift from above. You don't know who he is, you just assume he's connected to Hamilton as he speaks to him, but none of you realised his true identity.'

'You even make a song and dance of Malcolm suggesting they get the "real" bow for the shoot when there was never a swap. You wanted the police to believe Sam Hardy, on Alex Hamilton's orders, killed Montgomery Pryce. But you didn't know one important part of the story until the following day. That he was Pryce's bastard son.'

Flick glared at Declan as he spoke.

'Bloody Hamilton and his stupid revenge plans,' she hissed. 'And bloody Pryce and his penis.'

'And then we have the opening ceremony,' Declan leant closer. 'You've had to plan this off the cuff, but it's pretty solid, as plans go. You stand in the corner, at the back, one of the white-fletched longbow arrows in your hand, Nigel's recurved bow with it. You told Pryce to walk out, said it'd get a laugh, and he was nervous, needing something to give him back some pep. You knew the exact spot he'd move to. You were counting on it.'

'And why was that?'

'Because you intended the force of that arrow to punch through Pryce and carry on into Margot Trayner,' Declan replied calmly. 'The "imposter" you really hated.'

He pointed at the bow, still on the mannequin.

'Problem with the bow, though, is that it's a recurve, as they lost the longbow at the last minute, when the bar staff broke it on the Thursday night,' he said. 'Which meant you hadn't considered the changes it would make to the longbow arrow you needed to use. It's not the same bow you were used to, especially on the show all those years back, and you hadn't been practising with it, because you expected to have the longbow. The draw strength wasn't enough, and you killed your first target, but not the second.'

'In the confusion, you replaced the bow.' Anjli took over again. 'And now you played the part of an angry manager with John Moss, "forcing" him to keep the convention open. Which you both needed, as you had to set up Alex for the murders.'

Derek looked at John now.

'That explains so much,' he said. 'You used this convention, our years of sweat and tears, for your own revenge?'

'It wasn't your daughter he molested,' John hissed. 'Yeah, we kept the event open. We needed to have Peter found.'

'Because by this point, Peter was already dead,' Anjli looked at Nigel. 'Killed by you.'

'Oh, come on!' The accusation shocked Nigel, but Anjli turned to face him fully now.

'Peter was killed in his tent, at close range,' she said. 'Anyone with a bow could have done it. But, when you killed him, you rummaged around in the tent to find anything that linked him to you, including the letter, which you tossed into the fire as you left. On your knees. On the grass. Or, perhaps, as you said to us Friday, you were having a little prayer for him? Either way, you did this, using Alex's room pass to open and shut the door just in case it was registered. It wasn't, by the way.'

Nigel sighed theatrically.

'He'd ripped me off for thousands, and I committed a perfect crime,' he said. 'Why wouldn't I do it?'

'And here's problem three,' Declan continued, looking at Flick. 'Because Saturday morning, you learn from Margot Trayner who Sam is. And so, you start a new story, that Peter Crock shot the arrow, gaslighting Sam into believing he saw it, knowing this might help him when he's arrested for the murder.'

'But Peter Crock can't shoot the arrow, because he had a separated shoulder,' De'Geer said, surprising everyone as he spoke to Flick. 'The only possible archer there ... was you.'

'Two arrows down, and one to go.' Declan looked back at Luna. 'You wanted Standish dead, didn't you?'

'Malcolm paid his penance for this,' Luna nodded. 'Peter

and Pryce were dead, Standish was third. We had to find a different way to do it, though, as we wanted Alex to be found with the arrow.'

'Clever move,' Anjli replied. 'Give him a twin room, and the second bed would never need to be checked. How long was the arrow hidden in there?'

'Friday night, during the confusion,' John spoke now. 'I did it.'

'So, with no arrows left, how were you going to kill Standish?' Declan asked.

Luna looked at Flick sadly, moving closer to her.

'Sorry I let you down,' she said, placing an arm on Flick's shoulder ... and then pulled away the speargun, spinning it around, turning it to face the now terrified Robert Standish.

'Like this,' she said, firing the weapon.

25

SWORD PLAY

THE POWER IN A PNEUMATIC SPEARGUN COMES FROM compressed air, and a specified pressure that forces the spear, or harpoon, from the weapon. Within the speargun there is a chamber to store the air, and a piston that compresses as you load it. In fact, if a chamber has been compressed, a speargun could be used repeatedly for weeks, underwater.

The Nemrod Corbeta speargun, however, hadn't been pressurised in over a decade, and because of this, although the compression was still there, as the trigger was pulled, the spear itself didn't have the power and speed that it once had.

That was to say, it still had power and speed, and could have seriously hurt the elderly Robert Standish, if Ryan Gates hadn't selflessly dived in front of the director, taking the spear in the shoulder as he fell to the floor.

As Luna, shaken back to reality by this selfless act, dropped the speargun and ran to her husband, Flick McCarthy grabbed at the bow on the mannequin, already pulling an arrow to notch against the string, spinning it around to aim at the others. However, that was as far as she went, as Doctor Marcos, moving in quickly from behind, slashed at the bow cord with a scalpel, slicing it into two, the arrow falling to the floor as Cooper barrelled into the woman, sending both her, and the now useless bow to the floor.

Malcolm Stoddard had already made his choice and was also clambering to the floor, hands in the air. However, Nigel Cummings, realising the end had arrived wasn't content to go quietly, still with his combat-ready "Sheriff of Nottingham" sword in his hand and, with a yell of anger, swung it down at Cooper before she could rise back up. But then he stared in shock as Declan, grabbing something, anything, off the prop table to block this, suddenly broke the downward swing with a sword of his own.

'Hey!' Nigel glared at him. 'Be careful! That's expensive!'

Declan was going to reply to this when there was a commotion behind him. John Moss had been arrested by DCI Sampson, which, considering he was the father of his girlfriend, would not end well, but the ensuing racket had distracted Declan for a split second. As he looked back, he realised Nigel had run for another door to the room, hidden behind the mannequins and unused over the weekend, but was now visible and available for Nigel's escape.

As Jess also ran after him, Declan, with the sword in his hand, began sprinting after the slim, elderly man chasing him down the hotel corridor, yelling at him to stop as they ran past confused hotel guests pressing to the walls, and eventually catching up with Nigel in the hotel's lobby, still currently filled with attendees – although now they were simply hotel guests.

'Give up, Cummings!' Declan shouted as the actor, realising he'd run into a chokepoint, spun around to face his pursuer. 'You're under arrest for the murder of Peter Crock!'

'I'm too delicate for prison!' Nigel cried, hacking down with his blade at Declan, forced to block again with the sword, which he'd now realised had EXCALIBUR etched down the blade. 'I'd rather die!'

Declan had lost Jess in the chaos, and in a way was glad for this, as it meant she wasn't within reach of Nigel's sword, and so he carried on blocking Nigel's swings, pushing slowly back at him with each blow. Nigel was obviously trained in the blade's use, but luckily for Declan this was more for stage fighting than as a military or martial arts discipline, and Declan knew he simply had to keep Nigel moving and hope to God the man ran out of steam, or hope his adrenaline rush would suddenly stop. He even got in a couple of moves himself, catching Nigel with the flat of his blade, trying not to get distracted by the hotel guests currently watching, many of whom were filming the scene on their phones.

Nigel didn't seem to be stopping any time soon, and Declan's arms were feeling heavy. He realised with mounting concern that although Nigel's sword looked the same as Declan's, it was actually lighter and easier to wield, whereas the Excalibur he used was more of an unweighted display prop.

Dammit, he thought to himself, blocking another swing, *I should have just gone for my extendable baton.*

Nigel had realised, however, that this wasn't ending well, and as he'd retreated across the lobby, towards the bar area and the patio to the outside, he grabbed a small child, pulling her in front of him like a shield holding the sword against the child's throat, as her mother screamed in horror.

'Drop it,' he said hoarsely, gulping in breaths as he spoke.

'This might not be real, but it's still sharp enough to cut her throat.'

Declan held the sword up, stopping where he stood.

'What are your demands?' he asked softly, taking a moment to gather his own breath.

'I want immunity from prosecution!' Nigel hissed. 'I didn't kill Monty Pryce. And Peter Crock deserved everything he got!'

'He deserved death?'

Nigel paused as he tried to find an answer that didn't damn him more, and in the end, decided not to bother with it.

'I'm not an evil man!' he shouted, looking around the bar and lobby as he spoke. 'I just play one on television!'

'Put the sword down, Sheriff,' a fresh voice spoke, and Declan glanced to the side to see Sam Hardy, now released from the photo ops room, with Jess beside him, standing amid a now clearing group of people. In his hand was the only weapon he had to hand: his Larp bow, an arrow with a foam head notched to the drawn-back bow string.

'You've lost,' Sam continued, taking a step closer. 'Give up and let the child go.'

'No!' Nigel cried, his wild eyes darting from Sam to Declan, and then back. 'I'm not scared of that thing! You won't kill me—'

'I don't need to *kill* you,' Sam said, loosing the arrow.

The foam head wasn't the same foam as a sponge had and was under a solid latex covering. And, as it soared in the air towards Nigel, in the split second it was free, Declan recalled De'Geer's line about how such weapons could still cause concussion, a thought that lingered as the wide arrow tip slammed into Nigel's face at speed, not doing enough to serious damage him, but causing enough force to make him stagger back, dropping his hold on the girl as he grabbed at his now bleeding nose. And, as the girl ran from the scary bleeding man, Declan moved in fast, knocking the blade to the side, and placing the tip of Excalibur against Nigel's throat.

'Drop. Your. Sword,' he growled, and Nigel Cummings, realising he'd lost, let his sword fall out of his hand as the audience went wild.

This, as far as they were concerned, was the entertainment they'd expected.

As Declan turned Nigel around, handcuffing him, Sam walked over, Jess beside him.

'Thanks for believing me,' he said.

'Thanks for saving the girl,' Declan smiled. 'I think you don't need to worry about the fandom anymore.'

As Sam looked around, seeing the audience watching him, he smiled faintly. And, called over to the bar by a group of fans, he turned to leave through the main doors.

Declan, however, stopped him.

'Ladies and gentlemen!' he shouted out in his loudest, most military voice. 'Put your hands together for Sam Hardy, the son of Carol Hardy and Montgomery Pryce!'

At this revelation, the audience in the bar area went crazy, practically mobbing Sam, half-carrying him to the bar and away from the exit.

'Not a bad way to be outed,' Declan smiled, looking at Jess. 'As you save a life with a bow and arrow.'

'You're just a hideous romantic,' Jess grinned, looking to the back of the lobby. A hush had gone over the crowd, and everyone watched as, in a handcuffed procession, Luna Hedlun-Gates, Flick McCarthy, Malcolm Stoddard and John

Moss were escorted out by DCI Sampson and Thames Valley Police.

'Got one more for you,' Declan called out, pulling Nigel around to face the others. 'I'm guessing you're doing this one by the book?'

DCI Sampson's face was tight as he nodded, one of his officers moving out to grab Nigel, pulling him into the line as they walked out of the hotel. Monroe, having followed them out from the costume room, sauntered over to Declan and Jess, noting the sword on the floor.

'Always about the bloody performance with you, laddie,' he said, now frowning at the foam arrow.

'Sam Hardy,' Declan smiled. 'Finally came out from under his father's shadow.'

Monroe looked over at the bar.

'Do they know he's Samantha Hardly yet?' he smiled slightly. 'Because that will blow their minds.'

'I think that's for him to tell.' Declan gave Jess a hug. 'I'm guessing you were behind the bow and arrow?'

'He was in the corner,' Jess shrugged. 'He didn't know if he was still arrested or not, nobody had come to find him so he just left, he had his stuff with him, and the bow was beside his bag. I just made a suggestion.'

'It was an excellent suggestion,' Declan grinned, looking at his watch. 'And once we've settled everything up here, I reckon we can get home before midnight.'

'We're not staying the night?' Jess frowned, and Declan shook his head.

'Don't want to miss your lunch with Prisha's parents, do you?' he replied, ruffling her hair. 'Call her. Tell her it's still on because you cracked the case.'

'How did you know?'

Declan tapped his nose.

'Because, apparently, I'm the second-best detective named Walsh on this team,' he winked. 'And that's good enough to work things out.'

'Anjli told you.'

Declan was about to reply but paused as, from the back of the hotel, Ryan Gates emerged, being walked by two first aiders to the main doors. He had a bandage strapped to his chest, and as he saw Declan, he nodded curtly at him before walking out.

'Apparently there's an ambulance on its way, but he reckons it's just a scratch,' Monroe said. 'Wants to go to the station and make his statement first and has declined to press charges against his wife for his attempted murder.'

'Well, he did dive in front of the spear.' Declan puffed his cheeks out as he considered the moment once more. 'I saw she went to him, after.'

'Aye, love conquers and all that,' Monroe smiled. 'Still won't stop her being charged for everything else.'

Declan saw Anjli and Billy enter the lobby now as they walked over.

'Well, I think DCI Sampson and Jenny Moss are over,' she said. 'Jenny wouldn't even speak to him as they arrested her father.'

'Understandable,' Monroe replied as Doctor Marcos, finishing up talking with Bullman to one officer, joined them. 'Love and family are very emotional things.'

'On that matter,' Declan pointed at Doctor Marcos's blue latex gloves, 'would you mind removing your left glove?'

Doctor Marcos gave a shy smile, the first time Declan had ever seen her look that way, as she pulled off the glove to show a thin, white-gold engagement ring on the wedding finger.

'We wanted to wait until this was all done,' Monroe explained. 'No point talking about us as we're trying to sort out who killed who and everything else.'

'He asked me this afternoon,' Doctor Marcos said, back to business now. 'He had a big thing planned, but when this came up, he just bottled it all and blurted everything out at me like a terrified schoolboy when he thought he was being fired.'

'I did no such thing!' Monroe exclaimed. 'I was calm and reassured.'

'Sure you were,' Doctor Marcos kissed Monroe on the cheek. 'I'm going back with the forensics team, as I have to explain to them some of my discoveries now they're taking over.'

'They're still taking over?' Declan was surprised at this. 'I thought we'd still get the case win. Sampson was used because they thought they could control him.'

'Yeah, and that didn't go too well,' Anjli smiled. 'He'll actually be harsher on them than we would have been. Only downside of all this is Alex Hamilton gets to walk free.'

'Maybe of this crime.' Declan looked across the bar at the remaining attendees. 'But I think you'll find every little dark secret he has will come out over the court case, and he'll be damned by public opinion. He won't be able to hide from any of it.'

'I wonder if this has soured De'Geer's love of Robin Hood?' Billy asked, looking around. 'Actually, where is De'Geer?'

'And Cooper, for that matter?' Anjli laughed.

DE'GEER WAS IN THE COSTUME ROOM, STARING AT THE REMAINS of the prop table, when Cooper found him.

'You alright, Sarge?' she asked carefully. 'Everyone's gone now. You don't have to guard this.'

'Derek McAfee's getting some people to put this into storage,' De'Geer said, looking back at Cooper. 'This might be the last time I see all this. Cummings is likely to sell it all to cover his legal bills.'

He picked up one of the longbow arrows, staring at it.

'I never bought one of these,' he said. 'The ones Nigel signed. I'd considered it, but there was always next time.'

'Did you want one?' Cooper asked, with a slight hint of nervousness in her voice.

'Bit of a moot point, really,' De'Geer forced a smile. 'I don't think he'll be doing conventions for a while. The only "con" in his future is "convicted". Why?'

'Because I bought you one,' Cooper made a slight shrugging motion, but it seemed a little too awkward to be casual. 'This morning. Before everything went mad and we found Peter Crock. It's up in your ... *our* room, by the big stick.'

'Quarterstaff.'

'Whatever. But yeah, he signed it for me, gave me a healthy discount for being police, and I put it with your things. I didn't realise then it was going to be ... well, you know. So dark.'

De'Geer genuinely smiled at this.

'You bought me a murder weapon, signed by the killer?' he stroked his beard. 'Which at the same time isn't, and is linked to my childhood love? Esme Cooper, you might have just bought me the greatest present ever.'

It wasn't intentional, but De'Geer leant over and hugged Cooper in a gesture of thanks, but paused, pulling back awkwardly.

'We should find the others,' he said.

'Yes,' Cooper replied, straightening her vest.

'I need to wait for the organiser,' De'Geer pointed at the items on display.

'I'll catch you later, then,' Cooper grinned, backing out of the room.

And then De'Geer was alone, walking around the mannequins. For the first time all weekend, he was able to properly examine them.

And, with nobody around, De'Geer paused beside the Little John costume, pulling out his phone to take a selfie.

There was a message on the screen from DC Davey; it'd arrived half an hour ago, but in all the confusion, he hadn't realised.

> Thanks for checking in, M. I'm good, let's grab coffee soon. X

De'Geer stared at the message, then at the door, and then back to the message, before placing the phone away.

The moment had passed, and he no longer wanted the photo.

EPILOGUE

DECLAN PULLED HIS COLLAR UP AS HE SAT ON THE BENCH IN ST James's Park. The early October weather meant although it was a sunny day, it was also getting cold. And Declan had made the mistake of not bringing his overcoat out to the meeting.

He'd been late, but he knew his companion wouldn't be. And, beside him, sipping on a coffee, Ryan Gates stared out across the lake, wincing at a twinge in his shoulder. It'd been just under a month since a speargun shot him, and the wound hadn't been that deep, but it was enough to ache, especially when it was cold.

'So, did she get the deal?' Declan asked, watching the ducks on the lake as he spoke.

'They're still inking the page,' Gates nodded. 'But she's got a good case. Death of her mum, being convinced by Flick to help, she's able to show some serious diminished responsibility. And Alex actually manned up and refused to blame her for anything, wouldn't press charges, none of that. So, we're looking at probation, maybe a suspended sentence ...'

Declan fought the urge to argue this. Luna Hedlun-Gates might not have killed Pryce or Crock, but she was definitely involved in the planning of it. But Flick McCarthy, not Luna, had been the one that pulled the bow, shot the arrow and killed Montgomery Pryce, and although she'd also claimed credit for the death of Peter Crock, Thames Valley Police were still pushing forward with charging Nigel Cummings for that. John Moss, his daughter Jenny and Malcolm Stoddard were all being charged with perverting the course of justice, or something similar to lessening degrees, but Declan wasn't sure what the charges were now, to be honest. The moment Sampson took the case, it was no longer classed as a Temple Inn remit, and they'd simply returned to the crime unit on the Monday, ready for the next case.

The only one who hadn't had this was Jess, as DCI Sampson, most likely as an apology for being duped by the whole thing had written up an incredibly complimentary report on how she'd helped. In fact, it was so complimentary, she seemed to have now performed half the tasks Billy had over the weekend, a fact that Monroe and Bullman had taken great delight in reminding Billy about, every time they'd dealt with him on something over the last three weeks since the report arrived.

Declan realised at this point he'd become distracted, and looked back at Gates, now blowing on the top of his coffee to cool it down.

'Are you two okay?'

Gates rubbed at his shoulder.

'We've been better,' he said. 'But she had secrets, I had secrets ... you wanna know the funny bit? I don't mind her having this whole revenge thing she kept from me, but the fact she was sleeping with Alex to sell it. That's the bit I'm finding hard to swallow.'

He sipped at the coffee again, nodding as he took another.

'I never knew I'd covered up her mum's death. And it never came up in conversation, so I never put two and two together. But I did far worse when I was in the military. I'm sure you're the same.'

Declan thought back to his time in the RMP and nodded.

'We had our moments,' he replied quietly.

'Anyway, Luna and me? We're trying to fix things,' Gates said, biting his lip as he thought. 'Could be worse, though. Could have been that copper.'

'Sampson?'

'Yeah. His missus never forgave him for arresting her dad, and they had a massive row a couple of weeks back, apparently. Seemed she thought he should have done what they said. Problem was, during this, she gave away she knew *more* than she'd said. So, as a breakup gift, he arrested her and charged *both* members of the family.'

'Ouch,' Declan grinned.

'How's your daughter doing?' Gates changed the subject.

Declan thought about this for a moment.

'First year A' Levels, more of a change up than she expected, but she's managing it okay,' he said. 'She met her girlfriend's parents a few weeks back, and now she's getting stick from her for not returning the favour.'

'And why isn't she?' Gates smiled. 'You don't approve?'

'Not at all, it's purely scheduling,' Declan shrugged. 'Her mum is getting married again later this year, so that's stressful, and me and Anjli have been non-stop on cases. We'll get it sorted soon. Hopefully, this year. So, what's next for you?'

'I'm signing at the New York Comic Con next week, then a

couple of East Coast conventions in the New Year.' Gates shrugged. 'They pay the bills. And Luna's going to need some excellent solicitors. Matty Daniels, one of the other managers, offered to take me on the moment it all came out. It's going to be me, Terry Leighton, John Standish and Sam Hardy.'

'Sam?'

'Oh aye,' Ryan smiled. 'Son of Robin Hood and Lady Eleanor, the man on the floor during the murder, who took down the Sheriff with one arrow? He's a massive draw. Supernova in Australia offered him a quarter of a million dollars to do their shows next year. Helps he does the sexy stories, too. He's on Margot's show this week, talking about it.'

Declan felt a little piece of resentment at that. Sam might have been the one who shot the arrow, but Declan had been the one sword fighting across the whole bloody hotel. *He* should get a little of that cash.

'They'd probably invite you too,' Gates said, smiling, reading Declan's expression. 'And as the case was taken off you, I reckon you could probably talk about it. Added to the fact you're the guy who saved the Prime Minister, all that stuff, you're quite the media-friendly Detective Inspector ...'

'I'm good,' Declan smiled back, stretching his arms as he sat back on the bench. 'I've had my fifteen minutes of fame. I'm happy to let someone else take it.'

'Well, if you ever change your mind, drop me a message.' His coffee finished now, Gates rose from his bench seat. 'I have to go now, I need to ... well, it's best you don't know. Government work.'

He tapped the side of his nose in a knowledgeable way and Declan rose to meet him, shaking his hand.

'I hope things work out,' he said. 'If only so you can get your *Ahab* prop back.'

'Tell them to keep it,' Gates shrugged. 'I always hated that show.'

And with that, Gates nodded to Declan, walking off across the bridge. Declan watched after him for a moment, and then pulled out his phone, checking for messages. Seeing nothing of note, he turned left, heading towards The Mall, The Strand, and a cab back to the offices.

'HE MET HER FOR COFFEE?'

Billy turned from his desk monitor to stare in surprise at Anjli, currently at her own desk, leant back and reading from her phone.

'Apparently so,' she replied. 'Last week.'

'Does Cooper know?'

'She told him to do it.' Anjli shook her head. 'First person De'Geer asked once the message arrived was whether he should.'

Billy whistled through his teeth.

'That must have been a tough call,' he replied. 'Although they've been quite close over the last few weeks. Maybe she doesn't see Davey as a threat anymore.'

'Maybe De'Geer told Cooper that Davey wasn't a threat?'

Anjli rose from the desk, walking to the printer and grabbing some printouts.

'Worst part is, she didn't turn up. Ghosted him again.'

Billy laughed, looking back at his computer.

'Is it bad that I'm actually a little happy about this?' he asked. 'What with Marcos and Monroe now engaged, you and Declan doing okay and even Bullman having her not-so-secret tryst with David Bradbury in Scotland Yard, having De'Geer crashing and burning a little makes me feel a little better about my own life.'

'Still got problems there?'

Billy sighed.

'I still haven't told Andrade I'm not coming with him,' he said, spinning his gamer chair, so he now faced Anjli once more. 'It's really hard. And there's a part of me that wonders if I'm doing this because I do want to go with him.'

'So go,' Anjli suggested. 'Speak to Monroe, ask if you can take six months unpaid leave. A sabbatical of sorts. Go with Andrade to his next posting and see how you do. If you enjoy it, see a way to live like that, then you can stay. If not, you break up, come home, hug your butler and return to work.'

Billy considered the option for a long moment.

'I do like to hug my butler,' he mocked, 'but the other staff get jealous.'

'Look, it's a thought,' Anjli replied. 'You like Andrade, but the clock's running out. You've got less than three months with him, and then he's gone. If you want to be with him, you need to decide.'

Billy reluctantly nodded, and Anjli looked back at her own computer monitor.

'What do you think about that, by the way?' she eventually asked. 'Marcos and Monroe?'

'I think it's sweet, but at the same time I worry it's a knee-jerk,' Billy was reading his screen as he spoke. 'Monroe's got the ghosts of his last marriage to get rid of and Doctor Marcos ...'

He stopped, staring blankly.

'You know, I don't even know if she was ever married,' he replied. 'After all this time, and she's still an enigma.'

'Who's an enigma?' Declan asked, walking into the office now, blowing on his hands to warm them. 'Damn, it's cold outside.'

'Do you know if Marcos has ever been married before?' Anjli asked. Declan went to reply, frowned, and then shook his head.

'Sorry, no,' he replied, noticing for the first time the box on his desk. 'Gift from you?'

'Not me,' Anjli smiled. 'I don't like you enough.'

Declan blew her a kiss and then examined the long, slim box, before pulling a small folding knife out of his desk drawer and slicing along the seams. Pulling the flaps open and removing the bubble wrap inside, he eventually reached in and pulled out a sword.

'It's Excalibur,' he said, holding it up, staring at it. 'The one I used to stop Nigel Cummings.'

'Nigel sent it to you?' Billy asked, rising and walking over, checking inside the box. 'Here, there's a note for you. It's from Derek McAfee.'

'What's it say?' Anjli was walking over now, also eager to hold the sword.

'It reads, "*Dear DI Walsh, I'm currently selling the props Nigel Cummings owned to pay his legal costs, but I decided you should have the weapon that took him down. I hope you find a good use for it*",' Billy read.

'Wow,' Declan smiled as he held up the blade again, turning it. 'Not often I get something like this.'

'Actually, you didn't.' Billy turned the sheet. 'It continues. "*I also enclose Excalibur for your daughter, as she fought for truth, like you, but without being paid a pay cheque, which is the noblest of causes. I hope you enjoy both."'*

'Hold on,' Declan placed the sword down for a moment. 'I don't get Excalibur?'

'No,' Anjli grinned, reaching into the long, narrow box and pulling out a foam-headed arrow. 'I think, as the note said, you get the weapon that took Nigel Cummings down.'

'I took him down!' Declan protested, waving Excalibur. 'With this!'

'And I'm sure Jess will let you play with it whenever you want,' Anjli cooed.

Declan was about to reply to this when the door to Monroe's office opened and the man himself appeared.

'What's all the bloody noise—' he started, but one look at Declan, holding up the sword, stopped him in his tracks.

'I'm too old for this shite,' he muttered as he turned around, walked back into his office and shut the door behind him.

Declan looked at Anjli, placing the sword down, wrapping the bubble wrap back around it.

'So, what's on the docket?' he asked, moving the box off his desk.

'Well, we have a burglary at Cutler's Hall, a hit and run on The Strand, and a stabbing last night outside Ye Olde Cheshire Cheese ...'

And as Declan, Anjli and Billy started working out the Last Chance Saloon's next case, DCI Alex Monroe watched them through his office window.

'Bloody eejits,' he muttered with a smile, before returning to his day's paperwork. 'Nice sword, though.'

ACKNOWLEDGEMENTS

When you write a series of books, you find that there are a ton of people out there who help you, sometimes without even realising, and so I wanted to do a little acknowledgement to some of them.

There are people I need to thank, and they know who they are.

People who patiently gave advice when I started this back in 2020, the people on various Facebook groups who encouraged me when I didn't know if I could even do this, the designers who gave advice on cover design and on book formatting, all the way to my friends and family, who saw what I was doing not as mad folly, but as something good.

Editing wise, I owe a ton of thanks to my brother Chris Lee, who I truly believe could make a fortune as a post-retirement copy editor, if not a solid writing career of his own, Jacqueline Beard MBE, who has copyedited all my books since the very beginning, and our new editorial addition Sian Phillips, all of whom have made my books way better than they have every right to be.

Also, I couldn't have done this without my growing army of ARC and beta readers, who not only show me where I falter, but also raise awareness of me in the social media world, ensuring that other people learn of my books.

But mainly, I tip my hat and thank you. *The reader.* Who once took a chance on an unknown author in a pile of books, and thought you'd give them a go, and who has carried on this far with them.

I write Declan Walsh for you. He (and his team) solves crimes for you. And with luck, he'll keep on solving them for a very long time.

Jack Gatland / Tony Lee,
    London, September 2022

ABOUT THE AUTHOR

Jack Gatland is the pen name of #1 *New York Times Bestselling Author* Tony Lee, who has been writing in all media for thirty-five years, including comics, graphic novels, middle grade books, audio drama, TV and film for *DC Comics, Marvel, BBC, ITV, Random House, Penguin USA, Hachette* and a ton of other publishers and broadcasters.

These have included licenses such as *Doctor Who, Spider Man, X-Men, Star Trek, Battlestar Galactica, MacGyver,* BBC's *Doctors, Wallace and Gromit* and *Shrek*, as well as work created with musicians such as *Iron Maiden, Bruce Dickinson, Ozzy Osbourne, Joe Satriani* and *Megadeth.*

As Tony, he's toured the world talking to reluctant readers with his 'Change The Channel' school tours, and lectures on screenwriting and comic scripting for *Raindance* in London.

An introvert West Londoner by heart, he lives with his wife Tracy and dog Fosco, just outside London.

Feel free to follow Tony / Jack on all his social media by clicking on the links below.

www.jackgatland.com
www.hoodemanmedia.com

Visit Jack's Reader's Group Page
(Mainly for fans to discuss his books):
https://www.facebook.com/groups/jackgatland

Subscribe to Jack's Readers List:
https://bit.ly/jackgatlandVIP

www.facebook.com/jackgatlandbooks
www.twitter.com/jackgatlandbook
ww.instagram.com/jackgatland

Want more books by Jack Gatland? Turn the page...

DI Walsh and the team of the *Last Chance Saloon* will return in their next thriller

MURDER BY MISTLETOE

Order Now at Amazon:

My book.to/murderbymistletoe

THE THEFT OF A **PRICELESS** PAINTING...
A GANGSTER WITH A **CRIPPLING DEBT**...
A **BODY COUNT** RISING BY THE HOUR...

AND ELLIE RECKLESS IS CAUGHT IN THE MIDDLE.

JACK GATLAND

PAINT
— THE —
DEAD

A 'COP FOR CRIMINALS' ELLIE RECKLESS NOVEL

A NEW PROCEDURAL CRIME SERIES WITH
A TWIST - FROM THE CREATOR OF THE
BESTSELLING 'DI DECLAN WALSH' SERIES

AVAILABLE ON AMAZON / KINDLE UNLIMITED

EIGHT PEOPLE. EIGHT SECRETS.
ONE SNIPER.

THE
B⊕ARD
ROOM

HOW FAR WOULD YOU GO TO GAIN JUSTICE?

NEW YORK TIMES #1 BESTSELLER TONY LEE WRITING AS

JACK GATLAND

A NEW STANDALONE THRILLER WITH
A TWIST - FROM THE CREATOR OF THE
BESTSELLING 'DI DECLAN WALSH' SERIES

AVAILABLE ON AMAZON / KINDLE UNLIMITED

THEY TRIED TO KILL HIM...
NOW HE'S OUT FOR **REVENGE.**

NEW YORK TIMES #1 BESTSELLER **TONY LEE** WRITING AS

JACK GATLAND

THE MURDER OF AN **MI5 AGENT**...
A BURNED SPY **ON THE RUN** FROM HIS OWN PEOPLE...
AN ENEMY OUT TO **STOP HIM** AT ANY COST...
AND A **PRESIDENT** ABOUT TO BE **ASSASSINATED**...

SLEEPING
SOLDIERS

A **TOM MARLOWE** THRILLER

BOOK 1 IN A NEW SERIES OF THRILLERS IN THE STYLE OF
JASON BOURNE, JOHN MILTON OR **BURN NOTICE**, AND
SPINNING OUT OF THE **DECLAN WALSH** SERIES OF BOOKS

AVAILABLE ON AMAZON / KINDLE UNLIMITED

JACK GATLAND

THE LIONHEART CURSE

HUNT THE GREATEST TREASURES
PAY THE GREATEST PRICE

BOOK 1 IN A NEW SERIES OF ADVENTURES
IN THE STYLE OF 'THE DA VINCI CODE'
FROM THE CREATOR OF DECLAN WALSH

AVAILABLE ON AMAZON / KINDLEUNLIMITED